The Forgotten War Begins

A Novel of the Sea War in Korea

Archie T. Miller

ATM Consulting

ISBN-13: 978-1499330090
ISBN-10: 149933009X

Cover Photo
Republic of Korea minesweeper YMS-516 is blown up by a
magnetic mine, during sweeping operations west of Kalma Pando,
Wonsan harbor, on 18 October 1950. - *US Navy Photo*

Maps
Maps used in this book are derived from US Navy maps obtained
through the Korean War Project and are in the Public Domain.

Book Design by Archie T. Miller

To Judy

The Forgotten War

"Korea became the forgotten war largely because Americans didn't want to remember it. Coming so soon on the heels of World War II and with such an unsatisfying conclusion when compared to the unconditional surrenders of the Germans and Japanese in World War II, the country didn't want to think about it. Americans simply wanted to get on with their lives."

Admiral James L. Holloway III, USN

"We forget because the war was not a war. It was a police action that failed to find a resolution to the original crime."

Richard C. Kagan

TABLE OF CONTENTS

MAPS

Prologue

The Far East was left in turmoil at the end of World War II. The Empire of Japan had taken over large portions of Asia either by annexation in the early 20th Century or by conquest during World War II. With the defeat of Japan by United Nations forces in 1945, Communist and Nationalist forces in individual countries struggled for control of large portions of East Asia.

The Korean peninsula was governed by the Korean Empire from the late 19th century to the early 20th century, when it was annexed by the Empire of Japan in 1910. After the surrender of Japan at the end of World War II, the Korean peninsula was divided into two occupied zones. The northern half of the peninsula was occupied by the Soviet Union and the southern half by the United States. A United Nations–supervised election held in 1948 led to the creation of separate Korean governments for the two occupation zones: the Democratic People's Republic of Korea (DPRK) in the north, and the Republic of Korea (ROK) in the south.

China was a more complex case. Civil war between forces of the nationalist Kuomintang government, led by Chiang Kai Chek, and the forces of the Communist Party of China (CPC) led by Mao Zedong raged in China for most of the first half of the Twentieth Century

1

including the period when China was fighting Japan. Major combat in the Chinese Civil War ended in 1949 with the Communist Party in control of most of mainland China, and the Nationalist Kuomintang retreating offshore. The Kuomintang Republic of China (ROC) was reduced to the island of Formosa[1], Hainan Island, some islands along the mainland coast and some pockets of resistance on the mainland. On October 1, 1949, Mao Zedong proclaimed the People's Republic of China (PRC), which, during the cold war, was commonly known in the West as "Communist China" or "Red China". In 1950, the People's Liberation Army (PLA) succeeded in capturing Hainan Island from the ROC, occupying Tibet, and defeating the majority of the remaining Kuomintang forces in Yunnan and Xinjiang provinces.

During World War II, the United States had the largest Naval force the world had ever seen. At its peak, the US Navy was operating 6,768 ships including 28 aircraft carriers, 23 battleships, 71 escort carriers, 72 cruisers, over 232 submarines, 377 destroyers and thousands of auxiliary and supply ships. The Pacific campaign was primarily a naval amphibious war. The United States Navy was the major force in the defeat of Japan

With the end of the war, all of the American armed forces were scaled back to "peacetime" levels. The force levels were largely driven by the fact that the United States now had the atom bomb giving it a powerful superiority over any potential enemies -- including the Soviet Union. It was largely assumed that air power (primarily the B-36, six engine bomber) and nuclear weapons was all that was needed to either deter or win all future conflicts. At the same time, based on the lessons of WW-II, and the need for efficiency and cost reduction, the Congress passed,

---

1   The island was known to Westerners as "Formosa" from the Portugese "Isla Formosa" (Beautiful Island). Chinese and Japanese had always known it as Taiwan. By 1950, both names were in use -- I opted for Formosa.

and President Harry Truman signed, The National Security Act of 1947. This act established a unified National Military Establishment under a new Department of Defense. The Army Air Corps now became the independent United States Air Force on an equal footing with the Army and the Navy.

Passing the act was easier than implementing it. There was a great deal of squabbling between the three services about their "roles and missions". Despite many meetings and conferences, the Army, Navy and Air Force were not even close to an agreement about their individual responsibilities. The main sticking point was aircraft. The Air Force position was that only they should have aircraft — the Navy, Marines and Army disagreed. Finally, in disgust, President Harry Truman banished the service chiefs to Key West in March 1948 and told them not to come back until they had an agreement. When they finally returned to Washington, they had hammered out the Key West Agreement that evidently pleased none of them. The Navy and the Marines, however, would be allowed to retain their own combat air arms *"...to conduct air operations as necessary for the accomplishment of objectives in a naval campaign..."*. The Army would be allowed to retain aviation assets for reconnaissance and medical evacuation purposes only. They were not allowed any aircraft for tactical air support of their own troops. The Air Force would have control of all strategic air assets, and most tactical and logistic air assets as well.

The newly minted Air Force had a large number of supporters including President Truman, Secretary of Defense Louis Johnson and many members of Congress. In December of 1949 Johnson told Admiral Richard Connally: "Admiral, the Navy is on its way out. There's no reason for having a Navy and a Marine Corps. General Bradley tells me amphibious operations are a thing of the past. We'll never have any more amphibious operations. That does away with the Marine Corps.

3

And the Air Force can do anything the Navy can do, so that does away with the Navy," Johnson unilaterally cancelled the Navy's new super aircraft carrier that was designed to carry nuclear bombers, the USS *United States,* without consulting either the Navy or Congress. Shortly thereafter, Johnson announced that the aviation assets of the Marine Corps would be transferred to the Air Force. This plan was quietly dropped in response to an uproar in Congress. Johnson also barred the Commandant of the Marine Corps, in his role as chief of service, from Joint Chief of Staffs meetings including those dealing with Marine readiness or budgets. Navy budgets continued to be cut resulting in large numbers of ships being decommissioned and "mothballed". The policy was that there was only one enemy, the Soviet Union and the only potential battlefield was Europe. Risking their careers, the Navy's highest-ranking officers ranged themselves in flat opposition to the declared policies of the US Congress, the Secretary of Defense, the Joint Chiefs of Staff and the President of the United States. The "Revolt of the Admirals" ended when the Secretary of the Navy, John L. Sullivan and several admirals resigned and the Chief of Naval Operations Admiral Louis E. Denfeld was fired. The Air Force had won and the Navy and the Marine Corps took severe reductions in force, although not as much as the Air Force and Johnson would have liked. By June 1950, the Navy was down to 1 Battleship, 11 Aircraft Carriers, 4 Escort Aircraft Carriers, 13 Cruisers and 137 Destroyers, 72 submarines and various amphibious, mine force and auxiliaries. Most of these ships were in the Atlantic or the Mediterranean. Only 20% of the US fleet was in the Pacific.

When the Korean War started on June 25, 1950 , the naval forces in the Western Pacific comprised 1 Aircraft Carrier, 1 Heavy Cruiser, 1 Light Cruiser, 12 Destroyers, 6 Minesweepers, and 5 Amphibious Vessels home ported in the Philippines and Japan. Various auxiliary, transport and tenders were scattered around the Pacific from Alaska to Guam and

Okinawa.   The nearest backup combatant ships were in Pearl Harbor 4500 miles from Korea, with the majority of them being on the US West Coast, 7000 miles away.

Thus our story begins ….....

The Far East in 1950
Shaded areas show location of US Forces on June 25, 1950.

1 – Calm Before The Storm

Dawn was overcast and warm in Hong Kong on Sunday, June 25, 1950 as the USS *Percival* (DDE-452) swung at anchor in the harbor just north of the Causeway Bay Typhoon Shelter. It had rained overnight and the destroyer's deck was still wet despite the morning swab down by the deck force. The rain had also washed off most of the salt accumulated on the ship's superstructure after a week operating in a choppy South China Sea. And of course, being Hong Kong, the sides had already been cleaned by Mary Soo. Mary Soo was an entrepreneur who came aboard naval vessels as soon as they moored in Hong Kong. Her deal, usually made with the Executive Officer (XO), was that Mary Soo's girls could collect the ships food waste (for her pigs) and Mary Soo could sell Cokes on the fantail. In return her girls would come alongside in their little boats, scrub down the sides of the ship and paint a new black waterline. And so they did – they snapped a chalk line and it was the straightest the waterline had been since *Percival* came out of the shipyard.

Lt. j.g. . David "Hutch" Hutcheson, a six foot, blond, good looking, Naval Academy graduate, came out of the wardroom on the starboard side of the main deck and proceeded aft. The day was overcast and threatening, and low clouds were scudding around the Seven Dragons in Kowloon. "Probably have showers all morning." he thought, "Well, at least the the awning has been rigged over the quarter deck."

Percival's quarter deck was on the starboard side amidships.

He had just finished breakfast in the wardroom and was on his way to relieve the Officer of the Deck (OD) for the 8 to 12 watch. *Percival* and the destroyer *Radford* were nested together and shared a mooring buoy. The Essex Class Aircraft Carrier *Valley Forge* CV 45 was anchored to the east, off North Point in the Man-O-War anchorage.

Hutcheson greeted Lt. j.g. Benson, the Officer of the Deck, "Good morning Mark, what's happening?"

"Nothing much going on – Boiler 2 on line for Generator 1, Captain's ashore – his Gig is back alongside on the boom, XO's on board at the moment, liberty away at 1000 for Sections 1 and 3, holiday routine for everyone else."

"How's the liberty party going to get ashore?" Hutcheson asked. "All we have available is the whaleboat – it could take all day."

"HMS Tamar is supposed to send over a landing craft about 0930 to make runs to Queen's Pier in Central. Oh, and there is a note in the log that the old man wants the Gig to pick him up at HMS Tamar at 1700."

"Very well. You stand relieved." Hutcheson said and gave his best Annapolis salute. Benson and his Petty Officer turned over their guard belts and M1911 45 caliber pistols to the oncoming watch. David Michael Hutcheson III, "Hutch" came from a Navy family. His father and grandfather were both Naval Academy graduates. His father, Vice Adm. David Michael Hutcheson Jr., had a distinguished career in destroyers and was currently assigned to the staff of the Office of the Chief of Naval Operations in Washington.. His grandfather, David Michael Hutcheson, had been one of the pioneers in Naval Aviation, flying the famous Curtiss NC Seaplanes and retired as a Rear Admiral.

At 0800, Hutcheson mustered the duty section and found all present or accounted for.   After muster he told, Miller, the Petty Officer (PO) of the Watch, "Make sure that the bow and stern sentries are alert and watch out for any bum boats trying to come alongside to sell stuff."

Miller set off aft to check on the sentries.   Hutcheson mused that this should be a relatively easy watch – nothing much going on except getting the liberty party off.   He walked through the midships passageway to the port side and checked the mooring lines over to *Radford*.

Percival and *Radford* were both Fletcher class destroyers (DD) that were built by the Federal Shipbuilding Co. in Kearney, NJ in 1941. They had both served in the Pacific during World War II and had been decommissioned and put in "mothballs" on the West Coast in 1947.   In 1949, they were both recommissioned and converted to anti-submarine escorts (DDE) to combat the newer, faster and quieter submarines being built by the Soviet Union.   They were fitted with a larger rudder that gave them a tighter turning circle to maneuver against high speed submarines.   Three of the five 5-inch   gun mounts were removed and two dual 3-inch gun mounts were added on the   01 deck.   Anti-submarine Warfare (ASW) mortars (Hedgehog) and torpedoes were also added.   The new Anti-Submarine Warfare System was state of the art including the newest scanning sonar and a fire control computer. Hutcheson was glad to be on a DDE.   After graduating in the Naval Academy class of 1948 he had attended the Anti-Submarine Warfare (ASW) Officers course at the Fleet Sonar School, Key West.   What better assignment for a freshly minted ASW officer than a Fletcher class DDE?

As Hutcheson returned to the quarterdeck, he saw Lt. Frances X. Murphy approaching from the direction of Officers Country.   Murphy was the Command Duty Officer (CDO) that day. The CDO is the most senior officer, when the commanding officer is not aboard.   Francis Xavier "Frank" Murphy was a 6-foot, 2-inch, broad shouldered, red head who looked like the football player that he was. He was from a well to do family in Glen Cove Long Island.   His father was an Orthopedic Surgeon and Frank had grown up sailing his own 16-foot Comet on Long Island Sound. He was in the Naval Reserve Officer Training Corps (NROTC) program at Fordham, graduated and was commissioned Ensign in 1947. He had been in *Percival* ever since. Having been exposed to Jesuit philosophy and theology at Fordham, Murphy conducted Catholic services for the crew when the ship was at sea.

"The teletype bells are ringing like crazy" Murphy said. "Something is going on in Korea – the XO doesn't think it will effect us but just be sure everyone is alert."

"Yeah, well Kim Il-Sung just came back from a trip to Moscow and Beijing" Hutcheson said. "He must think they will back him up if he decides to go after South Korea."

"Let's hope not, just keep the lookouts and sentries sharp!"

As Murphy left, Hutcheson turned to the Watch PO. "You heard the CDO, stay alert – I want you to make a turn around the ship every hour – check the sentries and tell them to look out for any boats trying to make our side."

There was a light southwesterly breeze and the ships had swung on their anchor into the wind. Hutch could see the Star Ferry crossing the

10

harbor from Tsim-Sha-Tsui in Kowloon to Central on Victoria Island. There were lots of small boats and a few large freighters also transiting the harbor. Directly south there was a large number of small junks behind the breakwater in the Causeway Bay Typhoon Shelter.

At about 0945, Miller reported. "British landing craft headed our way."

"That's probably our liberty boat." Hutcheson said, "Have him make the accommodation ladder – you can call away liberty."

"Aye aye, sir." said Miller keying the 1MC PA. He put the bosun's pipe to his lips and sounded the short two note call Attention. "Now liberty commences for Sections 1 and 3 to expire at the Fleet Landing at Queen's Pier, Hong Kong at 2400 midnight." He said in his most authoritative voice.

The British LCVP approached *Percival* with the Brit bowman and stern-man doing their usual ceremonial boathook routines.

Hutcheson addressed the liberty party. "Listen up. As posted in the Plan of the Day, liberty is limited to Victoria Island. Do not take the Star Ferry to Kowloon. Kowloon is off limits, mostly lawless and extremely dangerous."

Hutcheson checked the liberty party off the ship and the LCVP was soon underway for Queen's Pier. He checked his watch – about 10:15 – only about 1-1/2 hours to go – this was pretty easy. A couple more runs of the P boat would get most of the Sailors ashore. It was mucky as hell and a bit warm but thus far no rain. He was not looking forward to his 8 to 12 watch tonight as the liberty party arrived back liberally lubricated with San Miguel beer. Naval folklore maintained that MacArthur's vow "I shall return" to the Philippines was not to liberate it but to rescue the San Miguel Brewery in which he had a financial interest. In any event San Miguel was widely available in Hong Kong and relatively cheap thus assuring it being the Sailor's favorite. Most of the Sailors landing at Queen's Pier turned left down Connaught Road and headed for Wan Chai, the red light district, where there was also a multiplicity of bars.

Miller returned to the quarter deck after his 1100 turn around the deck. "All secure," he reported to Hutch.

"Very well. Do you think those Seamen Apprentices on the bow and stern know how to use their M1's? They're just out of boot camp."

"I hope so – we took them over to the rifle range the last time we were in Subic."

"I hope so too, You go on liberty yesterday?"

"Yeah a few of us took a tour to the Peak, Tiger Balm Gardens, caught the Noon Gun at Causeway Bay and had lunch at the Repulse Bay Hotel – it was good."

"We will be here for a few days I hope to do the same, of course, that presumes this thing in Korea doesn't become a problem."

"Do you think it will?"

"Hard to tell – North Korea has a bigger army than the South and lots of Russian heavy tanks. And the people in the South aren't too happy with Syngman Ree and his government – could turn out to be a big mess."

About that time, Murphy, the CDO, arrived at the quarter deck, and by the look on his face, he was obviously concerned.

"The North Koreans' broadcast this morning that they invaded South Korea and are pushing southward. The American ambassador in Seoul estimates that about 100,000 troops have already crossed into South Korea – not good news."

Miller piped up, "The 1st Cavalry Division is in Japan – they could send them to Korea to help."

Hutcheson responded, "From what I hear, the 1st Cav is way under strength and they are all fat and lazy from being in Japan too long."

Murphy said, "The XO thinks that with all of the 7th Fleet being here in Hong Kong and in the Philippines, they will probably want to move us north closer to the action."

"Figures -- we leave before I get a chance to check out Hong Kong." said Hutch. "Have you heard from Emily?"

Murphy was engaged to Emily Sullivan who he had met when the ship was operating out of San Diego.

"No I haven't. I didn't get any mail here. If we don't go back to Subic, I hope the mail catches up to us wherever we go. She worries about me when we just go to sea off California. She'll really be upset when she hears about this."

"So will Peggy. All we can do is say a prayer and hope that this all works out."

Murphy turned and started forward to the Radio room.

13

Chief Quartermaster Alf Swenson stepped out on the starboard wing of the bridge to take a quick check that everything was shipshape before going ashore. The bridge was the crew cut Swede's personal fiefdom and he was obsessed that everything was kept in perfect order. He ran his finger along the splinter shield and, fortunately for the watch stander, didn't find any dirt or salt. QM3 Jones had just assumed the afternoon signal watch. Swenson looked up at the yardarm to confirm that the Captain's absentee pennant was flying.

He said to Jones "There is something going on in Korea and we may have to get underway in the next few days. When you get relieved at 1600, check in the chartroom to see if there are any new Notices to Mariners for the Formosa Straits and the approaches to Korea and Japan.

"OK – will do."

Swenson took another scan around the harbor then yelled ."Jones wake up! HMS Tamar is flashing D2 – that's us".

Jones jumped up to the platform for the 12-inch Signal Searchlight, pointed it at the signal tower at HMS Tamar and held down the shutter handle for a long dash. At the same time, he yelled to the bridge messenger, "Get the signal pad and stand by to write." HMS Tamar, the Royal Navy's base in Hong Kong, also includes the Headquarters of British and Commonwealth Naval Forces, Far East.

As each word was received, Jones called it out and acknowledged it with a dash on the signal lamp – being careful not to bang the shutter – there was to be no signal lamp noise on Swenson's bridge! Jones checked the message and then told the messenger to take it to the CDO.

The message was from the Captain requesting the Gig pick him up at HMS Tamar as soon as possible. He obviously had gotten the news about Korea – he wasn't due back until 1700.

A few minutes later the the Watch PO1 came on the 1MC, "Away the Gig Away."

Shortly thereafter Jones saw the Gig headed for Central to pick up the Captain. Commander Michael Brown was a product of the Navy V-12 program at Williams College. All of his time at sea had been in destroyers. He had been a lieutenant aboard the USS *Hoel* when it was sunk during a torpedo attack on the Japanese battleship Kongo in the Action Off Samar in WW-II. He had spent two days in the water before being rescued. *Percival* was his first command.

When Captain Brown reported back aboard *Percival*, he immediately called the XO, Charlie Cook, to his office. Lt. Cmdr. Cook had been an enlisted Naval Airplane Pilot during WW-II. As with many NAP's, he was eventually commissioned. He was later grounded when his eyesight degraded. In *Percival*, he was Executive Officer and also Navigator. When Cook arrived at the CO's office, Brown was reading through the pile of messages on his desk.

"Charlie this doesn't look good. What few US Naval Forces there are in the Far East are scattered all over. Our two destroyer types and the "Happy Valley" are here in Hong Kong. The cruiser Rochester and six more tin cans are in Subic Bay, Phillipines. The light cruiser Juneau, four cans and the Amphibious Group are in Japan. I suspect that they will be wanting to move us North, probably to Japan, rather quickly."

Cook said, "I have directed the Supply Officer to make sure that we

15

have 30 days of stores aboard. The SOPA[2] in *Valley Forge* notified us that a fuel lighter will top us off tomorrow. He also said that there will be a Captain's Meeting at 0900 tomorrow in *Valley Forge*."

"Yeah, I got the message on that – I want you to come with me."

At 2000, Lt. j.g. Hutcheson again assumed the deck watch just as the British LCVP was making the starboard side loaded with loaded Sailors. Fortunately the harbor was calm and the boat just bobbed alongside the accommodation ladder so it was unlikely that there would be any drunks in the water. As each Sailor arrived on deck, he saluted the ensign, saluted Lt. j.g. Hutcheson, turned in his Liberty Card and stumbled fore or aft to his berthing space. Obviously, the word on Korea had gotten around because there were many loud statements about "Fixing those gooks!" and "They don't know what they're getting into!" There was a definite miasma of malt flavored beverages in the air. Hutcheson looked at his watch – it was going to be a long evening.

Around 2200, Murphy, the CDO, was again making his rounds and stopped by the quarterdeck.

"Things are continuing to heat up in Korea. Some planes from the US 8th Fighter Group were fired on by a small North Korean convoy just south of the 38th parallel this afternoon. Also, down near Pusan, a ROK Patrol Boat sank an armed North Korean ship loaded with 600 troops, most of whom drowned. It certainly looks like this is turning into a naval war."

"It sure does and I am sure that we will eventually get pulled into it."

Both men could not help thinking of the possible dangers lying ahead.

---

2   Senior Officer Present Afloat

As Murphy continued his rounds, Hutcheson was thinking about Peggy back home in Columbus. The last time he had seen his wife was in March in Honolulu. Peggy's parents took care of Dave IV so she could fly out to Hawaii for a few days with Dave as *Percival* stopped in Pearl on its way to the Far East. It was a wonderful vacation at Waikiki but much too short. They had a great married life together starting with the post graduation wedding in the Naval Academy Chapel. The picture of them, leaving the chapel under the swords of his classmates, was on his desk. The way things were going, who knows when he would see her again.

2 – The Storm Breaks

The next morning,   Cmdr Brown and Lt. Cmdr. Cook went over to *Valley Forge* that was anchored in the Hong Kong harbor near North Point. As they arrived in *Valley Forge*, they were directed to the Flag Conference Room where the Captains conference would be held. Besides the Captains and Executive Officers there were *Valley Forge* Operations Officers,   Air Group and Squadron Commanders and members of the CarDiv 3 Staff.   Promptly at 0900 the command "Attention On Deck" was heard and Rear Adm. J. M. Hoskins, Commander Carrier Division 3 (ComCarDiv 3) came into the room and went directly to the podium. Admiral Hoskins was a World War II hero who lost his right foot when the aircraft carrier USS *Princeton* was bombed and blew up during the Battle of Leyte Gulf. He was awarded the Navy Cross and continued on active duty. [3]

"As you were" he said and everyone was seated. "As you know, the Democratic Peoples Republic of Korea launched a full scaled invasion of the Republic of Korea yesterday morning. These forces including heavy armor are pushing rapidly south and we would not be surprised if they took Seoul in the next day or so. NAVFE has received orders from Washington to insure safe evacuation of US dependents and non combatants from the war zone. Accordingly destroyers *DeHaven* and *Mansfield* are already on their way from Yokosuka, Japan to Korea to escort the evacuation ships. The entire Seventh Fleet has been ordered

---

3   The movie "The Eternal Sea "(1955) was about Hoskin's Navy career with Sterling Hayden as the Admiral.

to Sasebo, Japan to report to Vice Admiral Joy, Commander Naval Forces Far East (NAVFE). Our primary mission initially will be to neutralize Formosa, that is to prevent the Communist Chinese from crossing the Straits of Formosa and attacking Formosa. Carrier Division 3 will sortie from Hong Kong tomorrow morning at 0800. ComCarDiv 3 Operation Order 7-50 provides the details of this evolution. Captain McKloskey will go over the details of the OpOrder with you."

McCloskey started by saying "Escort Squadron 1 consisting of DDE's *Percival* and *Radford* will be responsible for providing anti-submarine and anti-aircraft protection for CarDiv 3 on the passage to the Straits of Formosa. It is planned that we will rendezvous with *Rochester* and six destroyers from Subic Bay in the Straits. At that point Task Force 77 will be formed from the combined ships and will proceed to Sasebo, Japan.

There followed a detailed discussion of the transit to Sasebo including planned air operations while in the Straits of Formosa. The air ops will be well within the range of the Chinese radars on the mainland so that the mandarins of the Peoples Republic of China (PRC) will understand that the US was keeping an eye on them. The flights will also overfly the Republic of China capital of Taipei to demonstrate the presence of the US forces in the Straits.

When the meeting was over Brown and Cook were having a cup of coffee with the Captain and Exec of *Radford* and some of the ComCarDiv 3 staff.

Elvin Ogle, Captain of *Radford,* noted "This is a really interesting development – never before, even during all of War 2, have aircraft carriers been put under the direct control of General MacArthur."

"Your right" said Brown "I guess this is the first test of how this new Department of Defense will work."

"Well I sure hope that it does" said Cook "Because NAVFE is going into this fight severely under resourced – not enough ships, planes or men.

"Speaking of NAVFE," Brown said, "I understand Vice Adm. Joy, COMNAVFE, is in Washington for his daughters wedding – wonder when he will be back?"

One of the staff guys said "My understanding is that he is going to stay in DC until after Admiral Sherman's meeting with the President today and should be back in Tokyo tomorrow with all the good news.   Vice Adm. Struble is also in Washington so our boss Rear Adm. Hoskins, ComCarDiv 3, is also temporarily Com 7th Fleet

The general sentiment among the destroyer captains and the air staff was that the Seventh Fleet had been kept in a better state of readiness than most of the other military units in the Far East.   In addition, recent training exercises this spring had put their ships and crews in a high state of readiness and they felt that the 7th Fleet ships could handle whatever tasks were placed on them.

On the way back to *Percival* in the Gig, the two men discussed the challenges facing their ship and its crew in the next few weeks.   As they approached *Percival* they could see a red Baker flag at the yardarm and a lighter was alongside delivering black oil bunker fuel.

"Well I guess our tank is full and we are ready to go." said Cook.

20

3 – Getting Ready

As the captains conference was going on in *Valley Forge*, back in *Percival*, QMC Swenson was supervising two QM strikers who were scrubbing down dirty paintwork around the door to the pilot house. The seamen had been grumbling about the fact that liberty had been cancelled today.

Swenson told them. "That's the way it is in the Navy – you never know what may happen. One day you're in port and the next day you're at sea. But in any event, we still need to keep things shipshape. You have to have pride in what you do and the ship in which you serve. What do you know about this ship and the man it's named after?"

The two strikers looked at him blankly.

"She is the second ship of the line named *Percival* – the first was a World War-1 four stack destroyer. John "Mad Jack" *Percival* was a legendary officer in the Navy during the War of 1812, the campaign against West Indies pirates, and the Mexican American War. In 1812 he was captured by the Brits and escaped, then made 3 cruises in which he captured nineteen British merchantmen and two warships. In the 1840's, he saved and restored the USS *Constitution* and then sailed the famous warship around the world, Old Ironsides' only circumnavigation. He so impressed the writers Herman Melville and James Michener that they based characters in their novels on him. Now that's the kind of tradition you have to live up to. OK – enough Naval

History for one day – back to your cleaning."

Swenson moved into the pilot house, the control center for the ship when underway. The forward bulkhead contained large portholes to provide forward visibility while being able to withstand heavy seas. In the center of the pilot house was the ship's wheel manned by the helmsman. The wheel was brass and Swenson insisted that it be kept highly polished at all times. Immediately to starboard was the engine order telegraph (also polished brass) manned by the lee helmsman and used to send ship's speed orders to the snipes[4] in the engine room. On the starboard side just forward of the door to the bridge was the Captain's chair. On the port side was a radar display and the chart table. The aft bulkhead contained telephones and radio controls on either side of the door that led to the Captain's sea cabin and the sonar shack.

Suddenly Jones on the open bridge called out "By your bag – PREP, EASY, VICTOR, ZERO, EIGHT."

Signalmen ran up the signal flags from the flag bag on the aft end of the bridge. They hauled them up to about 3-feet below the yardarm – at the dip.

Swenson called out from the pilot house, "That hoist means prepare to get underway at 0800. Two-block the hoist to show that we have received and understand."

With that the signalmen hauled the top flag right up against the yardarm. Swenson picked up the bridge phone and rang the quarterdeck.

---

4   Slang for engineering (Fire Room, Engine Room) ratings.

When the OD answered he said "*Valley Forge* showing flag hoist Prepare to get underway at 0800."

"Very well," the OD said "I will log it and notify the Captain when he returns from *Valley Forge,* although I am sure he already knows."

Swenson addressed his two strikers "Signaling by flag hoist is a another Naval Tradition going back to the days of Man-O-War under sail. It is also a very positive form of communication – when the recipient two blocks those same flags you know for certain that he received the message."

Swenson turned to his bridge crew and said "What that message means is that we will be leaving Hong Kong first thing in the morning – Special Sea Detail will probably be called away about 0700."

The news of their going to sea spread like wildfire through the ship. It was met with mixed feelings – disappointment that they were leaving Hong Kong early but also excitement that hostilities had started and they would probably be a part of it.

The two DDE's would have a big responsibility during the transit to Japan. At least for the present they would be the only anti-submarine protection for the aircraft carrier *Valley Forge.* No one understood this better than Lt. j.g. . David Hutcheson, *Percival*'s ASW Officer. When these Fletchers were modified to become DDE's, three of their five 5-inch 38 caliber gun mounts were removed and dual 3-inch 50 caliber gun mounts were added on the port and starboard side aft on the 01 level. Forward on the 01 level *Radford* had an anti-submarine rocket launcher "Weapon Able". *Percival* did not have Weapon Able but was instead fitted with a trainable hedgehog mount that could fire twenty four 7-inch anti-submarine "Hedgehog" mortar rounds in a cluster.

The whole mount could train in azimuth to point the mortar cluster directly at the submarine.   Both ships had four torpedo tubes that could launch acoustic, homing anti-submarine torpedoes.   Both ships could still drop a limited number of depth charges of a more streamlined, faster sinking, version than the traditional "ash cans". The ships also had the most up to date search and depth determining sonar equipment and a computerized fire control system.   These were formidable ASW ships designed as escorts to provide protection for aircraft carriers and battleships.   Hutcheson's concern was that even the best weapons systems are only as good as the Sailors that man them.

He passed the word for all Sonarmen to lay down to the Mess Deck at 1400.   The Sonar "Gang" consisted of a First Class Sonarman, two Second Class and three Third Class Sonarmen and four Seamen Sonar Strikers.   Because the ASW weapons were handled by the Gunnery Department, Hutcheson had asked Chief Gunners Mate Anderson to sit in on the meeting.   Also attending were Ensigns Matthews and Langan who were qualified as ASW Officers.

Hutcheson opened the meeting, "We are not sure what, if any, submarine capability North Korea has. There have been reports of four submarines in the port of Chinnampo, North Korea but this has not been verified nor do we know if they are Korean or Russian subs.   We do know, however, that two years ago, the Chinese Communist Party authorized the Peoples Liberation Army Navy (PLAN) to develop a submarine force.   The Russians have been assisting the Chinese in this effort. A couple of hundred Chinese have already received submarine training in Russia. Intelligence tells us that the Russians have built over 200 Whiskey class subs based on the German Type XXI design. We do not know if they have turned over any of these to the Chinese.   There have been as many as 12 Russian submarines spotted in the Yellow Sea at various times in the past.   We believe that there are currently about

24

50 submarines in the Siberian port of Vladivostok and there may be some closer by in Port Arthur on the Yellow Sea."

"CarDiv 3's first assignment is to patrol the Formosa Straits to insure that the People's Republic of China does not take any hostile action against Formosa under the cover of what is going on in Korea. It is entirely possible that the PLAN has submarines deployed in the Formosa Straits – either theirs or Russian. This is serious business and we are now on a wartime footing." He paused for a moment to let that sink in.

"Chief, if we go to ASW GQ, your Gunners Mates should be ready to shoot if ordered – I don't want to get ready to attack and find out your guys have hand grenades and dye markers ready because they thought it was a drill!"

"Aye Aye Sir" replied the Chief. "We'll be ready."

"We and *Radford* will alternate days on the Bathythermograph (BT) Guard." Hutcheson said, reminding them of the necessity of getting daily water temperature data to determine sonar range.

"Ensign Matthews will coordinate the schedule with *Radford*.

"When we finish here, I want all of the sonar systems lit off and completely checked out. Coordinate with the Gunnery Department and make sure that you can point the Hedgehog mount and that our target data is being transmitted to the torpedoes. Also verify that our firing signals operate to both Hedgehogs and torpedoes. Ensign Langan will be in charge of the testing. Any questions?"

PO1 Johnson, the Leading Sonarman, said "I am sure glad that we have the trainable Hedgehog mount rather than Weapon Able. From what I have heard from guys in *Radford*, they have not had great results with Weapon Able, and it's 250 pound warhead, even in exercises against a non-maneuvering sub. The Mk4 Attack Director isn't always able to complete a Weapon Able firing solution in the time between sonar contact and when the ship overruns the sub. I think we have a better system here where we can train 24 hedgehog rounds against a sub no matter how he maneuvers – and we can even do it using the Attack Plotter if the Attack Director can't get a solution."

"I agree with you." said Hutch, "Anything else?"

PO3 Mike Owen said, "As you know I just recently reported aboard and have never served in a ship that had anti-submarine torpedoes – how do we fire them and how do they work?"

"There are four torpedo tubes in the Torpedo Room back aft on the Main Deck. They use compressed air to launch the Mk-32 Mod 2 ASW Torpedo over the side. The Mk-4 Attack Director, in the sonar shack, decides when to launch the torpedo based on the subs location that it has calculated from sonar tracking data. The torpedo can operate either in passive (listening) mode or active (ranging) mode – I prefer active mode because it is more accurate even though the sub can hear it coming. Once in the water, the torpedo starts descending in a circular spiral path and sends out pings and listens for an echo. When it gets below 50 feet it arms the warhead and if it gets an echo it shifts rudder, stops descending and turns in the opposite direction. As soon as it loses the echo, it shifts rudder again. It keeps taking cuts on the sub until it runs into it and the warhead goes off."

"Oh," said Owen, "and it only arms below 50 feet so it can't sink the ship that launched it."

"That's right. And if it goes to the floor depth, that we usually set at 300 feet, it starts spiraling back up and if it gets to 50 feet it starts back down again.   It has enough battery to keep searching for about 20 minutes – when the battery dies, it sinks. And contrary to popular opinion, acoustic torpedoes have a success rate of over 20% contrasted with the depth charge's less than 10% success rate."

"Cool," said Owen, "Thanks."

"OK," said Hutcheson, "If there is nothing else – Dismissed."

They all left the Mess Deck to carry out their assignments.   In the sonar shack, Ensign Langan watched as the sonarmen powered up the equipment. The QHBa Scanning Sonar Set, is the basic search sensor that can detect subs at ranges up to 3750 yards. The QDA Depth Determining Set, is used to determine how deep the submarine is, and the OKA-1 Range Resolver corrects for the bending of the sound waves caused by water temperature changes. SO3 Green, at the Mk-4 Attack Director, had on sound powered phones connecting him to the Gunners Mate at the Hedgehog mount and the Torpedoman in the aft torpedo room. Everyone was taking this seriously and there was a lot of banter back and forth about what they would do if they detected a "real" enemy submarine.

After about an hour, Langan was confident that all systems were online and operable.   He caught up with Hutcheson in the wardroom, where he was having a cup of coffee and going over some papers. Langan drew himself a cup of coffee and sat down across the table from Hutcheson.

"All systems checked out OK." He said. "The only open item is the

27

sword transducer for the QDA. We'd prefer not to lower it in the harbor. As soon as we are in deep water tomorrow we'll check it out."

"Very well – We will probably be cruising at 20-knots going north – that is about the fastest we can go without making too much water noise for the sonar. As we get closer to Formosa, the Valley is going to launch aircraft to overfly Taipei and generally make a show of force in the Straits. Unless we get help from some additional cans, our two DDE's will have to cover plane guard and rescue duties – we sure are spread thin."

"Well" said Langan, " Isn't the rest of the Seventh Fleet also heading north from Subic Bay?"

"Yeah they are, however, we don't know when we are going to meet up with them on our way to Sasebo. I get the definite feeling that our leaders are making this up as we go along. Oh, I also just heard that *Mansfield* escorted a Swedish ship and *DeHaven* escorted a Panamanian transport out of Inchon with 700 Americans from Seoul on board headed for Sasebo."

"Boy – glad they got out." said Langan "You know, I have been thinking about something else – we will have to very careful as we go north. The South China Sea off the China coast is not very deep and it shoals up quite a bit as we get to the Formosa Straits. Most of the Strait is quite shallow – less than 200-feet. Our sonar is going to be getting echoes from things on the bottom that may sound like a submarine. All the sonarmen will have to be on their toes – check for doppler, echo quality, range rate and so on before they classify anything as a submarine."

"Your right." Said Hutcheson. " we don't want to send everybody to

28

General Quarters three times a day for false alarms or the crew will be ready to lynch the sonar gang.   I'll have Johnson talk to all of the sonarmen about contact classification procedures"

Langan finished his coffee and left; Hutcheson continued working over his papers interspersed with thoughts of home, his wife and son and when he would get to see them again.

4 – Assembling The Fleet

Captain Tom McKloskey, Chief of Staff for ComCarDiv 3 was in Flag Plot just below the *Valley Forge*'s bridge reviewing the current situation with Lt. Dave Brennan, the Staff Duty Officer. Flag Plot is the admiral's tactical and navigational control room aboard a flagship. It contains radio communication equipment, radar displays and status and plotting boards.

Brennan said, "This just came in – The United Nations recommended that their members provide assistance to the Republic of Korea as necessary to repel the armed attack and restore peace. Very shortly after that, President Truman issued an an order to Naval and Air Forces in the Far East to support operations of South Korean Forces and directed the Seventh Fleet to take steps to prevent an invasion of Formosa."

"That's certainly no surprise but now it's official and we're in it up to our necks. Any news about getting us some more ships?"

"I understand that CINCPACFLT[5] has tasked Rear Adm. Boone to organize reinforcements from ships on the West Coast and Hawaii."

"Well, I sure hope that they can get them underway fast."

"So do I. This also just in – we received a change in plans – we're not

---

5   Commander In Chief Pacific Fleet

going to Sasebo, Japan we're going to Buckner Bay, Okinawa. MacArthur is concerned because Sasebo is within bomber range of Russia – I guess he doesn't want a Pearl Harbor on his watch."

"Well, that's certainly understandable, however, we will still need to transit the Formosa Straits on our way Buckner – particularly so in light of the Truman order. What is the present position of the Heavy Cruiser *Rochester* and the tin cans?"

"*Rochester* and six destroyers sortied from Subic Bay in the Philippines yesterday afternoon and are now about 400 miles South of the Formosa Straits. The present plans are that we will rendezvous with them just south of Formosa. The Destroyer Tender *Piedmont* and the Fleet Tanker *Navasota* are also on their way to Buckner but with their slower speed, it will take them longer.'"

"Very well. I see that *Percival* and *Radford* have gotten underway and are now just passing Quarry Bay."

"*Valley Forge* will be underway shortly. When CortRon1[6] clears the Tathong Channel and are in the South China Sea they will conduct an ASW sweep to be sure that a sub isn't waiting for us on the outside."

"Good – When we rendezvous with *Rochester* and the small boys, the combined group will become Task Force 77 Striking Force."

Both men moved out to the Flag Bridge as *Valley Forge* got underway and proceeded south in Lei Yue Mun channel. The "Happy Valley" was a formidable weapon. On board was Air Group 5 considered the number one carrier and jet fighter trained group in the Pacific Fleet.

---

6 Escort Squadron 1 (*Percival & Radford*)

Air Group 5 consists of five aircraft squadrons. Two of the squadrons (VF-51 & VF-52) fly Grumman F-9F *Panther* jet fighters, the most successful Navy jet. Two squadrons (VF-53 & VF-54) fly the Chance Vought F-4U *Corsair*, considered to be the most capable carrier-based fighter-bomber of World War II. One squadron (VA-55) flies the single engine Douglas AD *Skyraider* that was possibly the best piston engine attack bomber ever built. AD's can carry a bomb load almost equal to that of the WW-II four engine Flying Fortress and can stay aloft for 10 hours. There is also a composite squadron of Special Purpose (Airborne Electronic Warfare, Anti-shipping, Carrier Onboard Delivery) AD's and F-4U's.

5 – Haze Grey and Underway

CarDiv 3 and CortRon 1 cleared Hong Kong harbor at about 0900 June 27 and were now proceeding northeasterly at 20 knots. *Percival* and *Radford* were the ASW screen steaming on parallel courses, 3000 yards apart about a half mile ahead of *Valley Forge*. The spacing between the two screen ships was a distance equal to 1.5 times the expected sonar range that day. With that spacing the two ships sonar coverage overlapped so technically a sub could not get through the screen undetected.

Radford had the Bathythermograph (BT) Guard today. Just after they entered deeper water in the South China Sea, *Radford* slowed to 12 knots and lowered the BT to measure water temperature from the surface down to about 300 feet. This data was used to compute the expected sonar range. *Radford* would repeat the procedure every four hours. Tomorrow would be *Percival*'s turn

On Fletcher class DDE's, the sonar room, or more popularly sonar shack, is in the after part of the bridge on the 02 level. The open bridge and pilot house are forward with the gun director room and the Captain's sea cabin directly aft of the pilot house and the sonar shack aft of the gun director room.

After being Relieved as JOOD on Special Sea Detail, Ens. Langan went through the pilot house and the director room to the sonar shack. As he entered, he could hear the QHBa ranging as the "stack" operator performed a standard beam-to-beam search.

"How's it going?" he said to Leading Sonarman Johnson. Johnson had enlisted in the Navy in 1945 near the end of World War-2. He went to boot camp in Great Lakes, attended the Fleet Sonar School in Key West and spent most of the following years in destroyers. He had a one year assignment to the Sonar Attack Teacher in the Destroyer Tender USS Dixie (AD 14) in San Diego. Because there are so few shore duty billets for sonarmen, tours of duty on AD's that rarely go to sea had to suffice in their stead. His wife and two year old daughter lived in San Diego.

"OK," Johnson said, "the South China Sea is pretty warm so we don't have the best sonar ranges but we are OK – if it got a little rougher, it would mix the water up a bit and make things better. Did you want to check the QDA?"

"Yeah – I think that we need to lower the sword transducer and see if it deploys and can tilt – I didn't want to do it yesterday in Hong Kong harbor."

"It is powered up – we just haven't lowered the transducer – Owen can do that now."

SO-3 Owen sat at the QDA Console and pushed the button to lower the transducer – the DOWN light came on. "It lowered OK and TILT seems to be working. We have had problems with it jamming in one tilt position – I understand everyone with a QDA has the same problem."

"But its OK now right?"

"Yes Sir – I sure hope that it works when we really need it – like in the Formosa Straits. By telling us how deep a contact is, it will help us decide whether it is a big rock or a submarine"

"I hope so too. Of course the depth determination will only be correct if the water temperatures from the bathythermograph (BT) data is entered correctly into the OKA. How are you sure that the most recent numbers are in the OKA?"

"Every time that we drop the BT," said Johnson, "or another ship sends us a Sonar Message containing BT data, we enter it into the BT Log that is in the pocket on the side of the OKA and update the OKA. Our watch change procedure requires the oncoming watch to check the log and the OKA numbers.

"Sounds like you've got it covered." said Langan, "Thanks!"

Cmdr. Mike Brown came out of his stateroom on the Main Deck, went past the Combat Information Center and went up the ladder to the 01 level where the Radio Room and the Navigation Office was located and continued up to the 02 or Bridge level. As he came through the starboard door and on to the Bridge, the Bosun announced "Captain on the bridge." The Captain proceeded forward and took his seat in the "Captain's Chair" on the starboard wing. It was a pleasant day and after hours reviewing the pile of teletype messages, Ops Orders and War Plans in his cabin, he felt like relaxing in the fresh air.

The messenger approached "Cup of coffee Captain?"

"That would be good – Thank you."

As the Captain was sipping his coffee and talking quietly to the OD, Lt.

Murphy, the messenger from the Radio Room brought him an incoming teletype message from COMNAVFE. He read it and when he finished he said to Murphy,

"This is not good news – the North Korean Army continues to push south and has captured Seoul. Not only that but the ROK Army has been routed – they are falling back rapidly trying to find a place to take a stand."

"And we are still a long way from being able to help – it sounds like they may be pushed off the Korean peninsula."

"Two shiploads of arms and ammunition have already been sent to Korea. COMNAVFE is loading the amphibious ships in Japan with US troops and supplies and they are probably going to try to make an administrative landing somewhere on the Korean east coast."

"Well, I guess all that we can do at this point is get to Buckner Bay as soon as we can."

"That's where everybody is headed. A destroyer tender and a tanker from Subic are on their way there and all the Seventh Fleet submarines have been ordered to Buckner. I just hope that we don't get tangled up in something with the Chinese in the Formosa Straits – I think they really need us up north in Korea." said the Captain as he finished his coffee.

36

6 – Formosa

Rear Adm. Hoskins was on the *Valley Forge*'s Flag Bridge surveying his newly formed Task Force 77 Striking Force shortly after dawn on June 27. CarDiv-3 and CortRon 1 rendezvoused with the *Rochester* group yesterday noon and they were now formed up in classic task force formation. *Valley Forge* was guide in the center of the formation with *Rochester* 1000 yards behind. Destroyers *Shelton, Eversole, Percival, Radford, Maddox* and *S.N. Moore* were arranged in a bent line screen at the front of the formation. Destroyers *Brush* and *Gearing* were in the "pouncer position" in the rear. Their responsibility was to attack any submarine that might get past the destroyer screen.

Hoskins looked down on the flight deck as aircraft were coming up on the elevator and positioned on the deck. At his direction, *Valley Forge* Air Group Five was preparing to demonstrate a show of force in the Formosa Straits. The Air Officer (Air Boss) directed aircraft positioning based on his planned launch sequence from his perch in Primary Flight Control (Pri-Fly). The planes were all piston engine propellor aircraft – F-4U *Corsair* Fighters and AD-1 *Skyraider* Attack Bombers. They made good radar targets and they were slower than jets giving all parties ample opportunity to observe them. One of the planes, from the composite squadron, was an AD-1Q Skyraider, an Electronic Countermeasures aircraft. It had a two man crew; an officer pilot and an enlisted electronics operator. The plane was equipped with an AN/APR-4 Countermeasures Receiver that could pick up radar signals over a wide frequency range and an AN/APA-11 Pulse Analyzer that could measure those signals and display them on a cathode ray tube (CRT). The AD-1Q's mission was to monitor and record any radar signals from Peoples Liberation Army (PLA) radars that tracked the American planes during their transit of the Straits.

Admiral Hoskins turned to the Staff Duty Officer. "Turn the task force into the wind and launch aircraft,"

"Aye aye sir."

He picked up the handset for the Talk Between Ships (TBS) radio and pushed down the key.

"Magistrate this is Jehovah – Turn Three Zero – Speed Two Five – Standby"

At the same time the signal flags Turn Three Zero, Speed two five were hoisted to the yardarm of the *Valley Forge*. On the other ships, the same flag hoist appeared – at the dip initially and then close up or "two blocked".

The Flag Quartermaster using his long glass was checking all of the ships in the task force. He turned to the Staff Duty Officer – "All ships two blocked. The OD picked up the TBS mike.

"Magistrate this is Jehovah – Turn Three Zero - Speed Two Five – Execute"

At the same time the flag signals were pulled down. The *Valley Forge* immediately started a left turn to change its direction by 30 degrees and the ship surged ahead as it picked up speed. *Rochester* turned to follow *Valley Forge*.

It was a lot harder for the destroyers – they had to dash out ahead of the carrier to reestablish the bent line screen.   In the few minutes between the "Standby" and "Execute" the JOOD on each of the ships worked on their Maneuver Boards to figure out the course and speed required for the station change.   After the course and speed was accepted by the OD (and possibly the Captain depending on his confidence in his deck watch) they awaited the "Execute".   At Execute, each destroyer came to their predicted course and sped up – most at speeds close to 30 knots. Some have described this evolution as a "Chinese Fire Drill" small ships going in every direction at high speed.   Actually it was quite dangerous and collisions have occurred.

On the destroyer bridges, the OD's and the JOOD's stood by the port and starboard peloruses checking that the bearing to all nearby ships was changing – a steady bearing means that you are on a collision course.   After a few minutes of excitement, the destroyers arrived on their new station and slowed to 25 knots.   Brush and Gearing, previously the "pouncers" were now astern of *Valley Forge* in the Plane Guard and Rescue positions in case a plane goes in the water.

Almost immediately *Valley Forge* started launching aircraft directly into the wind. The ship had two hydraulic aircraft catapults in the bow, one starboard and one port.   The combination of the catapults 80 mile per hour throw, the ships 25 knot speed and the head wind provided more than enough wind over the wing to get the plane airborne.

As the *Corsairs* and *Skyraiders* took off, they climbed to 5000 feet and formed up. Finally the formation of 29 US Navy aircraft proceeded northward in approximately the center of the Straits of Formosa.   The straits are only about 110 miles wide so they were surely being tracked by Peoples Liberation Army (PLA) radar from the West and the

Republic of China (ROC) radar from the East. The large formation of US Navy aircraft made a formidable looking blob on anybody's radar.

As the formation reached the northern limit of the straits, it turned east toward Formosa and was "feet dry" over Danshui. The purpose of this course was to insure that the population of Formosa knew that the United States Navy was here in force to keep an eye on the PLAN. The planes curved southward over the capital Taipei, proceeded south over the populous Hsinchu County and were back "feet wet" near Tongxiao.

Back on *Valley Forge*, Admiral Hoskins was in Flag Plot following the progress of the Air Group 5's show of strength over the Formosa Straits. Brennan approached, "Message from ComNavFE".

Hoskins read through the message and said, "This is really good news – the British Admiralty has placed Royal Navy units in Japanese waters at the disposition of ComNavFE. The cruiser *Belfast* which is the Flagship of Rear Adm. W.G. Andrewes, the aircraft carrier *Triumph* and destroyers *Cossack* and *Consort* are on their way to Buckner Bay. We will add them to the ships in Task Force 77."

"That is great news" said Brennan

"It gets better – all of her majesty's Australian ships in Japanese waters have been placed at our disposal and two New Zealand Frigates will be ready to leave Aukland on 3 July with more to follow."

At that point Task Force 77 was turning into the wind to recover Air Group 5. The recovery of the *Skyraider*'s and *Corsair*s on board *Valley Forge* was uneventful. As the last of the aircraft was recovered, the task force speed was reduced to 20 knots and turned into its course to Buckner Bay.

About two hours after the aircraft returned, Lt. Cdr. John Baldwin, CarDiv3 Intelligence Officer briefed Admiral Hoskins and his staff on the intelligence gathered on the overflight of the Formosa Straits. "We did not obtain any visual or photographic intelligence on this flight because we pretty much flew up the middle of the straits. The AD-1Q aircraft, however, did obtain some interesting electronic intelligence. We picked up signals from SON-4 "Whiff" radars at Dongshan in the south, Quanzhou about half way up the strait and Pingtan in the North. This radar is well known to us. It was reverse engineered by the Russians from a captured US SCR-584 radar that was developed by MIT and built by Western Electric for the US Army Signal Corps during World War-II. We had understood that the Russians had given some of these to the Peoples Liberation Army – now we know where three of them are. When we first picked up the signal on each of the three radars, they were operating in search mode with the antenna revolving at about 4 RPM. As we passed the one at Quanzhou they switched from search mode to tracking mode and locked the antenna on to one of our planes. The pilot of the AD-1Q warned the flight leader that a radar had locked up on them, however, nothing untoward occurred and the flight continued normally. Because these radars can both search and track, you can be sure that they are controlling anti-aircraft (AA) weapons. As we passed Xiamen, we picked up signals from a Miao-9 radar that is a Chinese improved version of the Russian SON-9 "Fire Can" radar. Although we have known for some time that the Chinese had developed the Miao-9 this is the first one of these that our guys have seen. We do know, however, that they are used as the fire director radar for 57 mm and 100 mm anti-aircraft guns. If we ever end up attacking China, all of these radars and their associated AA guns should be the first priority targets. We did not see anything that looked like naval shipborne radar emissions. That would be consistent with other intelligence we have that says that the Formosa invasion force is

41

made up of a few coastal patrol boats, thousands of junks and fishing boats and no "man-o-war" naval vessels."

"Well I am certainly glad that you didn't bring us any surprises – it is the last thing we need right now. Thank you commander."

Percival was on the western edge of the screen as the task force started to pass the northern coast of Formosa. They were on a heading of 080 that would take them just north of the Sakashima Islands and then around the southern tip of Okinawa to Buckner Bay on the east coast.

7 – Command Decisions

On June 25th when the Korean Conflict started, Vice Adm. C. Turner Joy, CINCNAVFE and Vice Adm. Arthur Struble, Commander US 7th Fleet had been in Washington meeting with Admiral Forrest Sherman, Chief of Naval Operations, and Vice Admiral Arthur W. Radford, Commander US Pacific Fleet. They had delayed their return to the Far East to await the outcome of a meeting on Korea at the White House on June 28th that included President Harry Truman, the National Security Council, State Department officials, Defense Department officials and the Chairman and Members of the Joint Chiefs of Staff. Admiral Sherman, who had attended as the Chief of Naval Operations, briefed Joy and Struble on the policy decisions immediately after the meeting. The two admirals flew from Washington to Tokyo and arrived on June 29 to confer with General MacArthur, and the other senior Far East service chiefs. The purpose of the next day's meeting was to discuss how the Navy's limited resources in the Far East could be most effectively used to implement President Truman's and United Nations policy directives.

Vice Admiral C. Turner Joy, a 1916 graduate of the Naval Academy, commanded a cruiser, a cruiser division and amphibious groups during WW-II. In 1949 he was made Commander In Chief, Naval Forces, Far East (CINCNAVFE).

Admiral Struble was a 1915 graduate of the Naval Academy who had commanded cruisers prior to World War II. During the war, he rose in rank and commanded amphibious and mine groups before becoming Deputy Chief of Naval Operations. Two months ago he was assigned as Commander Seventh Fleet.

General MacArthur convened the meeting on the morning of the 30th, with Struble, Joy, General Stratemeyer and members of their staffs, at his headquarters on the sixth floor of the Dai Ichi Building in Tokyo.

During World War II, MacArthur had been the Supreme Commander, Southwest Pacific Area responsible for the New Guinea Campaign, the Philippines Campaign, the Borneo Campaign and the Occupation of Japan. As the Supreme Commander Allied Powers, MacArthur and his staff helped Japan rebuild itself and institute a democratic government.

Lieutenant General George Stratemeyer, a 1915 graduate of West Point, was Air Commander of the Allied Eastern Air Command in China and the US Air Defense Command. In 1949 he was made Commander In Chief, Far EastAir Forces (CINCFEAF).

MacArthur opened the meeting.

"I was quite surprised by the order to commit US forces in Korea. This is really a complete reversal of our Far East policy. As a consequence, we have no plans for this kind of war. I was not consulted with regard to the decision to intervene before it was taken. The Joint Chiefs of Staff has assigned the Seventh Fleet to my operational control and in accordance with the Presidential Proclamation, we have committed these naval forces to the neutralization of Formosa.

Admiral Joy said, "Doug, Admiral Sherman reported to us, after the Washington meeting, that the President plans to announce a naval blockade of Korea in the next day or so. He also reported that the

44

President was visibly shocked when Admiral Sherman told him that the Navy no longer had sufficient warships to carry out such a blockade. That fact must remain Top Secret lest our enemies find out how unprepared we really are. I understand that the President still intends to announce the blockade and we will try to support it, however, it will in fact be only a "paper" blockade."

"Well," said MacArthur, "Defense Secretary Johnson and his Congressional buddies cut the hell out of the Navy and now we are faced with this fiasco. In five years we have gone from having the most powerful navy in the world to one that can't even muster enough ships to blockade a Communist third world country. Turner, we are going to have to do the best that we can with what we've got."

MacArthur turned to Struble, "At the same time, the situation on the ground in Korea demands that we provide naval gunfire support and, more importantly, naval air support to the ROK and United Nations troops. They desperately need the Navy's support to slow the North Korean advance southward."

"And we are ready to do this," said Struble, "Admiral Hoskins is prepared to sortie Task Force 77, including *Valley Forge* and the British carrier *Triumph*, from Buckner Bay on 1 July. Based on study of the problem and consultation with our allies, we feel that our naval striking power could be most effectively utilized by hitting military targets in and around Pyongyang. We plan to concentrate on airfields and aircraft and then on the railroads and bridges used to carry munitions into South Korea."

"Good," said MacArthur, "we need to strike at the Pyongyang area of North Korea as soon as possible to cut their supply lines and to show these guys that we mean business. And it's a big help having the Brits and other Commonwealth forces with us."

Stratemeyer added, "We have concentrated our fighter assets in the Fukuoka area of Kyushu, where they are closer to Korea, and General Partridge has set up an operations center there. We have also moved the B-29's of the 19th Bombardment Group from Guam to Kadena Air Base, Okinawa and are prepared to bomb North Korea."

MacArthur said: "I believe that those high altitude bombers should be used against cities and the carrier planes should concentrate on airfields, bridges and railroad yards. And besides supporting our badly outnumbered troops in Korea, we will still have to provide forces to "neutralize" the Formosa Straits. The signs are that the Peoples Liberation Army (PLA) is preparing to "liberate" Formosa. It is a pretty bad situation and Chiang Kai Shek is rightly concerned. Two months ago the Communist 4th Field Army landed on Hainan Island and captured 100,000 of Chiang's 160,000 troops and took over the island. Chiang was so badly shaken that he immediately evacuated 80,000 troops, a 25-plane air force contingent and a 7-ship naval force from the Chou San Islands near Shanghai. Our intelligence shows that the Communists have assembled 5000 vessels for the Formosa invasion and recruited 30,000 fishermen and other Sailors to man the flotilla. The PLA Third Field Army has swelled from 40,000 to 160,000 men and they are concentrated on the Fukian coast directly across from Formosa."

Struble said "I have been thinking about the Formosa problem. We have moved the 7th Fleet submarines from the Philippines to Buckner and I propose that we use them, at least initially, to patrol the Formosa Straits. In addition, the Seaplane Tender *Suisun* and a squadron of PBM *Mariner* seaplanes can be moved to the Pescadores Islands in the Formosa Straits. A squadron of PB4Y *Privateer* Patrol Bombers is being relocated to Naha Air Force Base in Okinawa where they can keep an eye on things in the Straits and along the China Coast."

"Very well." said MacArthur.

"General," said Admiral Joy, "I get the distinct feeling that the North Koreans surprised the Chinese with their invasion of the South. Is it possible that this may have put their Formosa adventure on hold?"

"It's possible but I wouldn't count on it" said MacArthur, I firmly believe that the Soviets are behind all this. North Korea would never embark on a major operation like this without the blessings of their long time benefactor Russia. I believe that the reason that Kim Il-Sung was recently in Moscow was to get that blessing. And then he went directly to Beijing to tell Mao that it was OK with the Russians. He probably also told them that while everyone is occupied with Korea, Mao could jump across the Straits and take Formosa. That's why we really have to watch what is going on in the Straits

"That may well be true," said Joy, "In any case, we are going to play hell fighting a war in Korea and at the same time keeping Mao on the mainland."

"Rip," said MacArthur to Struble, " you worked on the ROC Military Assistance Program and you know Chiang pretty well. When you get back to Okinawa I would like you to arrange to go to Formosa and reassure him that we will be keeping an eye on the Straits to discourage the mandarins in Beijing. Chiang's troops are holding quite a few of those small islands right on the China coast and there is a possibility that he may lose a few more of them before all of this is over. But Chiang also needs to know that we don't plan to go to war over those islands as long as it isn't part of an invasion of Formosa.

47

"Will do sir." said Struble, "I am sure that the ChiComms took note of our show of force in the straits a few days ago – they were sure tracking us on their radar I hope to hell that they got the message."

"So do I." said MacArthur, "Stratemeyer, what kind of fighter support can you provide in Korea?"

"We have a real problem here. Most of the aircraft we have in Japan are F-80C jet fighters designed for the air defense of Japanese cities. They are not designed for long range troop support missions and our pilots have not trained for those missions. We also have a some old piston engine F-82's that have been able to shoot down a few YAK fighters, however, we have been cannibalizing "hanger queens" to keep them in the air. They are all pretty tired and we don't have adequate spares. We have moved our F-80 Fighter Squadrons to Fukoka, Japan and a A-26 Attack Bomber Squadron to Iwakuni, Japan, putting them closer to Korea. Our problem is that the F-80's range is limited to about 100 miles so they can only loiter for a short time in Korea with a limited bomb load. Until we can get an airfield in Korea, some different aircraft or more "Misawa"[7] wing tanks, we are very limited in what we can do with jets.

MacArthur said, "The way things are going in Korea right now, your chances of finding a suitable airfield there are pretty low. In the next few weeks, the Navy will be sending additional aircraft carriers here from the West Coast. We are going to see if we can load some of your piston engine P-51 fighters on one of them and bring them out to you."

"That would certainly help. These jets are fast and can climb high but

---

7   Enlarged F-80C wing tip fuel tanks fabricated by mechanics at Misawa
    AFB, Japan that increased the planes radius of action to 350 miles.

they don't yet have the long range capability that we need. Some long range '51's would really work well for now in this situation. As soon as we get them, we will probably convert two F-80C jet squadrons to F-51's. We are also working furiously to get some of our new F-86 Sabrejet fighters out here – that would really solve the fighter problem. If our F-86's could hitch a ride on one of the carriers coming out, that would also speed things up."

Admiral Joy spoke up. "We'll see if we can help you out there."[8]

He then turned to MacArthur. "We currently have had the light cruiser Juneau and a couple of destroyers in the Yellow Sea near the frontline providing gun fire support. The problem is that they are all 5-inch gun ships with limited striking power and their range is limited to about 10 miles inland. As soon as we can get the USS *Rochester* up on the frontline, we will have nine 8-inch gun barrels with a range of 17-miles. We are also going to see if we can get some of Her Majesty's larger gun ships up there to help too. I have also asked the CNO to send the battleship USS *Missouri* (BB-63) to us, however, it is now in the Atlantic and will take quite a while to get her through the canal and out here."

"Well, " said Struble, "until we know what kind of naval forces we are up against, particularly with Russian naval units being in Port Arthur, I am reluctant to release *Rochester* from providing heavy gun protection for Task Force 77."

"That's understandable and I agree with that decision." said MacArthur.

---

8 In late November 1950, F-86 *Sabre* fighters were loaded on the US Navy aircraft carriers *Bataan* and *Bairoko* in San Diego and delivered to the USAF in Korea on December 6. Finally the Air Force had the jet fighters that they needed courtesy of the US Navy.

Admiral Joy said. "There is one other thing that everyone should keep in mind. One of the great advantages of aircraft carriers is that they are mobile and make moving targets. We lose that advantage, and in fact could put ships in peril, by staying in one place for more than two days at a time. If we are required to keep aircraft carriers on-station off Korea for extended periods, we will need many more destroyers to screen the carriers – and right now I don't know where they would come from."

Signaling that the meeting was at an end, MacArthur added. "While I have you all here, I want to say that I know that this war doesn't fit with what you were planning for after Key West. But, it is the war that we've got and we are going to fight it and win it. We are going to have to make it up as we go along and I expect all of you and your subordinates to cooperate with one another. – understood."

A chorus of "Yes Sir."

On that note, the meeting broke up. Struble headed for the airport to get a flight to Okinawa. In his car he was thinking "These Air Force guys that wanted to do away with the Navy, now need the Navy to save their asses in Korea – seems like some kind of poetic justice."

8 – False Alarm

In relatively calm seas, Task Force 77 steamed eastward toward Okinawa on the evening of the 29th. Other than the flight operations in the Straits, the transit from Hong Kong had been mostly routine -- just normal training exercises and drills. Their Estimated Time of Arrival (ETA) in Buckner Bay was 0600 tomorrow morning. *Percival* was at the northern end of the bent line screen of six destroyers.

In the sonar shack, Leading Sonarman Johnson was checking on the evening watch of SO3 Bill Tubbs and SOSN Ed MacDonald. The Sonar "Shack" was on the same level as and just aft of the pilot house. The narrow room ran athwart ships and the sonar equipment was lined up across the aft bulkhead. The QHB Sonar Console, or "stack" was on the port side and was a new scanning sonar that provided a 9-inch diameter video display of underwater targets in addition to an audio output of sub echoes. Next to the stack was the Tactical Range Recorder (TRR) that displayed the range to the sub for each ping on a paper chart recorder. The echo marks on the chart allowed calculation of the range rate -- how fast the surface ship was closing on the sub. Immediately to the right of the TRR was the OKA-1 that calculated the true range to the sub based on the temperature gradient of the sea water. Next to the OKA was the QDA Depth Determining Sonar that measured how deep the submarine was. Next was the Attack Director Mk-4, a mechanical analog computer that calculated the Course To Steer to go directly over the sub and times to fire weapons. In the corner was the anti-submarine Attack Plotter (ASAP) that provided a horizontal graphic video display of the anti-submarine tactical situation. The aft bulkhead contained weapon firing controls and status lights.

Tubbs was on the sonar stack and MacDonald was relaxing in a chair – they switched places every 30 minutes.

"Our NMC Fathometer is showing that it is only about 250 feet deep here." Johnson said "Yesterday in the Formosa Straits we were picking up some echoes off the bottom – fortunately nothing that looked anything like a sub."

"Yeah, we saw some of those last night," said Tubbs, "nothing to get excited about. The good news is that it is too shallow to drop the BT – it could hit the bottom and we would lose it. We're glad to be rid of that duty for a while"

"We are just south of the Kerama Islands and will be in reasonably shallow water all the way to Buckner – a good place for false echoes but also a good place for a sub to lurk, so keep alert"

"Sure glad to see that we're not doing anymore of those high speed flight operations – a few more hours of that and we would be on water hours with the showers turned off." said MacDonald.

"Yeah, more important to have water for the boilers than water for our showers."

Suddenly, Johnson cocked his head, "Tubbs, what's that little blip on your starboard bow?"

"Hmm – don't know, I'll slew over to it so we that can give it a listen."

As he placed the cursor on the blip and adjusted its length to get the estimated range, everyone in Sonar could hear the trailing reverb followed by a soft echo from the loudspeaker.

"Pretty solid – sounds like a little low doppler on it." said Tubbs.

"I don't hear doppler." said Johnson "Mac, what do you think?"

"I'm not sure – it might be a little low."

"OK Tubbs, go ahead and report it."

Tubbs put his toe on the foot switch to enable his microphone on the 1JT circuit that was connected to loudspeakers on the bridge and in CIC. [9]

"Sonar Contact bearing 105, range 2200 yards, echo quality sharp and clear, target width 10 degrees, doppler slight low – classified possible submarine."

On the bridge, the OD turned to the Bosun and said "Call away General Quarters ASW"

The Bosun keyed the 1MC and piped the long multi toned All Hands. "Now, General Quarters ASW, General Quarters ASW – All hands man your ASW stations." and the General Alarm sounded.

The OD picked up the handset for the TBS. "Jehovah this is Sofahound we have a sonar contact bearing 105 range 2200 yards , possible Goblin. We are turning to that bearing to investigate and pass through datum."

---

9   Combat Information Center

"Roger Sofahound – break – Gypsy Prince this is Jehovah.

"This is Gypsy Prince" the OD on *Radford* answered.

"Gypsy Prince detach and assist Sofahound – do you have contact?"

"We are seeing something near there – we are still evaluating."

"Roger"

Percival had turned to a heading of 105.   Sonarmen came bursting through the door. In a short time all of the sonar equipment consoles were manned by the General Quarters (GQ) watch.   Johnson stood behind them as the Sonar Supervisor. Lt. j.g. Hutcheson entered and took his GQ station between the Attack Plotter and the Attack Director as ASW Officer. Miller was on the JT phone circuit to the weapons stations and had the weapon arming and firing controls.

Dodge reported from the stack, "Bearing 110, 1550 yards, no doppler."

"CIC reports that their Dead Reckoning Plotter shows contact to be DIW.[10]" said Miller.

"Gypsy Prince reports no doppler and a target 20 degrees wide." reported Miller

Johnson said "Green what depth is the QDA showing?"

"I'm having trouble with it – the tilt control is erratic."

---

10 Dead In The Water

54

Dodge reported "Bearing 115, Range 1100 yards, target width 15 degrees, no doppler. – it seems to be getting wider as we get closer"

Johnson suggested "Why don't we roll one depth charge as we go over it."

"I don't think so." said Hutcheson "this is looking more and more like a piece of the bottom, not a submarine."

A s *Percival* got closer and closer the contact was getting wider and it was soon evident that it was a large rock or a reef formation.

Hutcheson reported "We are now classifying this contact non-submarine. Recommend securing from General Quarters."

Over the 1MC "Now, Secure from General Quarters. Set the normal steaming watch."

The OD on the TBS. "Jehovah this is Sofahound, sonar contact now classified non-goblin. We are breaking off and returning to station."

Hutcheson said, "While you are all here I think we need to review what happened -- Johnson do you have any comments?"

"We followed procedure -- two of us were hearing low Doppler."

"It had a sharp echo" said Tubbs "and the target didn't get wide until we got in closer."

"OK" said Hutcheson "Good job. If in doubt, we always want err on the safe side – classify as sub. Sonar contact classification is highly subjective and you have to rely on your training and judgement. There will always be promising looking contacts that turn out to be non sub – don't be afraid to report them. You are not alone – in the last few days there have been eight possible sub contacts reported by destroyers in the 7th Fleet. Keep up the good work – Resume the steaming watch."

Percival was increasing speed to 25 knots to return to it's place in the screen.

9 – Buckner Bay

Task Force 77 steamed up the east coast of Okinawa toward Buckner Bay as dawn broke on June30th. Buckner Bay, originally Nakagusuku Wan, is a well sheltered 85 square mile harbor on the southeast corner of the island of Okinawa. It was named Buckner Bay by the Americans for General Simon Bolivar Buckner who was killed in the Battle for Okinawa in 1945. He was the highest ranked American officer killed in World War II.

There was a large US Army presence at Buckner Bay during World War II, however, that had been reduced to a small Army facility, Tori Station. Typhoon Louise in October 1945 destroyed 80% of the buildings around the bay and most had not been rebuilt. There were, however, a few old abandoned Army buildings, stores of building supplies and other military gear left on the island at the end of the war.

The US Navy used Buckner Bay extensively during World War II because of its large sheltered anchorage. Literally hundreds of ships were sometimes anchored in the bay. Support facilities for the naval vessels were provided afloat by Destroyer Tenders, Submarine Tenders, Repair Ships, Cargo Ships and Tankers and there were still only limited naval support facilities ashore. There were only two piers capable of taking large vessels; Army Pier and the Navy Ammunition Pier, so most ships anchored out in the harbor. Many islands, reefs and shoal water surround the harbor entrances and protect the bay from storms -- an ideal fleet anchorage.

Percival had lingered behind the task force, off the southern tip of Okinawa, as a radar picket searching for hostile aircraft. The capital ships and the other destroyers continued toward Buckner Bay. Their air search radars were blocked by the Okinawan mountains to the west. Captain Brown was on *Percival's* bridge. The sun was just over the eastern horizon breaking through a bank of low clouds – it was warm and muggy. The ship had just secured from dawn alert. Lt. Murphy was the OD and Ens. Matthews was the JOOD and had the conn.

The TBS: "Sofahound this is Jehovah."

Langan picked up the TBS handset. "This is Sofahound."

"This is Jehovah. Secure radar picket duty and proceed inbound to Buckner Bay. Plan on refueling from *Rochester* after you arrive."

"This is Sofahound, Roger, will do."

Matthews turned to the pilot house. "Come to new course 350. make turns for two zero knots."

"Course 350 aye and the engine room answers 20 knots."

Captain Brown said to Murphy and Matthews. "It may seem a little silly to have us provide radar cover like this, except that the way things are at the moment we have no idea what the Chinese or the Russians are up to. If I were them, seeing the way the North Koreans are kicking our ass, I would just cheer them on and stay out of it."

"Boy, that sure is true." said Murphy "Things are not going well at all and the scary part is that our nearest large Naval resources are 7000

58

miles away."

"True, and what that means is that we are going to do whatever we can do with what we've got and try to hold on until help arrives. And the even scarier part is that although we have ships and planes here, we don't have the ammunition, supplies and fuel necessary to sustain a long campaign. Our having to fuel from Rochester because tankers aren't available is a good example of that "

Percival entered the Southeast Channel around Kudana Island and headed for the Heavy Cruiser USS *Rochester* CA 124 that was anchored in the center of the bay. *Radford* was just getting underway from alongside Rochester. As soon as *Radford* cleared, *Percival* requested permission to come alongside and tied up port side to *Rochester*. As soon as the mooring lines were doubled up,fuel hoses were brought over from *Rochester* and *Percival* began taking on fuel. Until fleet tankers arrived, the destroyers would have to refuel from cruisers, and aircraft carriers. After about an hour, fueling was completed, *Percival* got underway and tied up alongside *Radford* at anchorage D3 at 1000 hours. In port watches were established.

Around 1200, the Destroyer Tender USS *Piedmont* (AD 17) and the Fleet Tanker USS *Navasota* (AO 106) entered the harbor and anchored to mooring buoys in the North end of the bay close to White Beach. They had come from Subic Bay in the Philippines and had just now arrived because they were much slower than the man-o-war. Anchored nearby was the Refrigerator/Cargo Ship USS *Graffias* (AF 29) that had arrived from the west coast of the United States the day before. It was loaded with much needed food supplies.

Late in the afternoon, the British Commonwealth ships began to arrive in Buckner. Leading was the cruiser HMS *Belfast* (C35), the flagship of Rear Adm. W. G. Andrewes, RN. *Belfast* was a Town class light cruiser carrying twelve 6-inch guns and twelve 4-inch dual purpose guns and the first ship to be named after the capital of Northern Ireland. Belfast was followed by the aircraft carrier HMS, *Triumph* (R16), a Colossus class carrier and the 10th ship of the line to carry that name – the first being a 68-gun, sailing galleon in 1562. It carried the 13th Carrier Air Group consisting of the 827 Naval Air Squadron flying Fairey Fireflies, a two seat reconnaissance fighter, and the 800 Naval Air Squadron flying Seafires, a naval variant of the iconic Spitfire fighter. They were escorted by destroyers HMS *Cossack* (F03) and HMS *Consort* (R76). *Cossack* was a Tribal class destroyer carrying eight 4.7-inch guns, one quadruple 2 pounder and four torpedo tubes. *Consort* was a C-Class destroyer carrying four 4.5-inch guns, four 40mm Bofors and eight torpedo tubes.

Rear Admiral Sir William Gerrard "Bill" Andrewes KBE CB DSO was a Royal Navy officer who was in a battleship in Admiral Jellicoe's fleet in the Battle of Jutland in World War I, commanded cruisers in World War II and was now Commander, British and Commonwealth Naval Forces in Korea.

The rapidly increasing number of ships in the bay provided many juicy targets for possible Russian or Chinese submarine attacks. As a result, Seventh Fleet destroyers were put on a rotating daily schedule that kept a destroyer anchored at each of the three Sonar Guard Stations just outside the entrances to Buckner Bay. From these stations, their sonar covered the harbor approaches. The Sonar Guard destroyers set Condition 3 (wartime) watches and had two boilers on line so that they could immediately get underway and pursue any submarine intruders.

Percival and *Radford*, the only two DDE's in the Screening Group, were nested together at Anchorage D3. It was brutally hot. Okinawa at this time of the year averaged daily high temperatures of 85 degrees and humidity of 75 to 80%. The below decks berthing spaces had blower and exhaust ventilation fans but even after the sun went down it was stifling in the crew's bunk areas. The ship's steel absorbed the heat all day and then radiated it all night. Many of the crew brought their mattresses up to the 01 deck and slept there. Being that it was the tropics there could also be rain showers at night. Most of the crew had prickly heat or the infamous "jock itch". Most of the Sailors wished that they were back at sea where at least there was a breeze. They were soon to get their wish.

10 – First Air Strike

The newly reinforced Task Force 77 Striking Force , commanded by Vice Admiral Struble, had gotten underway from Buckner Bay two days ago on July 1st. The task force was made up of four Task Groups:

TG 77.1, Support Group - Rear Admiral Sir William Andrewes, RN
    Light Cruiser HMS *Belfast*
    Heavy Cruiser *USS Rochester.*
TG 77.2, Screening Group - Capt. C. W. Parker, USN
    Destroyers USS *Shelton, Eversole, Percival, Radford,*
    Maddox, S.N. Moore, Brush and *Taussig*
    HMS *Cossack* and HMS *Consort.*
TG 77.4, Carrier Group - Rear Admiral John M. Hoskins, USN
    Aircraft Carrier USS *Valley Forge*
    Aircraft Carrier HMS *Triumph*

The carriers were steaming abeam of one another about 1000 yards apart in the center of the task force with the two cruisers behind them as they proceeded north into the Yellow Sea. Eight of the destroyers were in a bent line screen in front of the carriers and the other two destroyers were in the rear pouncer positions. Since leaving Buckner Bay the task force had been performing various fleet evolutions including formation changes and flight operations. The mixed force worked very well together. The Brits had experience working with the US Navy in World War II and had recently participated in joint exercises with the US 7th Fleet in the South China Sea. The task force had gone to General Quarters twice when unidentified aircraft had flown out from North Korea and then turned back.

The task force was just south of the narrowest part of the Yellow Sea just west of Jeonbuk Province, South Korea. China was about 100 miles to the west and the major Soviet air base at Port Arthur was about 200 miles north. Not knowing what either the Chinese or Russians intentions were or the capability of the North Korean Air Force, Admiral Hoskins was seriously concerned about the possibility of attack from the nearby airfields. About 60 miles north of the task force, right in the narrowest neck of the Yellow Sea between Chaoyang on the Shantung Peninsula in China and Onjin, North Korea, was a point designated as Birddog Station Yoke. The destroyer USS *Mansfield* was steaming in a triangular course there while maintaining constant radar surveillance of the sky over the northern Yellow Sea and Korea Bay. *Mansfield* maintained radio contact with nearby Combat Air Patrol (CAP) aircraft and ComTaskForce 77. Should there be an intruder in their airspace, *Mansfield* controllers would vector the CAP aircraft to intercept and alert Task Force 77.

As the sky lightened in the east, the carriers prepared to launch attacks against North Korea. The sky was overcast with scudding clouds and raining lightly with a moderate sea. The weather forecast was for improving weather over Korea. The task force was steaming into the wind at 23 knots, the maximum speed for HMS *Triumph,* and preparing to launch aircraft. At 0500, *Valley Forge* launched two F4U's for Combat Air Patrol (CAP). They climbed to ten thousand feet, proceeded to Birddog Station Yoke and made contact with *Mansfield*. Two Anti-submarine AD aircraft were launched and they took up patrol positions ahead of the task force.

At 0545, the *Triumph* launched twelve Fairey *Firefly* two seat reconnaissance fighters and nine Supermarine *Seafires* armed with rockets. Their primary target was the Haeju airfield about 100 kilometers south of Pyongyang with secondary targets of railway and highway traffic and bridges. The Brits destroyed many planes on the ground, heavily damaged several hangers and started a number of fires in the fuel tank farm. They also damaged some bridges. There was very little opposing anti-aircraft fire.

At 0600, *Valley Forge* launched 16 F4U *Corsairs*, each with eight 5-inch rockets, and 12 AD *Skyraiders* with two 500-pound bombs each. Shortly thereafter *Valley Forge* catapulted eight F9F2 *Panther* jet fighters that were being used for the first time in combat. Although launched after the prop planes, the faster jets climbed above them and arrived at Pyongyang just ahead of the prop planes. The plan was to catch North Korean's Russian-built warplanes on the ground.

And catch them they did! They destroyed a number of planes on the ground including a large transport plane and destroyed hangars, ammunition dumps and plane shelter revetments including some with planes in them. They also scored direct bomb hits on the field's fuel storage farm starting enormous fires. All three hangers were destroyed and the runways were heavily cratered. Most of the planes caught on the ground were destroyed and those that were still flyable couldn't take off because of the severely damaged runways. Two Russian-built Yak fighters, that managed to get off the ground, were shot down in the air and a third was damaged. There was very little anti-aircraft fire, and what there was, was not very accurate. The aircraft started returning to the carriers about 0815. No aircraft had been damaged and all were recovered without incident. An excellent mornings work.

The afternoon flights were similar with Pyongyang rail yard and rail and road bridges as primary targets. The roundhouse, repair sheds and stations were destroyed. Fifteen locomotives were destroyed with ten others damaged and many boxcars set afire. Despite several bomb hits, the multi-span steel arch bridge over the Taedong River was still standing.[11] Although the strikes cause extensive damage in Pyongyang, no enemy planes came out to retaliate and anti-aircraft damage to the planes was insignificant.

When all aircraft were recovered, Task Force 77 steamed southward in the Yellow Sea to where there was more sea space. Originally, the strikes on North Korea were to be a one day operation. In view of the "rapidly deteriorating Korea situation", General MacArthur authorized another day of strikes. In *Valley Forge* and *Triumph*, crews worked through the night to maintain, repair and rearm all of the aircraft. Tomorrow was another day and a great day for the Americans, July 4th, Independence Day. What would the Founding Fathers have thought that 174 years after they declared independence from Great Britain, Brits and Americans would be fighting side by side against a common enemy in a land far away.

---

11 This bridge was bombed often during the war and destroyed. In 1951, a Max Desfor photo of refugees fleeing over the bridge wreckage won a Pulitzer Prize.

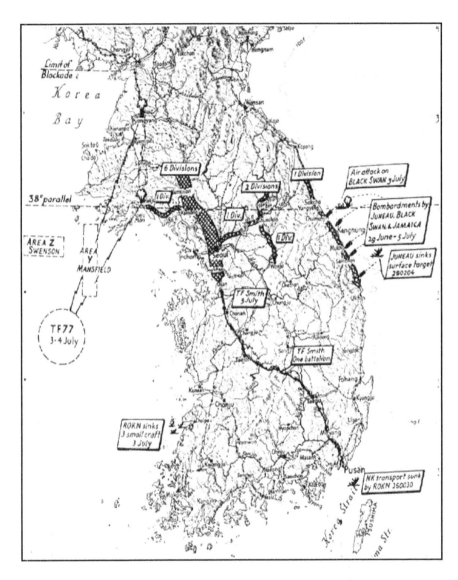

**Disposition of naval forces in the Korean War Zone in the
first two weeks of the war. Crosshatched areas show location
of DPRK (North Korean) troops.**

11 – One More Time

Overnight, Task Force 77 had retired southward out of easy range of Russian, Korean and Chinese aircraft. Around midnight the task force reversed course and once again headed northward. As dawn on July 4 approached, they were once again off the coast of Korea ready to bring the war home to the Communist enemy. MacArthur's staff had designated rail and highway bridges along the 38th parallel and some further north as the targets for the second day of attacks. Admiral Hoskins decided that his naval air assets could be more effectively utilized by returning to Pyongyang – and that is what they did.

As Task Force 77 turned into the wind and prepared to launch aircraft, *Percival* moved into the Plane Guard position 3000 yards astern of Valley Forge. The 26-foot whaleboat on the port side had been swung out on the davits and was now prepared for lowering. First Aid and Rescue equipment was loaded in the boat. The boat crew, including rescue and medical personnel, donned lifejackets and helmets and stood by on the main deck under the whaleboat. Any time that the carrier is launching or recovering aircraft, the crew is in the boat ready to go. If a plane goes into the water either on launch or while landing, the Plane Guard destroyer immediately goes to the scene and puts the whaleboat in the water to rescue the pilot. One thousand yards astern of the Plane Guard destroyer is the Rescue destroyer that backs up the Plane Guard.

Lt j.g. Hutcheson was the OD and had the conn on the 8AM to 12 Noon watch. Ens. Langan was the JOOD. Hutch had just maneuvered *Percival* into the Plane Guard position and was trying to get the correct stationkeeping speed. The task force was steaming at 23 knots into the wind in preparation for launching aircraft,

"Range to the guide." he called to his phone talker who relayed the request to the Radar Operator in the Combat Information Center (CIC).

"3100 yards to the guide." the talker called out.

"Add five turns." Hutcheson said to the the Lee Helmsmen.

"Engine Room answers 235 turns." said the Lee Helmsman.

Hutch said to the talker "Tell CIC radar to let me know when we close to 3000 yards from the Guide.

"CIC says will do"

Captain Brown was sitting in the port side "Captain's Chair" a short distance behind Hutcheson.

"It seems to me that blowing up North Korea is a very appropriate way to celebrate Independence Day."

"I agree." said Hutch. "The airedales sure had a good day yesterday -- they evidently really tore up Pyongyang."

"They did.   And I certainly hope that the speed with which the Navy got here and did the job is not lost on the Congress and others who wanted to do away with the Navy and more particularly Navy Air."

"I'll drink to that" said Hutch.

At that moment the Bridge Talker called out "CIC reports range to the Guide now 3000 yards."

"Roger that." Said Hutch. "Drop five turns."

"Engine room answers 230 turns." said the Lee Helmsman.

Hutch turned to Langan. "Mr. Langan, you have the conn, maintain station on the guide."

"I have the conn." responded Langan.

"Magistrate this is Jehovah, commence Flight Operations." came over the TBS.

Hutcheson turned to the talker. "Tell the crew to man the whaleboat."

"FOX flag two blocked on *Valley Forge*." the quartermaster called out.

The FOX (F) flag indicated that the carrier was conducting flight operations.

On the main deck, the Ensign Costa and the crew clambered up the ladder to the whaleboat. They settled into their assigned places and tried to get comfortable in spite of their bulky kapok life jackets and steel helmets. They were there for about 45 minutes as the AD-1 and F4U prop aircraft were launched and headed off to North Korea and flight operations ended.

69

On the bridge, Hutcheson said to the talker "Tell the boat crew that they can stand down until the returning aircraft start to land."

He walked into the pilot house to look at the radar display. The display was switched to show data from the AN/SPS-6 Air Search Radar. The Plan Position Indicator (PPI) display was set on the 200-mile range scale and blips from the departing aircraft could clearly be seen approaching the Korean coast. A few minutes later the blips disappeared as the planes went out of radar range.

Over the next hour everything was quiet. The task force continued on the same course that brought them closer to North Korea and a shorter flight for returning aircraft. As the returning aircraft appeared on radar the tension aboard *Percival* increased as it always does when aircraft return from combat. The whaleboat crew was standing by on the deck under the whaleboat.

Hutch told the talker "Man the whaleboat and tell the boat crew that four of the AD *Skyraider*s have been damaged by enemy anti-aircraft fire and we may have to rescue someone."

The planes started to land and aircraft recovery proceeded uneventfully. As each plane landed and caught an arresting wire with their tail hook, they came to a sudden stop. A steel cable barrier across the the middle of the flight deck was then lowered and the plane taxied forward over the barrier cables to join the other planes parked at the forward part of the ship. As soon as the plane cleared the barrier it was again raised to catch any landing plane that wasn't stopped by an arresting wire.

All planes were back aboard *Valley Forge* except for one AD whose pilot couldn't lower the wing flaps because of battle damage. Without flaps, he couldn't slow the plane down to normal landing speed. The Air Officer had kept him until last because if he crashed on the deck no one else could land. It also allowed the AD to burn off more fuel to reduce the fire hazard.

Finally, the troubled AD came up astern of *Percival*. He was about 800-feet high as he passed *Percival* to starboard. As he passed Valley Forge on the starboard side, he started a sharp descending left turn. As he continued the turn, he passed over *Percival* again at about 300-feet.

Hutch said to the Captain. "His landing gear and arresting hook are down but his flaps are definitely not extended."

"Yeah, and he's going pretty fast."

Both men were following the plane with their binoculars. Chief Swenson had a Long Glass[12] braced on the signal lamp so he could watch the landing area on the carrier.

The AD straightened out as the pilot lined the plane up with the flight deck.

Chief Swenson called out, "The Landing Signal Officer on the stern of the carrier is signaling to the AD that he is a little high."

As the plane passed over the stern of the carrier, the LSO signaled cut, the pilot pulled back the throttle and the plane started to drop to the deck. He hit the deck and bounced.

"Oh no." Hutch yelled. "He is going to bounce over the barrier."

_____

12 A Nautical Telescope

The AD went about 20-feet in the air, went over the barrier and crashed into the planes parked up forward.   As the AD came down, it's left landing gear collapsed and it swerved toward the port side of the ship pushing another plane out of the way.

"He's going over the side." said Hutch. "tell the whaleboat crew to standby"

Over the TBS: "Magistrate this is Bearcat. We have a plane and pilot overboard port side – am coming left to swing the stern away from him."

Hutch picked up the TBS handset. "Bearcat this is Sofahound we will backup your Lifeguard helicopter.   Our whaleboat will be in the water in the next six or seven minutes."

"This is Bearcat. Roger."

"Mr. Langan," said Hutch, "I have the conn."

"All ahead two. Make turns for 15 knots." called Hutcheson to the Lee Helmsman.

"Ahead two – 15 knots"

"Mr Langan." Hutch called. "Stand behind the helmsman and coach his steering. I want to be about 50 yards to the right of the pilot."

"Aye aye"

About a minute land a half later Hutch called " All stop."

72

"Engine Room answers All Stop."

The ship continued forward.

Hutch could hear Langan. "A little further right – we don't want to go too close. That's good . . . OK. Steady as you go."

The Captain had gotten out of his chair and was now standing directly behind Hutcheson.

"All back one" Hutch called.

"All back one."

Black smoke belched from the stacks and the ship started to vibrate as the engines reversed and the twin screws pulled back against the ship's forward motion. The ship was slowing rapidly.

The TBS: "This is Bearcat. Lifeguard One reports pilot in the water in life vest, however, he cannot lift his arms to get into their rescue sling."

"Bearcat this is Sofahound. We are coming up on the crash scene now and have the pilot in sight. We will have a boat in the water shortly."

"All back two." Hutch called. The ship vibrated even more and many of the metal fittings were rattling loudly. Water was boiling up around the stern, and the ship was now barely moving through the water.

"All stop. Launch the whaleboat."

"Engine room answers All Stop."

The pilot in his yellow "Mae West" life vest was about 60 yards off *Percival*'s beam.

Hutcheson looked over the wing of the bridge. The whaleboat was being lowered, the engine had been started and all hands were holding onto the monkey lines for safety. The ship was still moving slowly. When the boat was in the water, the Sea Painter became taught pulling the boat along until the boat's engine started moving it forward.

Hutch picked up the Loud Hailer.

"On the Foc'sle. Mind the Sea Painter we don't want to foul the whaleboat's screw."

The bow man and stern man pulled the release hooks freeing the boat from the davit's lowering lines and the bow man threw off the Sea Painter. The Foc'sle crew quickly pulled it aboard.

The Lifeguard One helicopter had moved off about 100 yards and Valley Forge was stopped about a mile away.

In short order, the whaleboat was alongside the pilot and hands grabbed his life vest to hold him. It was obviously very painful when they tried to pull his arms. One of the Sailors went over the whaleboat's side and into the water and held onto the gunnel with one hand while he lifted the pilot with his other arm. Others in the boat then grabbed his belt and pulled him aboard. He was kept face down until his back could be checked. The corpsman immediately looked to his injuries. In a few minutes, the signalman in the whaleboat blinked back to *Percival*:

"Pilots shoulder dislocated. Other than wet and shook up, appears OK.".

74

"Sofahound this is Bearcat, we are coming toward you now. Would appreciate your delivering our pilot back to us."

"This is Sofahound, Roger will do. Pilot has injured shoulder but otherwise OK."

"This is Bearcat. Thank you and tell everyone involved job very well done. We will have the ice cream ready for your boat crew and have them make our port side."

It is an old Naval tradition that crews returning downed pilots to their carrier are rewarded with ice cream.

"Quartermaster," Hutch called. "Send to the whaleboat to make the port side of *Valley Forge* and job well done"

Captain Brown though appearing nervous at times had not spoken during the rescue. "Hutch, that was an outstanding job. I would not have come in as fast as you did, but it was a great piece of ship-handling and you got the ship stopped on a dime in just the right place. Using Langan to coach the helmsman was a good idea. I hope you didn't rattle any of the wardroom china loose with your hard back down."

"Thank you sir. The boat crew also did an excellent job."

"Yes they did."

While the rescue was going on, Task Force 77 had turned around and was now proceeding eastward toward the east China Sea and back to Buckner Bay. After the pilot was returned to *Valley Forge*, the whaleboat came back alongside and was hoisted aboard. *Percival* then proceeded at 30 knots to rejoin Task Force 77.

At 1145, Hutch was relieved by Lt. Frank Murphy.

"Frank, we are steaming at 20 knots on course 170 headed to Buckner Bay. Boilers 1 and 3 are on line, Generators 1 and 2 are on line, OTC[13] is Task Force 77, Captain is in his cabin. Mr. Langan has the conn. We have been encountering a few junks – all of them seem to be fishermen. We are on the western side of the screen. The Chinese mainland is about 120 miles on our starboard side.

Murphy said. "I read the log. You certainly had an interesting watch this morning."

"Yeah, it was a bit exciting here for a while. *Valley Forge* lost a few aircraft besides the AD that went over the side. A jet *Panther*, two prop *Corsairs* and another AD. What a mess – fortunately there wasn't a fire."

"Well I, I sure hope that things are uneventful this afternoon." said Murphy. " You stand relieved."

Murphy looked over the task force spread out around him through his binoculars. "This is unbelievable." He thought. "The North Koreans make a surprise invasion of the South and here we are nine days later bombing the shit out of their capital with an American and British task force of two carriers, two cruisers and ten destroyers on Independence Day. I'll bet these guys didn't realize what they were getting into. I just hope that the Chinese and Russians stay out of it."

---

13 Officer In Tactical Command

Ensign Matthews relieved Langan and assumed the conn.

"Sir'" The Bridge Talker said to Murphy. "Sonarmen on the fantail request speed of 12 knots for scheduled BT drop."

"Roger" said Murphy, "Tell them to standby."

Murphy picked up the TBS handset. "Jehovah this is Sofahound, request permission to slow to 12 knots to drop BT."

"Sofahound, permission granted. Report when you are back in the formation."

"Roger"

Murphy turned to Matthews, "Slow to 12 knots so the sonarman can drop the BT."

"Aye, aye", said Matthews and then turned to the Lee Helmsman. "All ahead two. Make turns for one-two knots.

"12 knots aye."

It took the ship a few minutes to slow down.

Turning to the Bridge Talker, Murphy said. "Tell the fantail that we are at 12 knots and to drop the BT and do it smartly so that we can rejoin the task force."

"Aye – Fantail reports that they are dropping the BT smartly."

"Sonarmen are a bunch of smart asses." observed Murphy.

About five minutes later the phone talker said, "Fantail reports that the BT is back on board, the boom is rigged inboard and they have a good glass slide."

Murphy observed, "That actually was done pretty smartly. Tell the sonarmen well done."

Matthews turned to the Lee Helmsman. "All ahead full, make turns for two-five knots."

"Aye. 25 knots."

The ship surged ahead. At about that time the Bridge Talker said, "CIC reports that they have a Bogey[14] on radar at a bearing of 280 range 90 miles."

Murphy picked up the TBS handset. "Jehovah, this is Sofahound we have a Bogey bearing 280, range 90 miles.

Sofahound this is Jehovah designate Bogey Able, Sofahound tracks. Report CPA."[15]

"Roger" Murphy said.

Murphy called into the pilot house. "Switch the Radar Display to the Air Search Radar so we can watch this guy."

He turned to Matthews the JOOD after looking at the radar. "That Bogey looks like it's coming out of China."

---

14 Unidentified aircraft.
15 Closest Point of Approach

"Oh boy, that's all we need."

The Bridge Talker said, "CIC reports Bogey Able, bearing 282 range 79 miles and he is coming directly at us.

"Magistrate this is Jehovah, Turn 60, Speed 23, Standby."

Langan said "Jehovah is obviously also tracking Bogey Able, they didn't even wait for us to report that CPA was right at us."

Murphy had been calling the Captain every time there was a new development.

The Bosun called out. "Captain on the bridge."

"Good afternoon Captain." Murphy said. "It looks like they are getting ready to turn us into the wind and launch aircraft."

"Call away General Quarters."

"Aye Aye Sir."

The Bosun keyed the 1MC and piped the long multi toned All Hands "Now, General Quarters , General Quarters. All hands man your battle stations." and the General Alarm sounded.

Captain Brown said, "If I was a betting man, I would say that as soon as Bogey Able thinks that he has us all stirred up he will scurry back into China."

Murphy and Matthews remained on the bridge as OD and JOOD were their Battle Stations.

As Battle Stations were manned, the Mark 37 Gun Director above their heads noisily slewed around until it was pointed along the bearing to the bogey.

"Magistrate this is Jehovah, Turn 60, Speed 23, Execute."

Task Force 77 then executed the high speed maneuver necessary to get aligned for flight operations. About 5 minutes later Valley Forge launched two F9F *Panther* jets that immediately climbed out and turned toward Bogey Able.

The Fire Control Officer's voice came over the 1JP loudspeaker. "We have the Director pointed along the target bearing and we are searching up and down in elevation. We are getting occasional hits but nothing that we can track. It looks like he is just outside the Mark 25 Radar's 100,000 yard maximum range.

About 3 minutes later, CIC reported that Bogey Able had turned around and was now headed for China.

On the 1JP loudspeaker the Fire Control Officer said, "He was just getting into range and we were tracking manually when he turned away. He was definitely a fast mover. If he had a radar detector, our tracking radar probably lit up his lights."

"Magistrate this is Jehovah. We vectored two *Panthers* out after the bogey, however, he turned and ran and our pilots never got a visual on him. The bogeys speed says to us that it was probably a Russian-built MIG-15."

Captain Brown turned to Murphy and Matthews. "I should have put some money on it with you guys. At least enough for steaks in the Army O-Club in Buckner."

The next hour or so was taken up with recovering the two *Panthers*, reorienting the task force and getting back on the course to Buckner Bay.

The task force arrived back at Buckner bay on the afternoon of July 6. There were now more auxiliary ships anchored in the bay than when they had left. Like everything else, the Navy logistics system had been in catch up mode since June 25. The Destroyer Tender USS *Piedmont* (AD 17), the Fleet Tanker USS *Navasota* (AO 106) and the Refrigerator/Cargo Ship USS *Graffias*(AF 29) had arrived in Buckner a few days before. This was the first opportunity since leaving Subic for the Seventh Fleet ships to replenish stores. When the Landing Ship Dock USS *Comstock* (LSD-45) arrived at Buckner, its landing craft were quickly commandeered to deliver stores to the ships in the harbor. More cargo could be moved this way than by having the ships come alongside the *Graffias* or the *Piedmont* to load. The supplies situation was so critical that a decision was made to transfer all of *Graffias*'s cargo into *Piedmont* as quickly as possible so that *Graffias* could return to the US for another load.

Almost all of the 7th Fleet ships were undermanned because of the recent cutbacks of Navy funding.. Sailors were being pulled off ships in the US and flown out to Okinawa. With few naval facilities ashore, the *Piedmont* had quickly become a de facto receiving station for personnel reporting to ships in the 7th Fleet. In the last few days the destroyer tender fed 1200 Sailors a day. The *Piedmont* Repair Department also salvaged materials left near the Army facilities at the end of WWII to construct a much needed boat landing at White Beach.

Percival went alongside the tanker USS *Navasota* to take on fuel. They were then directed to go alongside Baker Docks in Buckner Bay instead of anchoring out as they had done before.

12 – Mission to Taipei

Hutch had showered and was getting dressed as he heard over the 1MC loudspeaker, six strokes of the bell and then: "Seventh Fleet Arriving."

"Holy shit," he thought, "that's Vice Adm. Struble coming aboard. No wonder we pulled alongside the pier last night." Hutch knew that they were scheduled to get underway on July 7 but thought that it was for some routine exercises off Okinawa. Obviously there is something much bigger afoot.

The 1MC announced "Now go to your stations all the Special Sea Detail." He quickly finished dressing picked up his hat and headed for the wardroom to get a cup of coffee to take to his station on the Main Deck amidships.

As he entered the wardroom there was no sign of the admiral but there were a couple of brown shoes[16] sitting at the table drinking coffee. Hutch introduced himself and found out that Commander C. F. Skuzinski was commander of Patrol Squadron VP-28 flying PB4Y *Privateer* Patrol Bombers and Lieutenant Commander M. F. Weisner was commander of Patrol Squadron VP-46 flying PBM *Mariner* Seaplanes. They were vague about why they were there other than to say that they had come with the admiral.

A Mess Steward came into the wardroom and said "Mr. Hutcheson, the

---

16 Naval Aviators wear brown shoes – the rest of the Navy wears black shoes.

Captain wants to see you in his cabin."

"Thank you" said Hutch and started down the Officers Country passageway.

"Come in – At ease" said Captain Brown. "You undoubtedly heard Admiral Struble piped aboard. We are going to make a high speed run to take the admiral and two aviators to Taipei, Formosa. Admiral Struble knows Chiang Kai-Shek, President of the Republic of China (ROC), quite well. General MacArthur has asked Struble to go to Taipei to talk to Chiang. The admiral is going to meet with Generalissimo Chiang Kai-shek, tomorrow morning. The aviators are going to meet with their counterparts in the ROC Navy. Because of our space limitations, the admiral came without staff – I have offered your services as aide to take notes and be otherwise useful to him during his time in Taipei. The crew knows that we have an admiral on board and they will soon figure out that we are going to Formosa. The meeting with Chiang is Confidential so don't talk about this to anyone. After we get to sea you will meet with the admiral to find out what he needs. I'll have the XO take you off the Watch Bill so that you can devote all your time to this. Any questions?"

"No sir – I will do my best to help Admiral Struble on his mission."

"Very well – carry on. Remember discuss this with no one."

"Aye aye Sir."

As Hutch came out on deck to go to his Sea Detail Station, he noticed that the mooring lines were singled up and line handlers were standing by on the pier.

The 1MC. "The Officer Of Deck is shifting his watch to the Bridge."

Shortly thereafter, *Percival* backed away from the pier and turned toward the Southeast Channel. As soon as they cleared Kudana Island, the ships speed increased to 25 knots and they secured the Sea Detail. Hutch went to his cabin, buffed up his shoes and put on a clean pair of khakis. He had been told to be prepared to meet Struble at 1000 in the wardroom.

Precisely at 1000, Hutch entered the wardroom. In a few minutes Admiral Struble and the Captain came in. "Attention on deck," said a steward. Hutch snapped to attention.

Struble said "At ease – Hutcheson I am glad to meet you. I know your father quite well – a good man."

"Thank you sir."

"Captain Brown told you generally what is going on. I have been involved with the Military Assistance Program for the Republic of China for some time and the Generalissimo and I are friends. The Generalissimo is concerned that we are moving naval forces to Korea and we will not be able to protect Formosa from invasion by the Peoples Republic of China. The two aviators, that are going with us, will talk to Chiang's Naval commanders about coordination with them while using the PBM's and P4Y's to patrol the straits and the China coast. We are also going to explain to them how we will use submarine patrols in the Straits. This should be a friendly meeting and is primarily to reassure Chiang that we still have his back while we are fighting in Korea. I would like you to take notes in the meeting. Robert C. Strong, the U.S. Charge d'Affairs in Taipei will be there and I am sure that he will prepare a report but I would like a record of my own. Can you do that?"

"Yes Sir, I certainly can."

"Very well, we will be in the port of Keelung, Formosa in the morning and our meeting is tentatively scheduled for noon at the Presidential Office Building in Taipei. The US Consulate is supposed to have cars for us at the pier. Any questions – if not I will see you in the morning."

"Aye aye sir."

After lunch, Hutch rooted through a stack of magazines in a corner of the wardroom looking for recent news magazines. He found a couple Times and a US News and World Report that had some articles about China and recent hostilities between the PRC and ROC over Hainan and other ROC claimed islands along the China coast. He returned to his stateroom with his reading for the afternoon.

13 – The Generalissimo

Percival had tied up to a pier in Keelung, the port for Taipei, at about 0700 this morning. Hutch was in the wardroom drinking coffee and talking to the two airedales about the upcoming mission to Taipei. Right now, they were all just killing time until their transportation arrived.

Hutcheson said to Weisner "I understand that your PBM's were scattered all over the Far East when this started."

"Yeah they were" said Lt. Cmdr. Weisner, "Five of PatRon[17] 46's 13 PBM Seaplanes were in Yokosuka, Japan and three were at Sangley Point in the Philippines. We had just relieved PatRon 47 and their planes were on their way home. Three had already gotten to Hawaii, one was in Guam and one was between Guam and Hawaii when we called them back. And just to make it a little more complicated, our Seaplane Tender USS *Suisun* (AVP- 53) was in Tanapag Harbor, Saipan."

"Well at least all of PatRon 28's PB4Y Patrol Bombers were together at Agana, Guam." Said Cmdr. Suzinski. "We got them in the air in a hurry and flew them to Iwakuni, Japan. We've got our planes in theater and now I guess we're going to find out what they want us to do with them."

"It seems to me" said Hutch "that they will probably want you to keep

---

17 Patrol Squadron

an eye on Mao to see if he tries to invade Formosa."

"Well," said Weisner, "We certainly have the planes to do that kind of a job. Both the PBM and the P4Y have a range of about 2500 nautical miles so we can certainly keep an eye on China even from Okinawa. There has been some talk of moving some PBM's to the Pescadore Islands in the Straits of Formosa. That would be good except during typhoon season when we would have to move them back to Sangley Point in the Philippines.

At that, the quarterdeck messenger came in and said: "Gentlemen, your cars are on the pier."

As they arrived at the quarterdeck, the OD said. "The admiral is going in the first car with the Charge d'Affairs – you guys are going in the second car."

The three officers got into their car and the two cars proceeded off the pier, through the port gate and on to Highway 1. The road wound through some fairly rugged hills as the highway climbed toward Taipei.

Hutch asked, "Who are you guys going to confer with?"

Cmdr.. Suzinski replied "We are supposed to meet with Chou Chih-jou, one of Chiang's aides, and some senior Navy and Air Force people about how we will keep an eye on China. It appears that the plan is to try to reassure them that we have got the straits covered."

"Good luck" said Hutch. "I understand that plans are being considered to move a couple of submarines into the Formosa Straits. That should help."

Just then the cars pulled up in front of the Presidential Office Building. It was a large six-story stone building with a 180-foot tower at its center designed and built by the Japanese in 1919 during the time when they ruled the island. Like many important Japanese buildings, it faced the rising sun.

Struble, Strong and Hutcheson were greeted on the front steps by two Chinese officials who Struble and Strong knew. Struble introduced Hutcheson and they entered the building. Two Chinese Naval Officers introduced themselves to the two US Navy aviators and led them into the building. The Struble group entered the building and took an elevator up to the sixth floor that contained the Presidential Offices. They went into a large fairly ornate room with groupings of easy chairs. As they entered, Struble and Strong were greeted effusively by Generalissimo Chiang Kai-shek and Madam Chiang. Struble introduced Hutcheson to the Chiangs and to Admiral Kwei. Madam Chiang, who had been educated at Wellsley College in the US, interpreted for her husband.

After the greetings and some small talk, all were seated, the official interpreter was brought in, and discussions began. Hutch sat next to Struble with his pad and pen at the ready. The Generalissimo said to Struble, "I am very happy that you came to Formosa. What is happening in Korea and what is the strength of Seventh Fleet in the Formosa area."

Admiral Struble said "Our naval forces are getting stronger. The addition of the Commonwealth ships has been a big help. Task Force Yoke consisting of the aircraft carrier *Philippine Sea*, two cruisers and eight destroyers plus some support ships is expected to leave the West Coast on the 15th and to be in Okinawa by August 4. As you know our patrol squadron commanders are meeting with your staff today to plan patrols by both PBM's and PB4Y's in the Formosa Straits. On July 18, the submarines *Catfish* and *Pickerel* are going to start patrolling along the China Coast including around the islands.

"Very good," said Chiang through his interpreter. "We would also like to use our naval forces to continue reconnaissance of the coastal areas."

"The US has no objection to that," said Struble. " because it is essential to your defense. I also have to say that we have had excellent cooperation with Chou Chih-jou and Admiral Kwei and his staff and the other ROC officials we have been dealing with."

"Boy oh boy," thought Hutch as he continued writing, "he is walking a tightrope here. It would be good for us if the ROC Navy would keep an eye on things along the China coast but we sure don't need them provoking the PRC into some aggressive reaction."

"As you know," said Struble, "the Secretary of Defense appointed Rear Admiral Jarrett to be Senior Military Attache' in Formosa along with officer representatives of the three US military services. We believe that this will strengthen the link between the Seventh Fleet and your government.

"We appreciate that, however, we still believe that the Communists are planning to attack us within the next 40 days." Said Chiang. "They will attack us even if they know that they cannot win. You must be vigilant because they will probably launch air attacks against your fleet."

"You can be assured that we are on the highest state of alert." said Struble.

Hutch was scribbling furiously.

I have to tell you, "said Chiang. "that I do not believe Admiral Cooke's assessment that Mao has abandoned plans to invade Formosa."

Adm. Charles M. Cooke (ret.), former Commander US 7th Fleet, had recently been in Formosa as a private citizen and had lunch with Chiang, an old friend.

Hutch was thinking. "Struble really can't say what he thinks about his predecessor's opinions on a matter this touchy."

Struble did not comment. Conversation continued concerning Military Assistance to the ROC and some logistics problems.

Struble said, "This was a rather quick trip, however, I want to come back in the near future in order to firm up some liasion details with you."

The Generalissimo recalled, "You know that I took over Formosa as Allied Commander of the Chinese theater pending a peace treaty while General MacArthur took over Japan and other areas as Supreme Commander Pacific.   Now the Chinese government is here on Formosa. I hope that despite this fact you would not feel that you were coming to foreign territory in visiting Formosa.

"Absolutely not." said Struble

Chiang said. "Admiral, I encourage you to return to Formosa anytime. I have a special regard and real friendship with the US Naval Commanders in the Far East. The Navy has always been willing to come to help friends in need."

91

"Thank you very much Generalissimo. I think that you will definitely be seeing more of me over the coming months."

On that pleasant note the meeting ended. Hutch continued writing and reviewing his notes. Struble and Strong made small talk with Chiang and his staff for a few minutes and then they made their way to a nearby office to call on Chen Cheng, Premier of the Republic of China. The meeting lasted about 40 minutes and was mostly an exchange of pleasantries. Hutch did not take any notes.

As they went down in the elevator, Hutch said to Struble. "I'll get these notes organized and typed up when we get back to the ship."

"Good. Mark them CONFIDENTIAL and don't make any copies. And remember, don't discuss this meeting with anyone."

"Aye, aye sir."

As they went on board *Percival*, the Special Sea Detail was being set and within a half hour they were steaming down the main channel and out of Keelung harbor.

Hutch was hard at work in his stateroom converting his notes into a report that could be typed up by a Yeoman. After giving the draft to the Yeoman in the Ships Office he went to the wardroom for dinner. The Admiral, the Captain and the two airedales were there in addition to the ship's officers. Dinner proceeded pleasantly with a lot of small talk, a few jokes and some sea stories. One of the Navy's great wardroom traditions is that there is to be no discussion of work, religion, politics or women.

After dinner, Hutch went to the Ship's Office and picked up his report.

He read it over carefully to make sure there were no typos or other errors. Verifying that it was OK, he thanked the Yeoman and went up the passageway to the admiral's cabin and knocked.

"Come in. Oh it's you Mr. Hutcheson – that was quick."

"Thank you sir. I hope it's OK."

The admiral immediately started reading the report. When he finished, he said. "Very good job. It certainly was an interesting meeting and you got to meet the two top men in the Koumintang government

"Yes sir, it certainly was interesting and I appreciate the opportunity to serve you on this mission."

 You were a big help and the next time you see your Dad, give him my best."

"I certainly will sir. Thank you."

Hutch went down the passageway to his stateroom. Fortunately he was still off the watch list so he could sleep through the night – which he did. In the early morning hours, *Percival* arrived in Buckner Bay and tied up alongside the tanker USS *Navasota* to take on fuel.

The Captain's Gig took the admiral over to the White Beach Navy pier. When *Percival* finished fueling they got underway and tied up alongside the USS *Piedmont* for some badly needed maintenance.

14 – Buckner Break

For two days *Percival* had been alongside the Destroyer Tender USS *Piedmont* (AD 17) receiving some repairs and routine maintenance. Tenders have facilities not available in destroyers such as machine shops, optical shops, electronic test facilities, calibration labs, etc. There is engineering and technical help available to assist with complicated repairs. The tender also has medical and dental facilities. When the repairs and maintenance were complete, *Percival* got underway and anchored in berth D-3.

About two hours later, a Landing Craft Medium (LCM) came alongside Percival with a load of stores. It was a very labor intensive job to heave the boxes up and out of the landing craft to the deck and then strike them below to the various storage lockers. There were dry stores such as sugar and flour and canned goods, fresh vegetables and refrigerated and frozen things like meat and milk. Storage was tucked into available space all over the ship. Some provisions were stored forward, some aft and potatoes were stored in a large ventilated box on the 01 deck. Getting all of these stores into all of the storage places on the ship is what the Navy calls an "all hands evolution." That means everybody gets to help. That also means that everyone got an opportunity to steal some goodies.

Each Sailor got a case of something to carry from the LCM to a storage locker. Storekeepers were stationed at strategic locations to direct the cases to the correct location. They were also there to assure that the

Fruit Cocktail, Peanut Butter, Jelly and Saltine Crackers made it to their storage location and were not diverted to crew coffee messes.

Although the crew was crafty, so were the storekeepers and most of the delicacies ended up locked in storage. However, being a crafty group, the Sonarmen, Radiomen, Radarmen and Fire Control Technicians (FT's), led by First Class Sonarman George Johnson, organized a cooperative to insure a supply of PB, jelly, saltines and fruit cocktail for their respective coffee messes. These four gangs' technical workspaces were in a vertical stack in the main superstructure. This made for convenient distribution of the spoils. The sonar shack was on the 02 level. Directly below sonar on the 01 level was the Radio Room and directly below that on the main deck was the Radar Room/CIC. The Plotting Room, where the FT's worked, was on the first deck right below the Radar Room.

A set of ladders (steep stairs), just outside each door, connected all four areas. The route to the main forward food storage area went right by the radar transmitter room on the main deck. The deal was that if during stores replenishment any members of the co-op got a case of the top four (Fruit cocktail, PB, jelly or saltines), they would head for the forward storage. As they passed the Radar Room, they would open the door and toss the case in. Hopefully there were no Storekeepers or Masters At Arm's in the area to witness the deed. They would then turn around and head empty handed back to the LCM for another load. The radarman on watch would stash the loot under the workbench or in the darkened confines of the adjacent Combat Information Center (CIC) to await distribution.

Each case of peanut butter, jelly and fruit cocktail contained four 1-gallon cans – one for each of the gangs in the co-op. The cases were cracked and the cans quickly disbursed to the coffee messes. The

95

saltine cases contained multiple boxes that were split four ways. For the next couple of days, the miscreants would be eating fruit cocktail out of their coffee cups and having PB&J on saltines with their coffee.

Or until Ed Cosgrove, Chief Hospital Corpsman caught them as he prowled about the ship. Chief Cosgrove was responsible for public health measures and that included "no food allowed in any operations spaces" and the chief enforced it with a vengeance. Submarines, destroyers and other small ships that have no doctors carry a Chief or First Class Corpsmen that has special training (including Public Health) and are certified for independent duty. Knowing this, the thieves kept their loot under cover and generally got away with it unless the chief caught them in the act of enjoying their ill gotten spoils.

There was a limited amount of liberty allowed while in Buckner Bay. There was an enlisted men's beach in the White Beach area with some athletic fields, changing facilities, showers and a beachside restaurant and several "geedunks" where beer was sold. Ships were allowed to send one duty section over each day. Even this type of liberty is important. Naval vessels generally and destroyers in particular have cramped and crowded living facilities. In this environment, especially when the ship has been at sea for a long time, people get on one another's nerves and tempers flare. So getting off the ship and letting off some steam is important for the general welfare. Each afternoon a liberty boat ran back and forth between Percival and the Enlisted Men's Beach to give a third of the crew some rest and relaxation (R & R).

The officers had a little more freedom. Lt. Frank Murphy, Lt. j.g. Dave "Hutch" Hutcheson, and Ensigns Walt Harris and Bob Langan walked into the Army's "Top Of The Rock Officers Club" perched atop a steep hill high above the White Beach area of Buckner Bay. It was early and they were able to get a table next to a large window overlooking the bay.   They took seats and gave their drink orders to the Okinawan waiter.

"Wow what a view." said Harris. "You can see the whole fleet, ours and the Brits, all spread out there."

"Has anyone heard how long we're staying in Buckner?" said Langan. "From the news that I've been hearing, they really need us in Korea."

Murphy spoke up. "My understanding is that the attack we made on Pyongyang was a quick strike to cut off some of the supplies going south and to show the Commie's that what they can expect in the future At the moment the 7th Fleet is committed to keeping the peace in the Formosa Straits until the airedales can get their planes here to patrol the Straits."

Langan asked. "Well when the hell are they going to take the load?"

"From talking to those airedales," said Hutch "it appears that within the next few days, VP-28, a PB4Y *Privateer* squadron, is transferring here to Naha Air Force Base from Iwakuni, Japan.   From Naha those long range planes can cover the straits pretty well. In addition, the Seaplane Tender, *Suisun* (AVP 53), that you can see out there in the harbor, is going to sail to the Pescadores Islands in the Formosa Straits next week. They will establish a seaplane base there for VP-46, a PBM *Mariner* Seaplane squadron who will follow shortly."

"I know what a PBM is" said Harris. "What the hell is a PB4Y?"

"A PB4Y" Murphy replied "is a Navy version of an Air Force B-24 bomber with a lengthened fuselage and more guns and its engines optimized for low altitude maritime patrol. You can tell them because

97

they have single vertical stabilizer instead of the bomber's dual stabilizer."

"Oh that's what those things are." said Harris.

The general opinion of his fellow officers (and a large portion of the crew) was that Yale grad Harris was not the brightest light on the street. In fact some of the crew referred to him as "Sneaky Pete". The waiter delivered their drinks.

Hutch proposed a toast. "To Commodore John "Mad Jack" Percival, for whom our ship is named. May we all follow his lead as seaman, officer and warrior."

"Hear, hear." all around.

"Well, things are really going down the tubes in Korea." said Langan. "Although there are now US troops in the front lines, there aren't enough of them and they appear to be no match for the North Koreans and their Russian Heavy Tanks. The last I heard, the Commies had taken over 60% of South Korea and are still pushing South. It's beginning to look like the good guys may get pushed into the sea."

Murphy said. "Yeah they keep falling back and it looks like they will try to take a stand at the Naktong River and form a perimeter around Pusan. There is a rumor that the only way that they can get enough troops into the Pusan perimeter to make a real difference is to make an amphibious landing somewhere on the east coast just north of Pusan. They would probably land the First Cavalry Division from Japan onto the beaches at Pohang. And of course that all pivots on whether UN Forces are able to hold on to Pohang until the 1st Cav is ready to land."

"Good luck with that. All I hear about the 1ˢᵗ Cav is that they are way below strength with only two battalions to a regiment instead of three and are undertrained and under equipped as well. Evidently after the end of War 2, the Army got rid of all their surplus weapons." Said Hutch.

Murphy continued. "A Regimental Combat Team with air support that has been organized from First Marine Division and the 1ˢᵗ Marine Air Wing is on its way from California. I heard that the first elements are supposed to be underway from San Diego today."

"Thank God for the Marines," said Hutch. "only the Marines stored and maintained their World War-II surplus equipment and weapons, and although undermanned, they are trained and ready for deployment."

"Sure as hell hope that they get here in time." said Langan. "This is not looking good."

"The biggest problem," said Murphy, "is that the troops have no close air support. The Air Force is trying to use F-80's based in Japan to provide their version of close air support. Their problem is that the F-80's have a very limited range, can only carry a couple of 100 pound bombs and ten minutes after they arrive over the front lines, they have to go back because they are low on fuel. The only way to do close air support is to have folks on the ground control the planes and direct them right to where they need the bombs – that's the way that the Navy and the Marines have always done it. The Air Force won't allow planes to be controlled by anybody on the ground. All of the Air Force controllers are in small AT-6 Trainer aircraft called Mosquitoes that don't have enough or the right kind of radio communications to handle navy/marine planes."

"Well, I hope that the situation improves when the Marines get here and can work with our carrier guys." said Langan.

"The biggest problem," said Hutch, "is that all the carrier planes are tied up down here in Okinawa keeping an eye on Chiang and Mao."

They ordered another round of drinks.

"And as if we don't have enough to do, yesterday Tokyo extended the blockade to include just about all of North Korea." said Hutch. "We don't have enough ships to blockade the South Korean war area no less the North. And today, as if reading my mind, the Chief of Naval Operations authorized reactivation of mothballed ships in the reserve fleet including 110 destroyers. We really need those ships, but unfortunately, it will be many months before we get to see any of them."

"Yeah, and who the hell is going to man them?" said Harris. "They may have to draft Sailors."

"I heard a rumor of a faster solution to the manpower problem." said Hutch, "President Truman is considering extending all Navy enlistments by one year."

"Oh that's a wonderful solution," said Harris.

"Since the war started, the anti-aircraft cruiser USS Juneau and a few US and Limey cans have been doing a yeoman job on the east coast of Korea trying to enforce the blockade and support the troops." said Langan. "But they really need a lot of help."

"As good as those ships may be" said Hutch, " They only have 5-inch guns. What they really need up there is a heavy cruiser with 8-inch guns or, even better, a battleship with 16-inch guns that can reach over 20 miles inland. Unfortunately, the only battleship still in commission, the USS *Missouri,* is in the Atlantic. Admiral Joy has asked for it but it will take a long time to get here. Even after it gets through the Panama Canal it is still over 8000 miles, or about two weeks, to Korea."

"And while we are talking about problems." Murphy spoke up. "There are not enough tankers available to do replenishment at sea. Right now, the ships up on the line on the west coast have to run back to Sasebo to refuel. And, as I am sure you have noticed, Task Force 77 sorties out and then returns to Buckner to refuel. What a mess."

"Before we get too drunk, why don't we get something to eat." Hutch suggested. "I understand that the steaks here are very good."

They called over the waiter, ordered steaks and another round of drinks.

"Yesterday morning at Officer's Call," said Harris, "The Captain said that Admiral Joy had authorized attacks on unidentified submarines either in self defense or if it looks like they might shoot. I guess that means if we get a good contact, we can blow the hell out of it."

"Yeah it does," said Hutch, "But enough of this war talk. Murph, did you ever hear from Emily?"

"Yeah, I got two letters when we arrived in Buckner. She's worried sick about the war over here and that I might get killed. I have tried to reassure her, however, there is a lot of shooting going on and this ship could certainly be on the receiving end of it before this is all over.

"Peggy feels the same way." said Hutch. "The more I think about it, the worse I feel. I miss Peggy, I miss my son and we have been gone for quite awhile. After four years in the Trade School, I sure as hell knew what I was getting into, however, I didn't really think we would be in a war this soon. We have been dishing it out in the last couple of weeks with not much response at sea, but this can't last forever. We could well take a torpedo from one of those Russian submarines. And the Commies aren't going to stand still forever while we shell them from the sea. They've got artillery and sooner or later they are going to start shooting back at us and there's not much armor on these tin cans. I also understand that the Russians have given the North Koreans thousands of mines including some magnetic ones. The sea war in Korea could really get nasty."

There was a general nodding of heads around the table. The waiter arrived with their steaks and another round of drinks was ordered. They dug into their meals with gusto – this was a lot better than the *Percival* wardroom. About an hour later with full stomachs and a little woozy they trudged down the hill to the Fleet Landing to await a boat back to *Percival* and the war.

15 – Brits at Buckner

On the morning of July 14, *Percival* and *Radford* weighed anchor and got underway from Buckner Bay. They steamed out through Tatsu Guchi and entered the Phillipine Sea. As they cleared the harbor *Percival* veered southward and *Radford* veered northward until they were about 3000 yards apart. The aircraft carrier HMS *Triumph* cleared Tatsu Guchi and was about 1000 yards behind the two screen destroyers. The screen was designated Escort Squadron 1 (CortRon 1) and its voice call was "Redhat". Being the senior captain of the two destroyers, Captain Brown of Percival was ComCortRon 1

Triumph was the guide for the task group and it took *Percival* and *Radford* about 15 minutes to get their positions and speed adjusted to maintain their 1500 yard station from the guide. The *Triumph*'s captain, Capt. A. D. Torles, DSO, was the Officer in Tactical Command (OTC) of the task group.

After she cleared the harbor, *Percival* secured the Special Sea Detail and set the Normal Steaming Watch. Ensign Walter Harris was the OD and Ensign Joseph Hagerman was the JOOD and had the conn. Harris had been standing JOOD watches and had just recently been qualified to stand OD watches.

The sun was just rising over the eastern horizon, the sky was cloudless and the sea was calm with a breeze from the southeast. It was predicted to be about 85 degrees later today.

"Perfect day for Triumph to practice flight operations." Harris said to Hagermen.

"Watching the Brits operate when we were bombing North Korea, I wouldn't think that they needed to practice."

"Practice is how you keep the fine fighting edge sharpened." said Harris. "They are going to do some flight ops this morning and then we are going to tow a target spar for their fighters to shoot at."

"Sounds interesting." said Hagerman.

At that moment the TBS radio came alive. "Redhat, this is Coaster. Corpen one one zero. Standby."

"We're turning into the wind to launch aircraft." said Harris. Hagerman, work the maneuver board and get our course and speed for the turn maneuver."

"Aye, aye."

"Captain on the bridge." called out the bosun.

Captain Brown walked out on the wing of the bridge and stood behind Harris. Until Harris had some more experience as OD, Brown was more comfortable being on the bridge during critical maneuvers. Actually today's exercises were good experience because they weren't nearly as complex or dangerous as maneuvers with the much larger Task Force 77.

Hagerman called from the Maneuver Board, "Course 115 at 25 knots."

Harris looked over at the Maneuver Board and Hagerman's vectors. "Very well."

"Redhat, this is Coaster. Corpen one one zero. Execute."

"Right Standard Rudder come to new heading one one five." Hagerman called out.

"One one five, aye."

"Make turns for two five knots."

"Engine Room answers 250 turns."

The captain walked aft to the flag bag and to watch where *Triumph* and *Radford* were going. Although *Triumph* had turned immediately on to the new course, *Percival* was already clear of a collision course and *Radford* was well to *Percival*'s port side. As the two destroyers came to their assigned screen positions they turned to the 110 heading and slowed to 23 knots.

Brown walked forward and said "Well done gentlemen." and returned to his sea cabin.

Harris turned to Hagerman. "Operations with Triumph is good practice for stationkeeping with Task Force 77. Remember, no one or two turn speed changes. With that big wheel on the throttle board, the best that the engine room can do is three or four turn adjustments. Besides, if you ask for one or two turns, it makes the snipes laugh. They just wait for your ones and twos to add up to three or four and then they adjust the throttle."

First Class Boatswains Mate Joe Sopchick was responsible for the Captain's Gig. The gig was a standard 26-foot motor launch that had a metal canopy over the forward part of the boat to protect the captain from the elements and had nicer seats. Sopchick trained the crew and was in charge of the maintenance of the boat itself. And much like Swenson on the bridge, this was Sopchick's fiefdom and he was very proud of it. He made sure that the paintwork was perfect, all of the coxcombing and "fancy work" was shipshape, the bell was shining and the crew's boat shoes were spotlessly white. With the beautiful weather today, Sopchick put two seamen to work sanding the mahogany gunwale in preparation for a new coat of varnish – a task that would take them a few hours.

The TBS: "Gypsy Prince this is Coaster. Drop back and take the plane guard station."

"This is Gypsy Prince. Dropping back."

Harris looked over at *Radford*. She had slowed and was now almost parallel to *Triumph*. When *Radford* was in plane guard position *Triumph* started flight operations. *Seafires* and *Fireflies* were launched for about 25 minutes.

The TBS: "Gypsy Prince this is Coaster. Return to your screen station."

"Gypsy Prince is returning to screen station."

The TBS: "Sofahound this is Coaster. Bear off until you are about 2000 yards off my port quarter. Stream the target spar and report when ready.

Harris answered, "This is Sofahound will bear off 2000 yards and stream target."

Yesterday a boat from *Triumph* had brought the spar target and it's 1000 foot tow rope over to *Percival*.   The deck force had passed the bitter end through the stern bullnose, shackled it into the towing pad and faked out the towing line free-for-running on the fantail deck.   As Percival arrived at the towing station, they put the spar overboard and the line started running out.   When the line was completely out and the spar came up to the ship's speed, a geyser shot about ten feet in the air above the spar.

On the bridge, Harris picked up the TBS handset. "Coaster this is Sofahound, spar has been streamed and is operating."

"Roger Sofahound, expect to get some company shortly."

From the west, a Seafire appeared low over the water and as it came closer, it opened fire.   Geysers of water from the bullets appeared just aft of the spar's geyser.   Wave after wave of Seafires and Fireflies strafed the spar for about 30 minutes.

"Sofahound this is Coaster, retrieve the spar. Thank you very much for your assistance."

"Gypsy Prince this is Coaster, drop back into plane guard station."

"This is Gypsy Prince, taking up plane guard station."

As Triumph began landing operations, Percival slowed to 5 knots so that the spar could be pulled in. Even with ten seamen on the tow line, it took another fifteen minutes to get the spar back on board and stowed.

By that time they were about 13 miles behind *Triumph* and *Radford*.

The TBS: "Sofahound this is Coaster. Stay where you are. We have our aircraft on board and are going to reverse course to return to Buckner."

"This is Sofahound, will do."

Harris told Hagerman to start a slow turn and come to a heading of 280 with about 5 knots on to maintain steerage way. The wind that had helped flight operations was now dead astern. In about 30 minutes, Triumph and Radford arrived and they formed up at 20 knots on the course to Buckner.

Sopchick's men had sanded down the gunwale all morning and now Sopchick himself started to meticulously brush on the varnish.

On the bridge, Harris was thinking that he only had about 15 more minutes to go before he was relieved.

The phone talker said, "After Fire Room wants to know if it is OK to blow tubes."

Navy ships burn a smelly black bunker oil that is little better than crude and when burned it leaves soot that collects on the boiler tubes. Periodically the fire room requests permission to blow steam through the boiler tubes to clean out the soot. This is usually done when the wind is on the beam so that the wind carries the soot over the side.

Harris turned to the talker and said, "Permission granted."

Almost immediately the sound of steam blowing through the tubes could be heard and Harris brushed a piece of soot off his sleeve. "Oh shit," he thought, I blew tubes with a following sea."

About 30 seconds later, Sopchick came storming up the ladder from the 01 level with the varnish brush still in his hand. He came up to Harris and waved the brush in his face, "You dumb son of a bitch. You blew the fucking soot all over the wet varnish on the Captain's gig." With that he stormed back down the ladder.

Hagerman had ducked into the pilot house – he didn't want to be a witness to this rank insubordination. All of the enlisted men in the pilot house and on the bridge were almost splitting their sides to keep from laughing out loud. Some of them, despite their best efforts were giggling.

Harris, stone faced, was looking straight forward with pieces of soot on him. At about that time, Swenson arrived on his normally spotless bridge and almost had apoplexy. "What the fuck is going on here?" He turned to his quartermasters. "Get some buckets of water and get this mess cleaned up."

He turned to Harris. "Mr. Harris, didn't anyone ever tell you that you only blow tubes with a beam wind? I would have thought that a Yale graduate would have been able to figure this out for himself."

Harris was speechless.

Leaving Harris to contemplate his sins, Swenson turned toward the pilot house and said, "And all you smart ass white hats, wipe the smiles off your face and mind what you are doing."

A few minutes later, Murphy arrived to relieve Harris. The word must have spread rapidly because Murphy ignored all the cleaning activity and went about relieving Harris with a straight face.

The most persistent rumor that spread through the ship was that both the XO and the captain reamed Harris a new one and promised him a less than excellent fitness report.   It was also rumored, that the XO had a discussion with Sopchick saying that he certainly sympathized with him but in the interest of good order and discipline they couldn't have First Class Petty Officers screaming and chewing out Ensigns no matter how dumb they were.

T h e *Triumph* Group returned to Buckner Bay in late afternoon. *Percival* refueled from the USS *Navasota,* anchored out in the bay. She then got underway and moored in anchorage D3.

16 – The Admirals

Task Force 77 Striking Force commanded by Vice Admiral Struble, whose flag was broken in Rochester, had gotten underway from Buckner Bay on 17 July. The task force was once again made up of four Task Groups; TG 77.1 Support Group consisting of two cruisers, TG 77.2 Screening Group, consisting of Eight US and Two Commonwealth destroyers and TG 77.4 Carrier Group, consisting of two aircraft carriers.

The first mission of the task force was to provide close air support for the landing of the First Cavalry Division at Pohang on the east coast of Korea. These troops, that had been stationed in Japan since the end of World War II, were critically needed to help hold the line in the Pusan Perimeter and, hopefully, to break out of the perimeter. Close air support for the troops would only be required if the Pohang beaches were retaken by the North Koreans before the landing could be made. In that case the 1st Cav would have to fight their way ashore and would need all the help they could get. Hopefully, if the line held and Pohang was still in UN control, the US troops could make an administrative landing and offload the ships in Pohang harbor.

The Task Force 90 Attack Force was commanded by Rear Admiral James H. Doyle, a 1920 graduate of the US Naval Academy. He had held numerous seagoing commands before World War II and during the war was involved in amphibious operations in the Pacific. In January

1950 he was named Commander Amphibious Group 1 in the Pacific Fleet. His amphibious force for the Pohang landing consisted of an Amphibious Command Ship (AGC), one Attack Transport (APA), three Attack Cargo ships (AKA), seventeen Landing Ship Tanks (LST), six Landing Ships Utility (LSU) and assorted support vessels. It was a rather motley fleet pulled together from vessels immediately available in Japan and Korea. Two of the AKA's were Military Sea Transportation Service (MSTS) ships with civilian crews normally used to carry cargo from the US ports to ports in Japan. The shipyard in Yokusuka had quickly built boat skids and installed them on the two AKA's so that they could carry landing craft to offload their troops and cargo. Most of the LST's were former US Navy ships with Japanese crews and that were being used as commercial coastal freighters. The LSU's were pulled out of mothballs in Yokosuka and quickly made seaworthy – or so they hoped. There was a backup plan to tow the LSU's behind the LST's if their engines couldn't be made operable. Boat crews and other personnel with amphibious operations experience were flown in from the states. The success of this rapid deployment was largely a result of the experience and leadership of Admiral Doyle for which he was later awarded the Distinguished Service Medal. On the morning of the 17th, Task Force 90 was in the Sea of Japan steaming toward Pohang.

The Light Cruiser USS *Juneau* and the destroyers USS *Kyes*, *Higbee* and *Collett* and HMAS *Bataan* continued to provide shore bombardment support. These ships had been pounding North Korean forces just north of Pohang to slow their advance southward until the 1st Cav could be landed. They continued their bombardment day and night.

Recently there had been more and more reports of mines being used by the enemy. Because of this possible danger, two squadrons of US and Korean Navy minesweepers had swept the Pohang harbor and its approaches. Fortunately, they found no mines.

This morning Rear Admiral John M. Hoskins, Commander Carrier Division 3, had flown to *Rochester* by helicopter from *Valley Forge* to meet with Vice Admiral Struble, Commander Task Force 77.   Rear Admiral Sir William Andrewes, RN had also arrived by helicopter from HMS *Belfast*.   Sir William was a decorated hero of both World Wars.

The meeting was held in Admiral Struble's quarters in Flag Country. Struble greeted Hoskins warmly "Good to see you again "Peg Leg" your aviators have been doing a great job."

He turned to Andrewes, "Bill, I frankly don't know where we would have been without Her Majesty's Naval Forces.   This thing has definitely been touch and go."

"Always glad to help our friends in the colonies." Said Andrewes.

"Well Rip," said Hoskins,   "I hear that you have been traveling a bit trying to clarify the interservice roles and missions."

"Yeah and it hasn't been easy.   Met with MacArthur, Admiral Joy and General Stratemeyer in Tokyo.   We discussed strategies about how to make the most effective use of Naval Air and Air Force resources."

"And how did all of that come out?" said Andrewes. "It seems to me that the Navy came up a bit short in your battles with your new Air Force."

"The discussion was OK, I guess. As you know, about a week ago, in response to an urgent request from General Dean, Commander, 24th Infantry Division for carrier air support, I volunteered Task Force 77 to

Admiral Joy to help out. I told him that we could either do two days of close air support at the front lines or do strikes on targets on the west coast. Because we will be short of ammunition until shipments arrive in Okinawa on July 18, he preferred to hold us in reserve for support of the Pohang landing."

"Yeah." said Hoskins "and as a result we have been sitting in Buckner for a week while General Dean's guys have been getting pushed all over South Korea."

"Well, I worked out with Joy and Stratemeyer that Task Force 77 would provide two days of support for the Pohang landing and for northward strikes against the enemy on the east coast. If, as we hope, this is an administrative landing, I expect that Admiral Doyle will release us early in the day on the 18th and we can get most of the two days on targets in the north. Then we will steam southward, replenish in the Tsushima Straits and head up the west coast for two more days of air operations in areas cleared with Far East Air Force."

"As you know," said Andrewes, "When this started, *Triumph* was getting ready to return to Britain to replace all of it's aircraft. Our 24 *Fireflies* and *Seafires* are old and tired and have much shorter range than your *Panthers, Corsairs* and *Skyraiders.* Our lads were very keen to hit the North Koreans in those first two days of attacks, however, I also realized that we had to go close to shore in order to effectively utilize our planes. I would like to propose that *Triumph* aircraft take over the defensive Combat Air Patrol and Anti-submarine Patrol work close by the task force thus freeing up all of your more capable aircraft to hit the enemy."

"Bill, " said Struble, "I think that is a great idea and makes the best use of our very limited resources. Thank you very much."

114

"Right now," said Andrewes, "Replenishment is also becoming a big problem. I have ordered our Fleet Auxiliary Tanker HMS *Wave Conqueror* to Sasebo." said Andrewes. "She will be available for underway replenishment of Task Force 77."

"That will be a big help." said Struble. "We also have one fleet tanker available, the *Navasota*. Our bigger problem is ammunition. The *Grainger* is on its way to Okinawa with the ammunition it picked up in Guam on July 14. It should get to Buckner tomorrow but then it needs to be up here by the 20th to support our replenishment at sea – it is uncertain whether it can make that schedule, particularly if Typhoon Grace crosses our path."

"Afraid I can't help you on that one." said Andrewes

Hoskins said "I know that in the Key West roles and missions agreement, the Air Force is in charge of all air operations but in this kind of situation it really doesn't work very well."

"It doesn't." said Struble, " And the primary reason is that the Air Force is not prepared to fight this kind of war and particularly this kind of war in this theater. The majority of their planes in the Far East are B-29 heavy bombers that they planned to use against Russia. The next war wasn't supposed to be in Asia so they didn't have a lot of fighters here and the F-80's that they have are primarily air defense fighters to protect Japanese cities. A couple of their war-weary F-82's[18] from Japan shot down three Yak's on the second day of the war but they are having trouble keeping the F-82's in the air for lack of spare parts. They have been trying to provide close air support with short range, small bomb capacity F-80C fighters flying from Japan but they can only loiter for a

---

18 F-82's were basically two P-51's bolted together making a twin engine fighter.

short time over Korea. And when F-80's show up at the front lines, the Air Force ground controllers give them priority and our naval aircraft orbit around loaded with tons of bombs waiting for targets. They have finally been able to move a few of their fighters to a small air strip near Pohang and that should help some. They also plan to move a squadron of A-26 light bombers from Iwakuni to South Korea as soon as a suitable airfield can be recaptured. The Air Force guys have also been trying to bomb strategic targets in North Korea from 30,000 feet with B-29's flown from Okinawa. My understanding is that they have been churning up more rice paddies than factories. If the Commies ever bring on some Mig-15's, that are designed to attack long range bombers, the B-29's will be in really big trouble."

"And to further rub salt into our wounds," said Hoskins, "we had to make space in our aircraft carrier *Boxer* to bring the Air Force 145 of their War-2 P-51 *Mustang* propellor fighters, 6 Stinson L-5 *Sentinel* observer aircraft, 2000 tons of parts and tools and over 1000 pilots, mechanics and other support personnel. Where the hell would the Air Force be without the Navy? Fortunately, they were also able to find space in *Boxer* to bring us 19 *Corsair* fighters,which we badly need. Incidentally, it looks like *Boxer* is making a record-setting crossing of the Pacific in something under 9 days and should arrive in Yokosuka by the 23rd."

"Remember," said Struble, "there was a lot of blood left on the floor in Key West to get the agreement that the Air Force was responsible for the interdiction of enemy land power and communications. And now they are not able to perform that function and are assigning targets to the Navy that we never planned for. As you know, interdiction of land communications requires a continuous effort. In the current environment, not knowing what the Chinese and Russians will do, we cannot keep carriers on station for more than two days -- and the Air

Force knows that. We bombed the hell out of the Pyongyang, because no one else could do it, and now Stratemeyer is giving us target priorities beginning with rail and highway bridges and running down through petroleum facilities and airfields – all clearly strategic targets and Air Force responsibilities."

"And my Air Group Commander," said Hoskins, "reports that when his guys try to report in to the the Air Force controllers, in their little airplanes circling over the front lines, they are either too busy to handle them, or they don't have any targets or don't have the right radio frequencies. My guys end up going away to bomb secondary targets – it's a shame. And because the F-80's are always short of fuel, the controllers give them priority with their couple of 100 pound bombs and my guys with loads of rockets and 500 pound bombs have to wait. In one case, recently, two of my AD's ended up following some Air Force F-80's that had been given targets and dumped their bombs on the F-80's targets. But more fundamentally we and the Air Force have completely different concepts of close air support. The Air Force thinks that hitting anything within five miles of the front lines is close support. As you know, the Navy/Marine concept is that you hit the enemy right in front of your battle line with everything you've got and if the good guys get some dirt blown on them it was a good run. And the thing that really pisses me off about this whole mess is that after the Air Force guys got the responsibility for close support, they didn't buy the planes and radios that they needed to do it, or train any of their people as controllers."

"Well, tomorrow bright and early, we will cover the landing at Pohang." said Struble. "It appears at this point, that the landing will not be opposed so I expect that, after a short time, Task Force 77 will be released by Admiral Doyle. My plan then is to strike railroad facilities, industrial plants and airfields in the north. One of our primary objectives will be that huge oil refinery at Wonsan."

"Oh yeah," said Hoskins. "that's the one that the AF guys bombed with B-29's the week of 6 July and didn't hit anything vital. We are looking forward to really giving that place a pasting."

"So am I." said Struble. " Our intelligence says that the refinery is still producing at its normal capacity. If everything works out, we will strike the north tomorrow and the next day and then have a replenishment day on the 20th. The only problem with those plans is where will Typhoon Grace be by then – the weather guys are keeping close track of her and we will probably have to maneuver the fleet to get out of her way".

The admirals continued their discussion of issues unique to the carrier group, task force day-to-day operations and Typhoon Grace. About an hour later helicopters returned Andrewes and Hoskins to their ships.

17 – Strike The North

Task Force 77 was about 60 miles NE of Pohang by 0500 on the 18th preparing to provide   air support for the landing of the 1st Cavalry Division on the beaches at Pohang. The task force had turned into the wind in preparation for launching aircraft. *Percival* was in the Plane Guard station behind HMS *Triumph* steaming at 23 knots.   Lt. j.g. Hutcheson was the OD and   Ensign Langan was the JOOD and had the conn.   Captain Brown was on the bridge.   *Triumph* was launching *Seafires* for the dawn anti-submarine patrol and the dawn Combat Air Patrol (CAP).

Brown said to Hutcheson.   "You could come a little right -- pay attention to this too Langan.   You really want to be off the carrier's starboard quarter not following in her wake. It's not too important now, however, when they are recovering aircraft the pilots don't really need our mast sticking up in their flight path."

"Aye, aye sir."

Langan went into the pilot house and coached the helmsman right to a parallel course.

"Good.   That's much better." said Brown.   "You know this operation is touch and go.   The North Koreans have actually pushed south of Pohang inland behind our front lines and are only a few miles from the landing beaches. The Commies know we are trying to land troops and

119

have a major offensive going on north of Pohang where the line is held by ROK troops."

"Well, I sure hope that the ROKs can hold on." said Hutch. "I am sure that the flyboys are chomping at the bit to get released from here so that they can get a crack at those juicy targets up north."

"I'm sure that they are, however, it is vitally important to get these troops ashore to hold the line."

Triumph signaled that flight operations were complete and Hutcheson had *Percival*'s boat crew stand down.

At about the same time, *Valley Forge* launched *Corsairs* for the CAP over the landing area. At about 0545, *Valley Forge* launched *Corsairs* and *Skyraiders* that were the attack force to support the landing if needed.

Several miles to the north of Pohang, the Light Cruiser USS *Juneau* and the destroyers USS *Kyes*, *Higbee* and *Collett* and HMAS *Bataan* were steaming slowly in a column parallel to the coast providing gunfire support as required to the embattled ROK forces. Almost all of the US Navy ships now had ROK naval officers on board to translate and provide liasion with ROK Army and Naval Forces.

The Third ROK Division was in a tough battle with North Korean forces about seven miles north of the Pohang landing zone. Overnight they had repulsed an attack and were able to hold their ground and stop the DPRK advance. Based on this news, at 0558 Admiral Doyle in the Amphibious Command Ship *Mount NcKinley* ordered "Land the Landing Force" and executed his alternate "No Opposition" landing plan. Landing craft loaded with 1st Cavalry Division troops, from the transports, now headed for the Pohang inner harbor rather than the less-than-optimum landing beaches.   Shortly thereafter the Landing Ships Tank (LST) and Landing Ships Utility (LSU) pulled alongside the inner harbor piers to discharge their cargoes of tanks, trucks, artillery and other heavy equipment.   The troops were greeted by Lieutenant General Walton H. Walker, Commanding General, Eighth Army, whose troops were being pushed down the peninsula and who desperately needed the reinforcements.   Railroad trains were standing by to rush the troops and their equipment to the front and into the line.

About the time that the troops started to land and it was clear that they would not be opposed, Admiral Doyle released the Seventh Fleet aircraft from their support role. As soon as this order was received both *Triumph* and *Valley Forge* began recovering aircraft. The only aircraft left flying over Pohang were two *Valley Forge Corsairs* flying CAP. The   recovery evolution proceeded uneventfully and Task Force 77 turned northward to attack targets in Wonsan, Pyongyang, Hamhung and Hungnam, North Korea.   In mid-morning, *Valley Forge* launched seven Panthers that hit rail and airfield targets around Wonsan inflicting substantial damage.

Triumph   launched *Seafires* and *Fireflies* against targets in Pyonyang and Hamhung. *Triumph* also launched a rather ungainly looking *Sea Otter,* a single engine, amphibian, biplane used for air sea rescue.

The primary target in Wonsan was the largest oil   refinery in North Korea with an annual output of 1,700,000 barrels.   The refinery was originally built by the Japanese to support their continental expansion. After the war, the refinery became inactive but in 1947, a joint Russian/North Korean enterprise had been formed to operate it.   By 1948 the refinery was delivering oil to Russian tankers.   Recent reconnaissance flights had shown that the refinery was in full operation despite attacks by nine US Air Force B-29's on July 6 and forty-nine B-29's on July 13.[19]

About 1700, Task Force 77 turned into the wind and *Valley Forge* launched a group of 11 S*kyraiders* armed with 500 and 1000 pound bombs and 10 *Corsairs* armed with High Velocity Aircraft Rockets (HVAR) all bound for the refinery. The *Corsairs* came in at 4000 feet from two different directions launching HVAR rockets in pairs and firing their 20mm cannons. The *Skyraiders* followed and their bomb patterns covered the whole refinery. As the aircraft pulled away, it was difficult to see the damage because of the enormous clouds of belching smoke. There were constant explosions as the fires spread to unbombed areas. Planes returning to their carriers at an altitude of 3000 feet reported still seeing the smoke from 60 miles away. All aircraft returned to the carriers and were recovered without incident. Planes were refueled and rearmed for more operations on the following day. Naval Intelligence reported that the refinery continued to burn for four days after the raid. Analysis of after-action photos estimated that 12,000 tons of petroleum products were destroyed.

At 0200 the next morning, Percival was detached from the task force and assigned radar picket duty at a Bird Dog station about 50 miles north of the task force operating area. Their mission was to detect any aircraft flying out from North Korea, about 200 miles away or from the large Russian naval base in Vladivostock about 275 miles away. *Percival's* CIC was fully manned with active radio circuits to the CAP aircraft, the *Sea Otter* Rescue Amphibian and ComTF77 (Jehovah). Shortly after dawn, Task Force 77 turned into the wind to launch aircraft including the *Triumph's* venerable *Sea Otter* that would play an

---

19 - Postwar interviews with refinery managers determined that only 3 Air Force bombs had hit the refinery in those raids and the rest had dropped without damage in nearby fields.

important rescue role later that day. Both carriers launched full strength sorties against multiple North Korean targets.

In Percival, Ensign Robert Langan was the CIC Officer.   Enlisted Radarmen manned the VK Radar Repeater for surface targets, the VJ Radar Repeater for air targets and the VF Precision Radar Repeater.   It had been a quiet morning. They had tracked the flights of *Valley Forge* and *Triumph's* aircraft as they flew into North Korea earlier.   There had been no other radar contacts.

At about 1115, Radarman Varone said, "My VJ display is just starting to show returning aircraft coming out of the North Korean land clutter, they should be feet wet in a few minutes."

At that moment over the ARC1[20] came "Any Station, any station this is Biscuit on 121.5.[21]   Mayday, Mayday, Mayday. I have been hit by ground fire and am leaking fuel badly.   I am trying to make it to the Wonsan outer harbor before ditching.

In *Percival's* CIC, the Air Plotter called out, "Biscuit is an F-4U *Corsair* from *Valley Forge.* According to our list of radio calls, Biscuit is Lt. j.g. Boyd Muncie. "

Langan picked up the handset, "This is Sofahound, understand Biscuit heading for Wonsan harbor. We will vector Neptune's Daughter, the Brit Sea Otter,[22] to you."

"Neptune's Daughter this is Sofahound. Biscuit, a Corsair, is ditching in

---

20 AN/ARC-1 Air to Ground Radio
21 121.5 is International Distress Frequency.
22 The Supermarine Sea Otter, although ungainly looking, is a very rugged single engine, amphibian bi-plane

the Wonsan outer harbor. Come to new heading 320. Wonsan is about 80 miles."

"Roger, Heading 320. Be advised my max speed is about 100 knots, so it is going to take us almost an hour to get there."

"Roger, understand. Sofahound now proceeding toward Wonsan at 20 knots."

"Sofahound this is Banger1 flight of two Corsairs. We will stay with Biscuit as long as we can. He is definitely streaming fuel."

"Banger1, Sofahound, As you know Wonsan is enemy territory, so keep an eye out for the bad guys."

"Roger will do. So far, no boats in the outer harbor where Biscuit is heading."

Varone said, "I have a cluster of 3 contacts near Wonsan that's probably Biscuit and friends."

"Roger," Langan said, "work with the Fernandez to to get Biscuit on his VF scope so that we can get precision range and azimuth data to pinpoint the ditching location latitude and longitude."

Sofahound this is Biscuit. "My engine just stopped, I am out of fuel. I believe that I can clear the next ridge and make it to Wonsan. I'm going to try to get about midway between those islands because I doubt that the natives are friendly."

This is Banger1. Make sure that you have dumped all your weapons, that your canopy is all the way back and that your harness is cinched up tight. We will follow you down -- Good luck.

"It looks pretty rough down there with whitecaps. I'm headed into the wind and will try to stall into the back side of one of those waves. "

A minute and a half later, "This is Banger1. Biscuit is down -- beautiful job -- plunked it right down on the back of a huge wave. Plane is floating and he is getting out of the cockpit."

A few minutes later. "Biscuit is OK. He deployed the life raft, inflated his life vest, got out on the wing and went into the ocean just as the plane sank. He climbed into the raft and is waving to us.".

"Sofahound, Banger2, Small boat carrying guys with guns started out from the shore of the largest island headed toward Biscuit -- a couple of long bursts with my 20's sank the boat and hopefully discouraged any copy cats."

"Roger, Break -- Neptune's Daughter this is Sofahound, the wind seems to be getting you. Come to new course 315."

"Roger, three-one-five."

The two *Corsairs* stayed on station for about 20 minutes. "Sofahound this is Banger1, we are low on fuel and have to leave. Biscuit has put out some dye marker in the water so he is pretty visible from the air. Good day!"

"Good day -- thanks for your help."

"Sofahound this is Ajax, flight of one *Seafire*. Have Biscuit in sight and I will take over babysitting."

"Roger, Thanks."

About ten minutes later. "Neptune's Daughter, this is Ajax. I am going to climb to about 1500 feet and circle over Biscuit. Let me know when you get me in sight. I am looking for you."

"I am about 5 miles away -- should be there in a few minutes."

"Oh yeah, I've got you in sight. As a fellow Brit I can tell you that is one ugly airplane."

"We may not be pretty, but as an old girlfriend said "I can do tricks that you'll love.""

About 5 minutes later the *Sea Otter* made a low pass over Biscuit and circled around to come up into the wind. The Seafire made a low pass around the harbor looking for enemy boats and found none.

"Neptune's Daughter, Ajax, Looking at the sea, I estimate the wind is about twenty knots with higher gusts and with a sea of four to five feet. Do you think that you can put that thing down in this -- it's pretty rough?"

"It is a marginal situation but we need to get this guy and I'm going to give it a go!

The pilot made his approach into the stiff wind holding the nose high slowing the plane to just above stall speed. At just the right time, he stalled the plane and it dropped into the trough between waves with a terrible thump that slightly damaged one of the wingtip floats.

126

"This is Ajax, he is down OK and is taxiing toward Biscuit. He came up alongside and his Petty Officer hauled Biscuit through the rear hatch. He is turning around into the wind to take off."

In a few minutes, Ajax called, "He is going up one side of the waves and down the other but he is picking up speed. Oh shit! -- a wave just broke completely over his upper wing and the engine but he is still going -- Wow he bounced off the top of a wave and took off."

As the awkward amphibian gained altitude, "This is Neptune's Daughter, I thought we had bought the farm when that wave went over us. The engine sputtered but thank God it caught again with full power and we took off."

"This is Ajax, I am low on fuel and am proceeding directly to *Triumph*."

"So am I", said Neptune's Daughter. Lt. Muncie, who we picked up, is from *Valley Forge*, however, they can't trap[23] an amphibian so I'll have to land on *Triumph*. We'll ferry him over to the Happy Valley by helicopter."

About two hours later the a helicopter from *Triumph* delivered Lt. j.g. Boyd Muncie, the first US Naval Aviator to be shot down in the Korean War back to *Valley Forge*. The *Sea Otter* crew of Lt. Cane and Petty Officer O'Nion were rewarded with the traditional ice cream and a commendation from their Captain.

As the attack aircraft returned to Valley Forge, each of the pilots was debriefed. Two of the pilots reported seeing a sizable freight train disappear into a tunnel south of Songjin and not come out. The pilots

---

23 An arrested landing on a carrier.

thought, and the intelligence officers agreed, that the train was being hidden in the tunnel until after dark.   Because neither of the carriers had aircraft equipped for night fighting, they recommended that a destroyer be sent to attack the train as it came out of the tunnel.

A short while later, *Percival* received an Operational Immediate message from Comm 7th Fleet saying that because they were already about 50 miles north, they were to proceed to a small fishing village south of Songjin to destroy the hiding train.

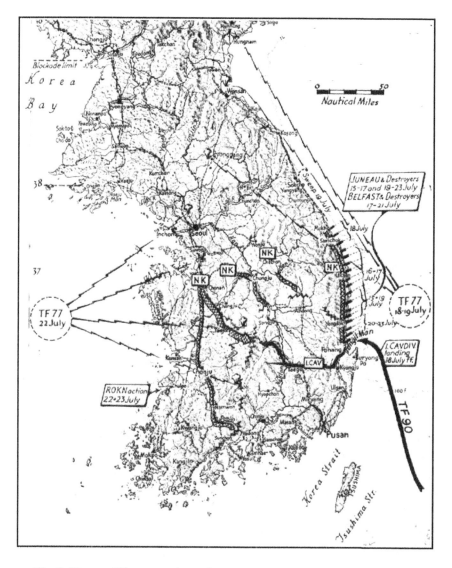

**Task Force 77 operations from the East & West Coasts of
Korea during late July 1950.
NK indicates North Korean Army lines.**

18 – Train Buster

The east coast of the Korean peninsula is very rugged with mountains extending to the waters edge for much of the coastline leaving very little coastal plain. As a result, the almost 1100 miles of railroad track along the east coast of Korea has 956 bridges and 231 tunnels. That works out to be about one bridge every 1.2 miles and one tunnel every 5 miles. The average tunnel is cut through solid rock and is about 1200 feet long.

After *Percival* was detached from Task force 77, she proceeded north to a point in the Sea of Japan about 5 miles south of the port of Songjin, North Korea just off the village of Ssangnyong.   Lt. Cmdr Cook, the XO and navigator had plotted a course to take the ship about 4 miles off shore from the south entrance of a long railroad tunnel.   This morning, pilots from *Valley Forge* had seen a long southbound freight train disappear into the north end of the tunnel and not come out the south end.   It was common practice for trains to hide in the tunnels during the day and then sneak out southward after dark. *Percival* had been dispatched to wait off shore until after dark to attempt to destroy the train when it tried to resume its journey.

Ssangnyong was a small fishing village with most of the houses lying between a main north-south highway and the beach. The north end of the village extended to a small peninsula that jutted out about a quarter mile into the Sea of Japan. The tunnel entrance pierced a steep rock face at the bottom of a mountain that was about two hundred yards west

130

of the north end of the village. The railroad tracks curved southward out of the tunnel and then ran parallel to, and about 100 yards west, of the highway. The tracks were about 20 feet above the level of the highway. About a mile further south, the tracks ran into another tunnel. Midway between the tunnels was the small Ssangnyong railroad station.

At 1700 *Percival* had gone to General Quarters. The captain was on the bridge. Lt. Murphy was the OD and Ens. Matthews was the JOOD and had the conn. The XO was at the chart table plotting the ship's position by piloting. Piloting involves taking bearings on identifiable land marks and plotting where they cross on a nautical chart. Quartermasters were stationed at the port and starboard peloruses to take bearings. At the moment they were taking bearings on the mouth of the tunnel and the cupola on the railroad station.

The XO walked out on the wing of the bridge and said to the captain. "I cannot believe that the North Koreans are at war and still have navigation lights on. Look on our port bow there is a single flashing light on the shore about a mile south of the village and on the starboard side there is a triple flashing light at the tip of the peninsula. Our position using those lights agrees with our position on radar and piloting on the tunnel and the station so I assume that they are where the chart says they are."

"Well if that's so," said the captain, "It will certainly simplify our navigating tonight when we go in close."

The captain turned to the Bridge Telephone Talker "Tell Plot 1 that the the entrance to the tunnel bears about 345 from us. See if they can get the Fire Control Radar for the 5-inch guns to lock up on the stone edge of the entrance."

131

"Plot1 says that they will give it a try."

Above their heads the Mark 37 Gun Director slewed about until it was pointed toward the tunnel entrance. The Mark 37 director is connected to the Mark 1A Fire Control Computer four decks below in the Plotting Room (Plot 1).   Also in Plot1 is the Mark 6 Stable Element that provides corrections for the ship's Roll and Pitch.   This equipment provides pointing and firing information for the two 5-inch 38 caliber guns.

The Mark 56 Fire Control System located on the 02 level aft provides pointing and firing information for the two dual 3-inch 50 caliber gun mounts. Directly below the Mark 56 Director is Plot 2 that contains the control, computing and radar equipment for the system.   The Mark 56 system can also control the 5-inch guns and is a backup to the Mk 37 Director.

The computers for both systems are mechanical analog computers. The insides of them are jammed with mechanical differentials, gear multipliers, ball and plate integrators and hundreds of steel shafts and gears.

The phone talker: "Plot 1 says that the optical range finder has a good view and a solid range and that the radar has locked up on the tunnel edge and they have solution plot. In fact, the optical view is good enough to see wisps of smoke and steam coming out of the tunnel entrance – sure looks like our train is in there."

"Ask them if they think that the radar will lock up on the train as it comes out of the tunnel?"

"They are pretty sure that it will but they are going to watch the scopes for any indication of motion and will track manually if necessary."

The phone talker: "Plot 2 reports that their Mark 56 Director is pointed at the tunnel entrance and that their radar is locked on the entrance and they have solution plot."

"Very well."

Captain Brown told the bosun to pipe All Hands on the 1 MC. Captain Brown then took the 1 MC.

"As you may have heard we have a Commie train trapped in a tunnel. We have our fire control systems locked on the tunnel entrance. Sunset tonight is about 2007. After dark, we are going to move in closer at darken ship and lay to and wait for the train to come out of the tunnel. As the train comes out, we are going to let him go about three-quarters of a mile and then Mount 55 will illuminate with star shells. Mounts 51, 31 and 32 will open fire on the locomotive with High Explosive – HE rounds. As soon as the locomotive is stopped, we will transfer our fire to the freight cars. We are going to swing around now and head slowly south as if we are leaving the scene while we maintain fire control radar contact. You may stand easy at your stations."

"Mr. Murphy," the Captain said, "come to a heading of 185 at 5 knots. We want to just go to the horizon from the tunnel. Make sure we keep radar contact. I will be in my sea cabin. Call me when the sun goes below the mountains or if the train makes a move."

"Aye aye sir. Mr. Matthews, make it so."

"Aye, aye."

133

At 1948, Murphy called into the sea cabin Voice Tube. "Captain the sun just dropped behind the mountains."

"Very well. Thank you."

In a few minutes, Captain Brown came through the door into the pilot house. He paused to look at the display on the radar repeater and then came out on the starboard wing of the bridge. The sky above the mountains was red and getting darker by the minute.

"Mr. Matthews, come right to new course 005, speed 10 knots."

"Aye aye sir."

"Bosun, pipe darken ship." Brown said.

As the bosun finished passing the word, the ship's running lights and all above deck white lights went out. The only lights left on were dark red to allow the crew to walk safely around without destroying their night vision. As the ship swung around to go north, the Captain, Murphy, Matthews and the phone talker walked around to the port side of the bridge.

Brown turned to the Bridge Talker. "All hands resume General Quarters stations. Also check that all darken ship door switches are operating correctly. I don't want any flash of light giving us away."

"Bosun. Secure the 1MC until further notice. Loudspeaker sounds carry a long way across the water, especially at night."

"Aye aye sir."

The sun had set and it was now completely dark. The Captain was looking through his binoculars toward the tunnel.

"Commander, I see that your two lights are still bright."

"They are. And we have been using them to take cuts – I still can't believe what I'm seeing."

"Remember that old saying about gift horses."

"Oh, I'm thankful, believe me."

The phone talker: "Plot 1 reports bearing to the tunnel is 335 range 7200 yards. They have a firing solution for Mount 51 and a star shell solution for Mount 55."

"Aye."

The Mark 1 Star Shell Computer generates gun angles so that the star shell bursts over the target area and it generates firing times to keep two of the parachute flares in the air at all times.

The phone talker: "Plot 2 reports range to the tunnel is 7100 yards and they have a firing solution.

"Mr. Murphy, speed 5."

"Aye aye sir."

Brown turned to the talker. "Tell Plot 1 to keep those bearings and ranges coming."

"Bearing 334, Range 6800."

Every pair of binoculars on the ship were trained on the bearing to the tunnel. Chief Swenson had a long glass propped on the port signal light to steady it so that he could look at the tunnel entrance.

"Bearing 333, Range 6650. Plot1 also reports that watching through the optical sights and the range finder they are occasionally seeing a faint yellow glow from the tunnel. They think that it is probably caused when the furnace door is opened to shovel in more coal."

"That probably means that they are getting ready to come out." said Brown.

A minute later, the phone talker almost shouted, "Plot 1 reports they are locked on the locomotive as it is coming out of the tunnel."

About a minute later Brown said. "Illuminate the target."

A loud boom and bright flash from Mount 55 and a star shell was on its way. A few seconds later an intense white light appeared over the fishing village. The train could be seen approaching the train station

Brown to the talker: "My intention is to let him get a quarter mile past the railroad station."

The locomotive and its train of box cars were starkly visible in the bright white light.

As the locomotive passed through the station, Brown said "Standby Mounts 51, 31 and 32, high explosive rounds."

A few seconds later. "Commence fire!"

A loud boom from Mount 51 rattled the bridge and the air was filled with the sharp smell of cordite. A few seconds later there was a large explosion on the cliff directly behind and above the locomotive, showering it with rocks and gravel. Shortly after that there was a smaller explosion from a 3-inch round on the first boxcar behind the locomotive.

"Correct and continue firing." shouted Brown.

Mounts 51, 31 and 32 continued firing and suddenly there was an enormous blast, steam billowed high into the air and the train skidded to a halt. The locomotive's boiler was completely ruptured and the forward truck was lying alongside the tracks. The first three cars had derailed and were lying alongside the track. Mount 55 continued to keep the scene illuminated.

Brown picked up the handset on the talkers chest set. "Check fire, check fire. Now that the train is stopped, Mount 51 train back to the tunnel and start shooting up the cars and work your way forward. Mount 31 start at that box car you already hit and work your way back. Mount 32 work over the cars in the middle of the train. Resume fire, resume fire."

All mounts started firing again. When the third 5-inch round hit the boxcar just outside the tunnel, there was an enormous explosion and a huge fireball rolled into the air. A few seconds later a huge shock wave hit the bridge, followed by cheers from all over the ship.

"Holy shit" said Murphy, "that was definitely an ammunition

explosion."

"Hopefully that blast destroyed any cars still in the tunnel." said Brown.

Three cars immediately in front of the blasted car were blown off the tracks and were laying on their sides and burning. Percival's guns continued to work their way through the train until it was a mass of blasted and burning rubble. The train station was also destroyed.

"Cease fire, cease fire." said Brown.

Brown picked up the handset on the talkers chest set. "CIC, you need to keep a really close watch on the air search radar. We've made huge disturbance here and there are plenty of North Korean and Russian air assets not too far away."

"Aye aye sir." answered Ens. Langan, the CIC Officer.

"Commander," he said to the XO. "Give us a course to rejoin Task Force 77. As far North and as close to the Commies as we are, I think that the better part of valor right now is to get the hell out of here."

"I recommend course 180 at 20 knots." said the XO.

"Mr. Matthews," said the Captain. "Make it so."

"Aye aye sir"

The XO said to Brown. "I recommend that we stay at General Quarters until we are well clear of the coast in about an hour."

"I agree" said Brown.

Just then Lt. j.g. Hutcheson came out of the pilot house on to the bridge and came over to the Captain.

"Captain, permission to relieve Mr. Murphy so that that he can finish up his Action Report. He has briefed me. I understand that we will be at GQ for a while longer."

"Very well, the jobs not done until you finish the paperwork. I will be in my sea cabin."

"Aye aye sir."

Hutcheson was on the starboard side of the bridge looking at the shore through his binoculars. It was a clear night with a smooth sea. A full moon had just risen in the east over the Sea of Japan. There were few lights along the shore except for an occasional fishing village. He thought of his wife Peggy at home in Columbus. "I sure as hell would much rather be home in bed with her than in this God forsaken place." He thought about the great times he and Peggy had when he was going to Sonar School in Key West. Friday evening Happy Hour at the Echoasis with the other young officers and their wives and lazy weekends on Truman Beach at the Fort Taylor Officers Club. "Oh boy, those were the days."

Suddenly, the 1JP speaker came alive.

"Bridge this is CIC, we have a Skunk bearing 260, range 15,450 yards, assigned Skunk Item."

"Roger." Said Hutcheson.

"This is CIC. Skunk Item is on course 085 speed about 30 knots, CPA is collision. We are designating target data to Plots 1 and 2."

Hutcheson opened the cover on the sea cabin voice tube. "Captain, we have a fast moving Skunk heading toward us. Could be a torpedo boat. I am calling surface action starboard."

"Aye, I'll be right out."

Directly above Hutch, the Mark 37 Director slewed to come to bear on the Skunk. Both 5-inch gun mounts followed the director. Back aft, the Mark 56 slewed out to bear on the Skunk followed by mounts 31 and 32.

The Captain came out on the starboard wing of the bridge and immediately focused his binoculars on the Skunk.

"Can't see much of it but with the speed and the bow wave it's probably some kind of a torpedo boat. Have Radio challenge them on the international frequency and have a Quartermaster challenge them by blinker light".

"Aye, aye." said Hutcheson.

In a few moments, a signalman was transmitting "Able, Able" over and over toward the Skunk.

"A week or so ago," said Hutcheson, "four North Korean torpedo boats took a run at the USS Juneau and some Brit frigates south of here. The Juneau and friends sunk three of the four. The remaining one ran for his life. Then the next day North Korean Radio said that their Torpedo Boat 21 had sunk the USS Baltimore. That would really be great

140

shooting inasmuch as the cruiser Baltimore has never been in the Far East!"

"Oh, I remember that." said the Captain. "We are in the blockade zone so any surface targets are fair game and we haven't gotten any response to our challenges."

"Captain," Hutch said. "I recommend we come left about 10 degrees to give Mount 31 a better field of fire."

"Make it so." the Captain replied.

Phone Talker: "Plot 1 and 2 both report solid track and that they have solution plot."

"Bring all gun mounts to bear. Standby with VT rounds for the 5-inch and HE rounds for the 3-inch."

VT rounds have proximity fuzes that detonate when they detect that they are near a target or the surface of the sea.

"Mounts 51, 55, 31 and 32 are designated."

"Commence fire, commence fire." Said Brown.

Immediately all guns began firing. A well trained 5- inch gun crew can get off about 12 rounds a minute. A dual 3-inch 50 gun crew can get off 40 to 50 rounds a minute.

Shells burst in the air directly above the torpedo boat and a mass of splash geysers blew up in front of it. The torpedo boat turned violently trying to evade the barrage. As the gun directors corrected and the boat

141

continued to swerve, there were a few explosions on the boat and then a few seconds later there was a massive explosion and flames billowed into the air.

"Cease fire, cease fire." shouted the captain, "We must have hit one of their torpedo warheads."

In the distance there was a large oil fire burning on the water.

"With just the light from the fire and the moonlight, I can't tell if there is still a boat out there." said the captain. "Mr. Hutcheson, come right to 200 and slow to 5 knots when we get within 500 yards."

"Aye aye sir."

As they approached, the flames had died down some and they could see that the water was filled with debris. There was no sign of life or bodies.

"Mr. Hutcheson, stop in the wreckage. Pass the word for the deck force to break out boat hooks and grappling lines and see if there are any bodies or recognizable wreckage that they can recover."

"Aye aye sir."

As they arrived on the scene the fire had pretty much died out. The signal lights were used to illuminate the scene. The XO had come out on the wing of the bridge. "No one must have been wearing life jackets because I can't see any bodies. Also, there's not much wreckage, the boat must have been completely destroyed."

"Not surprising," said the captain. "with the number of rounds we hit them with and the torpedo that exploded.

Down below on the deck there was a bit of a commotion as a piece of wreckage was hauled in. The Chief Boats held it up toward the bridge. It was a piece of wood that looked to be part of a name plate that was marked "P-21".

The captain shouted. "Hutch come over here and take a look. When you do your Action Report you can say that we destroyed the torpedo boat that sank the USS Baltimore." And they all laughed.

"Mr. Hutcheson,"said the captain, "Resume course and speed to get us back to Task Force 77."

Percival picked up speed as it headed south to find Task Force 77 that was now headed east to try to avoid Typhoon Grace.

19 – Typhoon Grace

Task Force 77 was trying to work its way around the worst part of Typhoon Grace, a Category 1 storm, with winds of 70 miles an hour. Grace formed in the Pacific Ocean, tracked northward just south of Japan and was now heading directly for a landfall on the south coast of South Korea. The task force speed was reduced to 15 knots and course was adjusted eastward to go around the typhoon as it headed northward. Nevertheless, since early this morning, at about the time *Percival* rejoined the task force, the ships had been battling high winds and heavy seas.

The aircraft carriers were rolling heavily but but with their high freeboard they were mainly taking sheets of spray on board. Most of their aircraft (including the jets) had been struck below in the hanger deck. The few planes remaining on deck had cowl covers on to protect their engines and all of their tie-downs had been doubled up. The cruisers, and particularly the destroyers, were taking green water over their bows. In *Percival*, the lifeguard lookouts, normally on either side on the main deck amidships, were in the port and starboard three-inch gun tubs on the 01 level. The bridge lookouts were brought down from the flying bridge and were now standing in the slightly sheltered aft section of the bridge. Sonar searches were secured because the water under the ship was filled with air bubbles that quenched the transmissions. Captain Brown, the OD, Lt. Murphy, the JOOD, Ens. Matthews and the telephone talker were standing in the pilot house for the moment with water dripping on the deck from their foul weather gear .

The Captain turned to Murphy. "Look at the way Seamen Sullivan steers the ship. Like most good helmsmen in rough weather, he depends less on the compass than he does on his feet. He feels the way the ship moves under him and turns the rudder to meet it. I'll bet that if you went out and looked at our wake you would find that it is almost perfectly straight despite the weather. That is a skill that no one can teach you – you get it by long experience at the helm of a cranky tin can. Good job Sullivan."

"Thank you sir."

Brown said to the pilot house generally. "Well I have certainly seen a lot worse weather, however, we are taking it on the port bow which certainly throws us around quite a bit. We are making turns for 15 knots but I bet that we are making no more than 12 knots good. The radar isn't very helpful. There is so much clutter on the scope from signal return from the high waves that it is difficult to see the other ships. Fortunately, it's a fast moving storm and we should be out of the worst of this in a few hours."

"Hope your right." said Murphy. "I never get seasick but this is pushing things a bit."

Murphy was not alone. There were buckets strategically tied down around the ship including one in the corner of the pilot house.

Percival's bow buried deep under the water and the ship shook from side to side as tons of water poured over the side of the main deck and slammed against the superstructure as the bow came back up. The bow continued up until it's bottom was completely out of the water and then it fell back with a sickening thump and more side to side motion as the ship burrowed its way back down into the sea. With the wind on the port bow, the ship was also taking some pretty large rolls to starboard. Every time it took a big roll, all eyes in the pilot house turned to the Clinometer mounted on the pilot house after bulkhead in the center of the ship. The pointer swung over to 15 degrees, 20 degrees, 22, 30 and hung there until the ship started to slowly right itself.

In weather like this, no one got much sleep. The crew bunks consisted of a rectangular aluminum frame with a piece of canvas lashed to it with white clothesline. In rough weather, Sailors would loosen the lashing so that the canvas (and they) would sag within the frame. There was a limit to how much you could loosen it, however, because of the proximity of your bunkmate below. There were rough weather straps on the bunks but most Sailors had trouble sleeping with them tight across them.

Eating was also difficult in heavy weather. *Percival* used the mess deck to berth the mess cooks. During the day the mess cook's bunks were folded up against the outer bulkheads. Most of the bench seats for the mess tables were free standing and not fastened down so that they could be stowed away under the tables when not in use. The crew tried lashing them to the table legs but in very rough weather only the fixed benches along the bulkhead were really usable. Chow was served from the steam table in one compartment and eaten in the next compartment forward. A critical operation in rough weather was stepping over the foot high hatch coaming between compartments while carrying a fully loaded food tray. This spot became increasingly slippery and hazardous as Sailors spilled food while navigating the hatch. Another complication was that the mess deck was not level but sloped up toward the bow. It was literally an uphill fight on a slippery deck to get to a table. As soon as someone got to a table a slice of bread

146

was slipped under the tray to keep it from sliding all over the table. A table mate was asked to watch your tray while you went back to get a cup of the drink du jour. Glass salt and pepper shakers had long ago been replaced with ones improvised from plastic bottles that wouldn't break when dashed to the steel deck. Those sitting on the benches lashed to the table had to use their feet to maintain their seat. As the ship rolled one way you extended your foot under the table to brace yourself. As it rolled back you bent your knee and braced your foot under the bench. These were folding benches that had a brace that hooked into the legs to keep them from folding up. All this foot motion often resulted in the fold-up benches' leg brace being kicked loose. After a while everyone's ear was attuned to the sound of a brace popping out. If you saw four people on a bench suddenly jump to their feet you knew the brace had been kicked loose and the bench was in imminent danger of collapsing. The rule was that whoever kicked it loose had to grovel on the deck to refasten it while the others held on to his tray. Of course in rough weather some Sailors lost their appetites so there wasn't as much demand for seating in the mess deck.

One of the major problems with Fletcher class destroyers in heavy weather is that they had no inside fore and aft passageway. Those living back aft generally traveled fore and aft on the lee side of the main deck and hoped for the best. As the seas become rougher, both the lee and the weather sides of the main deck start taking green water over the deck. In that case, the safest way fore and aft is up on the 01 level and you would still get wet – there is spray everywhere. Over the day as watches were changed and people had to go fore and aft a large part of the crew were salty, damp, cold, uncomfortable and surly.

As the captain had predicted, the weather gradually became better over the next few hours as the task force went east and Grace moved north. The seas got calmer and by that evening the moon actually came out.

Task force speed had increased to 20 knots as they enter the Tsushima Straits between Korea and Japan and headed for the Yellow Sea.

The British aircraft carrier HMS Triumph was detached from the task force and headed for a ten-day maintenance availability in Sasebo. Now Task Force 77 was down to a single aircraft carrier with commitments to provide close air support for the troops in the Pusan Perimeter and to bomb targets north of Seoul. The close support operations were particularly frustrating for Admiral Struble who continued to try to negotiate ground rules for Air Force control of Naval aircraft at the front lines. He felt that despite all of the talk he still did not have a workable plan.

Task Force 77 headed northward through the Yellow Sea to a point northwest of Kunsan, South Korea. On the morning of June 22, *Valley Forge* launched F9F jets northward to strike targets in North Korea. Shortly thereafter AD's and F4U's were sent off eastward to work under airborne controllers from the Fifth Air Force to provide close support for ground forces. As the propellor planes reached the frontline area, they were unable to reach the AF controllers on the assigned radio frequencies. After a number of tries the Valley Forge flights gave up in disgust and launched attacks on secondary targets near Seoul. In the afternoon, AD's and F4U's were launched again and proceeded to the battle area. The results were the same. They were unable to contact the Fifth AF controllers in their little Mosquito airplanes and dumped their bombs on secondary targets. As soon as the aircraft were recovered, the task force headed southward to meet the tanker *Navasota*.

20 – Replenishment

In the mid-morning, bright sunshine *Percival* was slowly overtaking the fleet tanker, USS *Navasota* in the Korean Strait near Cheju-do Island. There were still a few clouded remains of Grace in the far nothern sky. The sea was calm with only a medium swell from the typhoon. *Navasota* was about a mile dead ahead and *Valley Forge* was already fueling from her port side. It would take several hours for the aircraft carrier to refuel. She was taking Navy Special A Black Oil onboard for her eight boilers through two hoses, amidships and aft. She was also taking Aviation Gas through a hose from the tanker's forward fueling station. The aircraft carrier's AvGas was almost exhausted from the recent high level of air operations. Since the F9F *Panther* jets had been aboard, gas consumption was very high. The aircraft carriers had not yet been modified to install storage tanks for jet fuel so the new jets had been burning AvGas instead of kerosene – and they burned a lot of it.

Percival was slowly closing on the tanker at 20 knots – they were the tanker's first destroyer "customer" of the day. The Captain was on the bridge, Lt. Murphy was the OD and had the conn and Ens. Matthews was JOOD. Both were observing the tanker with their binoculars

The quartermaster called out. "Tanker is showing speed flags for one five knots."

"Roger" said Murphy. "Make turns for two two knots."

"Engine Room answers 220 turns."

Captain Brown turned to Murphy. "That's OK to close on the tanker faster – there are others behind us that need fuel.   Just be sure that you end up 100 yards behind the tanker at about 17 to 18 knots.

"Aye, aye sir."

" I have to be a little nervous about this." said Murphy. "We haven't done underway refueling in a couple of months and we may be a bit rusty."

"I agree." said Brown. "But we do have all of our best people in the critical jobs and I am sure that we will be OK."

As they talked, *Percival* slowly closed the distance to *Navasota*.

Matthews, the JOOD called out: "One thousand yards to the tanker."

"Roger" affirmed Murphy. "Turns for 20 knots."

"Engine Room answers 200 turns."

As an exercise, Captain Brown had Matthews taking ranges to the tanker with a stadimeter, an old sighting device that mechanically calculates the range to a ship if you know the height of it's mast.   The captain required that all of his deck officers know how to use the stadimeter in case the radar failed.

"Very good Mr. Matthews. What mast height did you use?"

"I looked up the AO-106 in the OPNAV and it gave me 72-feet."

"Very well."

Murphy turned to the Bridge Talker. "Status for both fueling stations and the highline station."

"All stations report manned and ready."

Chief Swenson came around the bridge and addressed the Captain. "Excuse me sir, any preferences in movies?"

"Yes Chief, see if they have "All About Eve"."

"Will do sir."

The tankers used the midships highline to deliver mail and exchange movies from their large library of 16mm films. By tradition, the quartermasters were in charge of obtaining the best movies available for the crew. They used their hands, instead of signal flags, for wig-wag communications with the quartermasters on the nearby tanker to negotiate movie trades while refueling was in progress.

The quartermaster reported. "Tanker has Roger two-blocked on starboard yardarm."

The Roger flag signaled that *Percival* was cleared to the tanker's starboard side to refuel. *Percival* had Roger at-the-dip at the port yardarm.

"Two block Roger'" called out Murphy.

The Quartermaster pulled the line to put the Roger flag close-up signifying agreement that *Percival* was coming alongside to refuel.

"Mr. Murphy your course looks good – you should be about 150 feet away from the tanker which is just about right," said Brown.

Percival was about one ship length behind the tanker. Murphy called out. "Turns for one seven knots."

"Engine Room answers 170 turns."

All of the crew above decks had helmets on to protect them from line throwing projectiles. Those at the fueling and highline stations also had lifejackets on.

As *Percival*'s bow passed the *Navasota*'s stern, Murphy called, "Turns for one five knots."

"Engine Room answers 150 turns."

Murphy turned to the Captain. "I always worry whether I am through the tankers stern pressure wave when I slow down – once I wasn't and got stuck back there."

"No – you're OK. We're closing nicely."

As *Percival* slowed and came even with tanker, the red helmeted gunner blew his whistle and fired the line throwing gun sending a brass rod attached to a light nylon line over to the forward fuel station on *Percival*. Sailors on Percival's foc'sle swiftly married a 21-thread messenger line to the nylon gun-line and the tanker crew pulled it in and connected it to the span line from the fueling boom. Percival's then hauled the span line cable over from the tanker. In short order the span line's pelican hook was shackled in above the fuel trunk and

Percival's on the foc'sle hauled the hose over on pulleys running on the span line.   A minute later fuel started to flow.   At the same time, a similar procedure connected the aft fueling station to the tanker.

At the midships highline station the highline was rigged and bags of mail were starting to come over.   Right alongside the highline was a light line rigged with colored pennants designating the distance between the two ships. Murphy was standing on the pelorus platform on the port side of the bridge where he had a good view of the distance flags.   The Captain was in his chair right behind him.   Seaman Sullivan, the *Percival*'s best helmsman, was at the helm.

"Sullivan, we are a little closer to the tanker than I want to be," said Murphy, "pull us out just a bit to starboard . . . . . Very well. Steady as you go."

Most of the crew were standing easy.   It would probably take about 20 minutes to top off *Percival*'s fuel tanks.

"So far so good." said Brown.

"Yes Sir." said Murphy.

"Just as well that *Triumph* left us yesterday. It would have been a waste given our problems with the Air Force ground controllers. And it's a shame because the troops really need our help."

"That's for sure." said Murphy, " Even with the infusion of troops from Pohang those guys have got their backs to the wall in brutal fight and don't seem to be making much progress. I heard that there are a couple of jeep carriers with Marine Air Groups and a Marine Regimental Combat Team due in Yokosuka next week – those guys certainly know how to work together.

"They sure do." said Brown.

Murphy was watching his bow in relation to the tanker. "Drop three turns."

"Engine Room answers 147 turns."

"I guess another big problem, is that the ammunition ship *Grainger* didn't get here today to rearm *Valley Forge* at sea." said Murphy.

"That sure is a problem. It probably means that the task force will need to go in to Sasebo to rearm."

"Well, I wouldn't mind a couple of days in Japan at this point." said Murphy.

"Don't get your hopes up – we may not be there for very long."

At this point, fueling was finishing up and the fuel rigging and hoses restored to the *Navasota*.

The bridge phone talker: "Both fueling stations and the highline station report that everything is clear and that they have secured."

"Roger" said Murphy. "All ahead full, make turns for 20 knots."

"Engine room answers 200 turns."

"Helmsman, steady as you go."

"Steady as you go aye."

Chief Swenson approached the Captain. "Captain, we were able to get "All About Eve"."

"Terrific. We'll schedule it for the wardroom tonight and the crew can see it tomorrow night."

"Aye, aye sir."

Percival returned to her position in the task force. *Navasota* continued fueling *Valley Forge* on her port side while one by one all of the destroyers refueled from her starboard side. In late afternoon all fueling was completed and *Navasota* and Task Force 77 turned and headed for Sasebo.

21 – Sasebo

At about 0500 on the 24th, Task Force 77 approached the narrow entrance to Sasebo Harbor in a long column with *Valley Forge* in the lead, followed by the two cruisers, followed by the destroyers. The carrier needed to get into port as soon as possible to begin the long process of rearming with aircraft bombs, rockets and machine gun ammo as soon as possible. The entrance to the harbor was protected by an anti-submarine net with a floating net boom gate. The gate was closed at sundown and reopened at dawn. Shortly after it became light, as *Valley Forge* approached, a small Navy Yard Tug (YTL) opened the gate.

After the narrow entrance, the waterway opened into several harbors, the largest of which was Sasebo to the north. The cruisers followed *Valley Forge* toward Sasebo with *Percival* and *Radford* close behind. *Valley Forge* moored alongside a pier at Tategamimachi and the two cruisers moored to a single buoy in the north end of the harbor.

Percival and *Radford* moored to a single buoy in the center of the harbor. *Percival* was moored starboard side to Radford's port side. The First Lieutenant established *Percival*'s quarterdeck on the port side amidships and put the accommodation ladder over the side.

Shortly after the ships were moored, a Landing Craft Medium (LCM), popularly called an "M Boat", from the Fleet Boat Pool pulled alongside. It would be *Percival*'s and *Radford*'s liberty boat, and the

156

two ships would supply it's crews, while they were in Sasebo. But, first things being first, the LCM was immediately commandeered for trips to pick up stores for both ships. Immediately following those trips, there was an all hands evolution to strike all the stores below with the usual thefts of PB&J, saltines and fruit cocktail. It was announced over the 1MC on *Percival* that liberty would begin as soon as all of the stores were struck below. It was the most expeditious stores loading operation in the history of the ship.

Mr. Harris was OD for the evening watch when the XO authorized liberty. He told the PO of the Watch to call away liberty.

"Aye aye, sir." said Miller keying the 1MC PA. He put the bosun's pipe to his lips and sounded the short two note call Attention. "Now liberty commences for Sections 2 and 3 to expire at Fleet Landing Sasebo at 2400 midnight."

Mr. Harris addressed the liberty party. "Most of you have been here before and know that it is basically a safe place, however, it is best to stay in the commercial areas of town or in the amusement areas catering to US servicemen. Remember, if you are not checked in through the gate of the Fleet Landing by midnight you are AWOL. Be careful, have fun."

The Sailors filed past the OD and down the ladder into the M Boat. Those in the duty section wistfully watched them go. Tomorrow would be their turn. For most, the first stop was the Bank of America Yen Exchange where the Sailors exchanged their Military Script dollars for Japanese Yen. Part of the fun of changing money was watching the young Japanese clerk's fingers fly over their abacus to calculate the conversion. In 1950 at 360 Yen to the US Dollar, Japan was real bargain for Sailors. The next stop was the closest place to the fleet

157

landing that served Nippon, Asahai, Sapporo or Kirin beer in those big one liter bottles for 200 yen (55 cents). Many sailors had their favorite hangout among the many bars lining Paradise Alley. These Sailors hailed a pedicab that traveled perilously close to the edge of the Benjo Canal to go uptown. Benjo is the Japanese word for toilet so that says it all about that body of water. Some went shopping for the many bargains available in cameras, china and silk. Some went to the Sasebo Enlisted Mens Club famed for its steak dinners. Whatever they did, however, it was all over at midnight. Because of the large numbers of US Navy ships visiting Japan and the limited number of overnight facilities, Sailors were limited to "Cinderella Liberty". Everyone had to return by midnight. Each ship could grant a few overnight passes but that required filling out forms in duplicate and applying to the XO. Also a Sailor usually didn't realize he wanted to stay overnight until he had been ashore awhile and had met an attractive young lady.

Of course there were segments of the Japanese economy that depended on overnight activity and had figured a way around the system. Almost all Japanese brothels had an arrangement with local water taxis to surreptitiously return Sailors to their ships anchored in the harbor early in the morning. For security reasons, no Japanese boats were allowed out in the harbor at night. A U.S. Navy Harbor Patrol enforced this rule. So at first light of dawn, as soon as they were legal, the water taxis shoved off with their cargo of smiling Sailors. The Sailors stayed out of sight in the water taxi cabin. The enlisted men on the destroyer 4 to 8 deck watch in the morning were well aware of the love boat system and kept watch for water taxis right after dawn.

Shortly after first light, Mr. Harris, who had the morning 4 to 8 watch, was taking a leisurely turn around the deck. Right now he was back aft and Miller, the Petty Officer (PO) of the Watch, had a worried look on his face. He had just spotted a water taxi coming across the harbor and it looked like it was coming toward Percival. He called to Harris.

"Mr. Harris, could you please watch the quarterdeck for me. I have to take a leak,"

Harris returned to the quarterdeck and Miller went aft as if going to the after head. He cut behind Mount 55 and waved to the water taxi to pull into the space between the sterns of the two ships. He quickly returned to the quarterdeck and kept Harris occupied with small talk as three Percival's climbed aboard over the screw guard and immediately disappeared down the aft companionway. Fortunately, the ship's ventilation blower noise covered up the taxi's engine sound.

Miller breathed a sigh of relief. Most of the officers who stood OD watches were well aware of the system and generally went along with being out of sight when the water taxis arrived, however, Harris had a reputation of being a hard nose and somewhat of a prude and Miller didn't want to take any chances.

Harris turned to Miller. "Well it's 0555 and in 5 minutes we get another day started. I think that there are probably a pretty good number of large heads this morning attached to bodies that won't want to get up.

"That's true." said Miller. "Have you noticed that *Valley Forge* and *Triumph* are gone and so are most of the tin cans. When I made rounds, the bow sentry told me that when he relieved the watch, the guy on mids told him that the task force had left a little after midnight."

"That's strange," said Harris, "*Triumph* was supposed to be here for 10 days for maintenance and the *Valley* came in with us yesterday morning to load ammo. They couldn't possibly have rearmed in those few hours. It's also strange that they left without us."

"Something must have hit the fan in Korea."

"I guess so." said Harris.

At exactly 0600 Miller keyed the 1MC and piped the long multi toned All Hands. Followed by, "Now reveille, reveille, up all hands, heave out and trice up, heave out and trice up, reveille."

Even up on deck you could hear some groans.

A few minutes later Miller keyed the 1MC and piped a warbled call.

"Now sweepers man your brooms. Clean sweep down fore and aft."

At exactly 0615, he piped Attention followed by:

"Mess Gear, Mess Gear, keep clear of the Mess Deck until pipe down."

And another day got started in Percival. And it was going to be a busy one. Breakfast was SOS[24] and home fried potatoes. As usual, the crew mustered at quarters at 0800.   The Sonarmen are part of the First Division and they mustered on the starboard side of the Main Deck near Mount 51. Although some looked somewhat worse for the wear of too many Asahais, all of the crew was back aboard – three courtesy of the early morning water taxi!   The Division Leading Petty Officer, Boatswains Mate 1c Joe Sopchick prepared the Muster Report and gave it to the Division Office, Lt. j.g. Walter Harris.

Mr. Harris and the other officers assembled on the 01 Deck for Officers

---

24 Cooked ground beef in gravy over a piece of toast. Popularly described by
   the crew as "Shit On a Shingle" thus SOS.

Call. They turned in their Muster Reports and fell in before the mast in reasonably even ranks. The officers made their reports to the XO. Captain Brown announced, "The hurried departure of Task Force 77, without *Percival* and *Radford,* during the night was because of the immediate, emergency need for close air support for the 8th Army in Korea. As you probably know, the Army is having a hard time holding on and are being pushed back by the North Korean Army. The Seventh Fleet has other plans for *Percival* and Radford. At this time it is uncertain when when we will get underway, but it will be soon. So, today has to be a maximum work day to take care of all those things that can only be accomplished in port. Dismissed!"

There was a lot of chipping and painting going on particularly on the foc'sle and other exposed areas of the weather decks. In mid-morning when the sun came out, the word was passed to "Air Bedding" and in short order the lifelines were covered with the crew's two-inch thick mattresses.

The M-Boat was kept busy all day making trips to the tender and the base picking up needed parts and supplies.

In early afternoon, the USS *Helena* (CA 75) arrived from Yokosuka where she had stopped briefly after her high speed transit from the States. *Helena* was a Baltimore class heavy cruiser armed with nine 8-inch, twelve 5-inch and forty eight 40mm guns. She moored to a buoy not far from *Percival.* Rear Admiral C. C.Hartman, Commander, Cruiser Division 3 broke his flag in Helena.

Lt. j.g. Hutcheson had the 1200 to 1600 OD watch on the quarterdeck. At about 1400, Lt. j.g. Murphy, the Command Duty Officer (CDO) came to the quarterdeck.

"Hutch, everybody is scrambling to get all of the work done. The XO wants to call away liberty at 1500. He wants those who had the duty yesterday to have an opportunity to hit the beach tonight because we may be getting underway tomorrow."

"Oh, what's up?"

"Well, there are signs that the Chinese may be getting ready to hit Formosa. There have been reports of a large buildup of junks along the coast and yesterday one of our PBM patrol planes investigating the reports was attacked by two fighters, Fortunately the PBM got away. Things are so tough in Korea right now that no major naval resources can be spared so they are sending *Helena,* who just arrived, and us and *Radford* to the Formosa Straits."

"I am impressed by their confidence in us. Do you think that two tin cans and a cruiser can hold off the "Yellow Peril?""

"I guess we'll have to. Have you noticed that ships are finally beginning to arrive from the States? *Helena* arrived today and a couple of carriers are due later this week along with another cruiser and some destroyers. I'm sure glad that help is finally getting here."

"Yeah, so am I."

"You had liberty yesterday. Were you able to call Peggy?"

"Yeah, they have a phone system at the Officers Club but it took about 30 minutes to get through. Peggy is really shook up – she was crying on the phone. All the news that they are getting in the States is about how badly the war is going. She is really worried. And I'm concerned too – how long are we going to be over here? I really miss my family.

My son is growing up and I'm not there to see it.

"Well," said Murphy, "I'm going over tonight and see if I can call Emily."

"Good luck."

The quarterdeck phone rang and Hutch picked it up. "Quarterdeck, Hutcheson."

He listened and made a note. "Aye, aye sir. Dodge, call away liberty." and handed him the piece of paper.

Dodge put the bosun's pipe to his lips and sounded the short two note call Attention. "Now liberty commences at 1500 for Sections 1 and 2 to expire at Fleet Landing Sasebo at 2400 midnight."

The M-Boat was alongside at the foot of the accommodation ladder. When the liberty party had gathered, Hutcheson said, "Listen up. Have a good time and enjoy yourself. The ship may get underway early tomorrow morning. Don't plan on riding Mama-Sans dawn water taxi back tomorrow because we may not be here. You would not only be AWOL but would have Missed Ship Movement, a very serious offense. Carry on."

The M-Boat made several more runs to take *Percival*'s and *Radford*'s ashore. And starting at about 2300 it started bringing them all back.

22 – Sub Sunk

Escort Squadron 1 (CortRon1) consisting of *Percival* and *Radford* slipped their moorings and started through the hot hazy harbor toward the East China Sea about 0700 0n the 26th. *Percival* was in the lead. The heavy cruiser *Helena* had also just gotten underway and was about a mile behind the destroyers. The three ship task group was going to the Straits of Formosa where they would take up patrol. Their objective was reconnaissance of the China coast looking for evidence of a Communist invasion force. It was also to show the Peoples Republic of China the US intention to keep the straits neutral.

In *Percival*, Captain Brown was on the bridge and Lt. Murphy was the OD, Ens. Matthews was the JOOD and had the conn. The XO was at the chart table plotting the ship's position in the harbor by piloting. Quartermasters were stationed at the port and starboard peloruses taking bearings on surrounding landmarks. They were steaming at 10 knots toward the harbor entrance in the fairly wide channel flanked by rugged mountains.

Murphy pointed to the rows and rows of terraced farmland on their starboard side. "Captain, every time we go through here I am absolutely amazed at how they cultivate this land and carry water up to the terraces. I guess when you have a mountainous country like this you have to make use of every scrap of land."

"Well," said Brown, "I grew up on a farm but I don't think that I could

164

do this. It certainly is a different country and these are hard working and resourceful people."

"And they certainly have bounced back after having been vanquished in war only five years ago."

The XO stepped out on the bridge. "Captain, Recommend new course 265 degrees to the harbor entrance.."

"Roger, make it so Mr. Matthews."

"Come right to 265, Matthews called into the pilot house."

"Right to 265 aye."

Percival was now pointed at the narrow entrance to the harbor and the even more narrow gate in the anti-submarine Nets. A few minutes later as they cleared the nets, Matthews ordered, "All ahead Full, turns for 20 knots."

Captain Brown said. "Set the normal steaming watch." and the bosun passed the word on the 1 MC.   In a few minutes the members of the Special Sea Detail were being relieved.

As the ships proceeded into deeper water between the Kuroshima and Oshima Islands, *Radford* came up abeam of *Percival* and they separated until they were about 3000 yards apart to form a screen. This spacing would do until they could drop a BT and determine more exactly the sonar range for today. *Helena* was directly behind the center of the screen and about 1500 yards back. They had just changed course to 225 degrees that put them on a course straight through the East China Sea to the Formosa Straits.

In the sonar shack, Leading Petty Officer George Johnson was checking to make sure that the steaming watch of Joe Green, SO-3 and Ed York, SOSN was established and that everything was working. York was sitting at the Sonar Stack.

"Stay alert. Do standard beam to beam searches and keep your ears open. Switch off on the stack every half hour. We are in deep water so there should not be any false bottom contacts. Understood?"

Johnson left, Green continued his reading and York continued searching. He was getting some return from Percival's wake to starboard and to a lesser extent from Helena's wake well astern off the starboard quarter – not unusual considering the calm sea. About 10 minutes later, York noticed a faint blip on the port bow. He slewed the audio cursor to it and measured the range to be about 3000 yards. As soon as he heard the faint echo, Green stopped his reading.

"That's weak but solid and it sounds like low doppler to me – whatever it is, is going away from us" he said.

"That's what it sounds like to me. I'm going to report it."

York put his toe on the foot switch to enable his microphone on the 1JT circuit.

"Sonar Contact bearing 135, range 3000 yards, echo quality sharp and clear, target width 5 degrees, doppler slight low – classified possible submarine."

On the bridge, the OD turned to the Bosun and said "Call away General Quarters ASW"

The OD picked up the handset for the TBS. "Buster this is Sofahound we have a sonar contact bearing 135 range 3000 yards, possible Goblin. We are turning to that bearing to investigate and pass through datum."

"Roger Sofahound – break – Gypsy Prince this is Buster.

"This is Gypsy Prince" the OD on *Radford* answered.

"Gypsy Prince stay on present course and speed and continue to provide ASW support for Gladiator in case other Goblins in area"

"This is Gypsy Prince. Understand steaming as before. We will maneuver so that we are directly forward of you."

Cruisers, were particularly vulnerable to sub attack because the sub can maneuver inside their turning circle. Also, cruisers had no sonar or anti-submarine weapons.

In a few minutes, all of *Percival's* sonar stations were manned by the General Quarters watch. Joe Dodge was at the QHB stack, Bill Tubbs at the Range Recorder, Joe Green at the QDA Depth Determining Sonar. When he came in, Mike Owen set up the Anti-Submarine Attack Plotter (ASAP) for the ASW Officer. He then initialized and prepared to operate the Mk4 Attack Director. George Johnson stood behind everyone as the Sonar Supervisor. Lt. j.g. Hutcheson entered and took his GQ station between the Attack Plotter and the Attack Director as ASW Officer. Tom Miller was on the JT phone circuit to the weapons stations, CIC and the Bridge and had control of the weapon arming and firing controls.

Dodge reported from the stack, "Bearing 135, doppler slight low, target

167

width 5 degrees."

Tubbs reported from the Tactical Range Recorder (TRR), "Range 2800 yards, not much data yet but range rate looks like about 18 knots."

"CIC reports contact is on course of 140 degrees, speed 3 knots" said Miller. CIC plotted the sonar data on the Dead Reckoning Tracer (DRT) that produced a plot of the ship's and the target's track.

Hutcheson called out. "Bridge, steer by indicator.[25] Johnson, challenge the sub on Gertrude."

"Aye, aye sir."

Johnson picked up the microphone for the AN/UQC-1 Underwater Telephone, popularly known as "Gertrude", and pressed the push to talk button.

"Abel Able, Able Able, Unidentified submarine this is an American Destroyer – identify yourself. Able Able, Able Able."

Johnson repeated the message several times and then went to CW Mode and transmitted Able Able in Morse Code over and over. No response.

Dodge reported, "Bearing 134, doppler medium low, target width 5 degrees, echo quality slightly mushy. I think he is going a little faster away from us and we are pinging through his wake."

Tubbs reported from the Tactical Range Recorder (TRR), "Range 1800 yards, range rate now looks like 15 knots."

25 In an ASW attack the helmsmen steers from orders on an indicator driven by the Mk 4 ASW Attack Director or the Attack Plotter (ASAP).

"CIC now reports contact on course 140, speed 5" said Miller.

Hutcheson said. "We are in a stern chase, which is ideal for a one-two attack. We will launch Hedgehogs from the ASAP and launch a torpedo from the Mk-4 Attack Director. I am going to increase speed to improve range rate. Miller tell Bridge to make turns for 22 knots. Green what depth are you showing?"

"I'll get a better solution as we get closer but right now it looks like 200 feet."

Owen reported, "I have set the ASAP up with the sub contact in the center of the screen and the Predictor Line set to 1000 yards."

"Miller" said Hutch, "Tell Hedgehog we will launch a full 24 round pattern."

"Aye aye sir, Hedgehog reports 24 rounds loaded, fuse caps and safety pins removed."

"Miller, Tell the Torpedo Room that we plan to launch a Mk-32 in Active Mode with the floor set at 300 feet.

"Aye aye sir, Torpedo reports that we will be launching from tube 1 and both of the Mk-32 battery switches are enabled."

"Bearing 145, range 900, range rate 17."

Owen called out. "We have a good Mk4 torpedo solution that is consistent with what we are seeing on the Attack Plotter. Set to launch from Tube 1.

"Bearing 143, range 500, range rate 17."

Owen called out, "ASAP Predictor Line switched to 220 yards for hedgehog launch."

"Range 500, Hedgehog standby." said Miller into the phones as he pushed the handle to sound the warning bell twice on the Hedgehog mount.

"Range 300, Hedgehog standby," said Miller as he pushed the handle for one long ring of the warning bell.

About ten seconds later as the sub blip on the ASAP screen just touched the Predictor Line; "Fire Hedgehog, Fire Hedgehog" yelled Miller into the phone as he squeezed the firing key.

Immediately there was a load thumping as the Hedgehog mortars fired sequentially in pairs.

Hutcheson called out. "Tubbs say your range rate."

"Range Rate 17" replied Tubbs.

Just then there came three sharp bangs from the Sonar Stack loudspeaker followed by cheers from the sonarmen.

"Belay that." yelled Hutch, "It does sound like we hit him but we still have more work to do."

Johnson said, "Miller, tell torpedo that you will notify them when the MK-4 launches torpedo and to standby to launch manually in case it doesn't go automatically."

"Bearing 140, range 250, range rate 17."

Miller called into the phone. "Standby torpedo."

"Lost sonar contact," called Dodge, "Slewing to starboard baffle."

"Fire torpedo," Miller yelled in the phone. And after a few seconds, "Torpedo reports Tube 1 launched normally on Mk-4 command."

"Aye, Roger," said Hutcheson

"I can hear the torpedo running," called Dodge.

Green reported, "I still hold contact on the QDA. I show that the sub sank to 225 feet after the hedgehog hits. Now I'm hearing noise that sounds like they are blowing main ballast tanks to try to surface and they actually came up a little."

"Miller," Hutcheson called, "Tell the bridge that sub is trying to surface and to standby for possible surface action starboard."

"Aye aye, sir."

"Right standard rudder. Bridge has the conn." said Hutcheson.

At that moment, there was a loud boom through all of the sonar loudspeakers followed by cheers from the sonarmen.

"We got him," yelled Johnson.

171

Percival was executing a right turn to try to regain sonar contact. Dodge had slewed the sonar around so he was searching behind the ship near the baffles that shielded. the sonar from the ships own propeller noise.

Dodge reported. "The water is so disturbed from the torpedo explosion that I can't find the sub in that mess."

"Keep trying," said Hutcheson. "Good job everyone. It sounded like we got three hits with Hedgehogs, and hopefully, their shaped charge warheads punched holes in the hull. We are going to go out about 1000 yards from where we fired and then circle back through datum.

Miller announced, "Bridge reports that there appears to be oil and debris right where we fired."

Dodge said, "I've got a no-doppler contact in the middle of that patch of disturbed water. Joe, do you have anything yet on the QDA?"

"Yes, as we've come around I think I see something there now and it looks like it's at about 250 feet – Holy mackerel now it's about 275 feet – It's sinking!"

"It appears that we got him." said Hutcheson.

Green reported, "Depth now 350, appears to be sinking faster."

There was aloud metallic bang through both the QHB and the QDA loudspeakers.

"Sound like the sub's breaking up." said Dodge.

172

Green reported, "Depth now 475, echo is weaker and target is going down faster."

Suddenly there was a loud crash and some crumpling sounds.

Sounds like it either hit the bottom or the hull collapsed from the pressure." said Hutch.

And with that silence descended on the sonar shack as everyone realized that they had just sent 100 or more seamen to a watery grave.

Hutcheson went out of sonar and stepped out on to the bridge.

"Captain, "I do think that we got him. The QDA followed the contact down and sonar has just now reported hearing what sounds like either break up noises or a crash into the bottom."

"Good shooting. Tell the sonar gang that they did a superb job. It is not often that you have an opportunity for a one-two attack with both Hedgehogs and torpedo and you certainly took advantage of the opportunity.

"Thank you sir and I will pass on your commendation to the sonarmen."

Brown continued. "We are going out to a 1000 yard circle in case another attack is required. If you think we sunk him, tell the weapons stations to stand easy and we will go in and take a look. There is quite a bit of debris and oil in the water."

As *Percival* moved into the debris field, the ship came to a halt and the crew used boathooks and grappling hooks to recover debris. There was a strong smell of diesel fuel in the air. A lot of the floating material looked like insulation. The Chief Bosun brought a paper document that looked like a newspaper up to the bridge.

"Captain, this looks like Russian writing to me – I think we got a Russian sub."

"Yeah, it looks like Russian to me. I have put Mr. Langan in charge of listing, photographing and taking custody of recovered material and told him to treat it as Secret. Try to retrieve anything that has any markings on it. Also see if you can get a sample of the diesel fuel -- the scientists may be able to figure out where it came from. And Chief, the fact that this appears to be Russian debris has to be treated as Secret information. Try to minimize the number of crew that knows about it and tell those that do to not talk about it – and no letters home about it. I will put out further direction to the crew on this later."

"Aye aye sir."

A short time later Captain Brown sent an encrypted Operational Immediate message to Com 7th Fleet with copy to ComCruDiv3 with a Summary Action Report including the tentative debris identification.

Percival remained in the area for about another hour, put their whaleboat in the water and retrieved floating material and some specimens of oily sea water. About 1300, *Percival* got underway at 25 knots to rejoin *Helena*. *Helena* and *Radford* had slowed to 15 knots after they cleared the sub contact area. *Percival* caught up with them in late afternoon and they resumed their 20 knot transit to the Formosa Straits.

The next morning Captain Brown received a copy of a Secret message from Com7th Fleet ordering the Submarine Rescue Ship USS *Greenlet*

(ASR 10) to the location of the incident. Their orders were to put divers down on the "Russian Sub"site and report their findings.

23 – Formosa Patrol

The next day, Rear Admiral Charles Hartman and his Chief of Staff, Capt. Ed Smith were looking out over the sunny calm of the East China Sea from *Helena*'s Flag Bridge.

"Ed, I think that we should lay to and have the captains of *Percival* and *Radford* join us and Swede to talk about how this patrol is going to work. We left so hurriedly, that I didn't get a chance to go over this op with them. I also want to talk to Captain Brown a bit further about his sub sunk incident."

"Yes Sir, I'll set that up."

About an hour later, all three ships were dead in the water and the Captains of *Percival* and *Radford* were in their gigs on their way to *Helena*. Captain Harold "Swede" Larson, *Helena*'s skipper, welcomed them as they came aboard *Helena* and brought them up to Admiral Hartman's Flag Quarters. The Admiral greeted the captains and introduced them to Smith and two other members of his staff. They were all seated around a conference table.

"Gentlemen," said Hartman, " we left Sasebo so hurriedly that we didn't have an opportunity to go over this mission. Frankly, I think that *Helena* could be much better utilized blowing up bridges near the front lines in Korea than trying to intimidate the Chinese down here, however, we have our orders. Two days ago, I reorganized the fleet to

176

concentrate the 8-inch gun ships on shore bombardment because the 5-inch and 6-inch gun ships weren't making a dent in some of the Korean's reinforced concrete bridges that really need to be destroyed. And now I end up down here making a show of force to the Chinese with *Helena* while the other half of my command, the heavy cruiser *Toledo* and a division of destroyers, are up north bombarding Korea."

"Unfortunately, the situation that we have here is that the ChiComs have been making aggressive noises about invading Formosa and we have to take that seriously. Basically our mission is to continue the 7th Fleet's Presidential mandate to neutralize Formosa. Our three ships certainly can't help much if Mao's folks decide to cross the straits in force, however, we can probably make them think twice before starting anything. Our plan is to monitor activity from Fancheng Island in the north to Swatow in the south and in doing so make sufficient radar and radio noise that the ChiComs know we are here. We will pay particular attention to the area around the islands held by Chiang's forces such as Tachen, Quemoy and Matsu. At all times, we must stay just outside the 12-mile limit of the Peoples Republic of China (PRC) but they will certainly know that we are snooping around. We are not alone in this operation.   Patrol Squadron VP-28 that flies PB-4Y's out of Naha, Okinawa is assigned to this mission as is VP-46 that flies PBM's out of the Pescadores Islands in the southern part of the Straits. We have set up coordination procedures with them and we all know where the others are at all times.   They have been and will continue to fly patrol missions along the China coast. If they find large groups of junks or boats in international waters or any other suspicious activity they will alert us and we will check it out. Now Captain Jim Evans, my Intelligence Officer, will brief you on what we know about the capability of the Peoples Liberation Army Navy."

"Thank you, Admiral. We don't have very much intelligence on the whereabouts of the PLAN's major ships – they have pretty much been staying in port. They may have one 6-inch gunned light cruiser, the former British H.M.S. Aurora that was given to Nationalists and renamed Chung King. In early 1949, the crew revolted and turned the ship over to the Communists who renamed her Tchoung King. In March 1949 she was sunk in Taku harbour by Nationalist aircraft. The ship has since been salvaged with Russian assistance but we do not know whether she has been repaired and made operational. Almost all of the Communist ships are ex Japanese vessels acquired by the Chinese at the end of World War II. They have two Escort Destroyer types and six Corvette types, all with 4.7-inch guns, and a number of gunboats, motor torpedo boats and Patrol Craft. We have not been able to observe any of these ships thus far and do not know their physical condition. I have given the Intelligence Officers on each of your ships data sheets with silhouettes of each of these ships. I believe that you already have data on the Republic of China Navy ships. Our intelligence says that the ROC five 5-inch gunned destroyers of the Yang class are in bad shape and not seaworthy. The 4-inch gunned Yang class former Japanese destroyers are operational. The Nationalists also have six former US, diesel powered, Destroyer Escorts and two ex Japanese Destroyer Escorts, all operational. They also have about 10 Corvette types. We have provided the Koumintang government our recognition codes so they should be able to identify themselves if we meet them at sea.

"Now for the rules of engagement," said Hartman "Any armed vessel in the straits is considered hostile and will be given an opportunity to either identify themselves or surrender. If they ignore our signals or try to get away, they will be sunk. Any aircraft from the PRC that comes within gun range will be fired on. As *Percival* has recently demonstrated, any submarine will be considered hostile and will be attacked."

"*Helena* and both destroyers have Electronic Counter Measures (ECM) equipment that can monitor PRC radio and radar signals. This equipment is to be manned 24-hours a day. All intercepts are to be logged with latitude and longitude location data and reviewed regularly by the Electronics Officer and the Intelligence Officer. Any new or different signals are to be reported to Flag Operations. Under no circumstances are electronic jammers to be energized – the ChiComs could rightly interpret that as an aggressive move. By the same token, if you use your gun director optics to look at China, insure that your Gun Fire Control radar is not radiating. It has a very distinctive electronic signature and we don't want the Chinese thinking that we are getting ready to shoot.

"The destroyer's primary responsibility will be to provide anti-submarine protection for *Helena* and in the event of an air attack to provide anti-aircraft support. Your 3-inch guns will be useful if we interdict hostile small boats. We don't know how long we will be down here and wish to conserve fuel. Because of this, we do not plan on doing anything that requires you to have more than two boilers on line. If we are here long enough, Helena can refuel the destroyers."

"Any questions?"

Commander Brown asked, "What is the latest intelligence that we have about activity in Fukian Province?"

"Over the last few months there has definitely been large troop movements toward the coast. There has also been an accumulation of junks and other small craft in the various ports along the coast. The recent attack on one of our PBM seaplanes by PRC fighter planes says to me that they are getting a little more sensitive about our

179

reconnaissance efforts. Chiang's people have always thought that August would be the month for an attack – we may get to find out. Two submarines, the *Pickerel* and the *Catfish*, have been snooping in close along the coast for the last week. Naval Intelligence in Tokyo is flying some intelligence photos and other material gathered by the subs out to us in a PBM. The PBM should arrive here about 1700.

"Captain Brown, could you give us a summary of your recent ASW action?"

"Certainly. We picked up the contact just after clearing Sasebo. As soon as the sub realized that we had him on sonar, he turned away and picked up speed. We challenged him and got no answer. We ended up in a stern chase with a low range rate that my ASW officer used to our advantage by executing a one-two attack using both Hedgehogs and a Mark-32 torpedo. We clearly heard three explosions that had to be hedgehog hits. I believe that she was slowly sinking with more than one hole in the pressure hull and then sonar heard sounds like they were blowing main ballast tanks when the torpedo got her. Debris collected afterward included some Russian language documents including a newspaper. I am convinced that we sank a Russian submarine."

"Well Captain," said the Admiral, "That is a very impressive performance. It is not very often that a sub is sunk on a single attack run. My compliments to your ASW gang on a job well done."

"Thank you sir."

"If there is nothing else Captains, you can return to your ships. "

The task group got underway headed south toward the straits. At about 1715 a PBM appeared from the north flying low over the water. The

180

PBM is a twin engine, gull wing, flying boat that has eight 50 caliber machine guns in five turrets and can carry two tons of bombs or torpedoes. *Helena* started a long sweeping turn leaving a calm "slick" on the ocean. The PBM landed in the slick and *Helena* came back around and stopped dead in the water. *Percival* and *Radford* laid to about 1000 yards away. A whaleboat got underway from Helena to pick up the guard mail from the seaplane. Besides its usual fenders, the crew had draped kapok lifejackets along it's gunwhale to prevent damaging the PBM's thin aluminum skin as it came alongside. Within a few minutes, the whaleboat was on its way back to Helena with the mail and the PBM had made a pounding, splashing take off.

Captain Brown was on *Percival*'s bridge, Lt. j.g. Harris was the OD and had the conn and Ens. Hagerman was JOOD. *Percival*, being dead in the water, had slowly come around into the troughs and was now rolling quite a bit.

"Mr. Harris," called the Captain, "Get underway and put our head up into the sea before you get everybody seasick."

"Aye, aye sir." answered Harris, his face turning red.

Harris issued engine and steering orders and got the ship settled down with its head into the sea and again dead in the water.

"Sorry about that Captain."

"That's OK Mr. Harris. But you have always have to consider that what you do from the bridge can affect others in the crew – like blowing tubes!"

Hoping to change the subject, Harris said, "It was pretty neat the way

Helena swept out a calm place for the PBM to land."

"Well they didn't really have to do that for a big twin engine seaplane like the PBM, however, cruisers used to carry two, single engine floatplanes. They had a catapult amidships to launch them and they did that sweeping maneuver to make a calm place for them to land. The floatplane landed alongside the cruiser and pulled up onto a landing mat towed by the ship that snagged a hook on the bottom of the float. Then while they were being towed alongside, they would use the crane to pick the plane up and return it to the catapult. Now all of the floatplanes have been replaced with helicopters. You should talk to the XO, he used to fly one of those OS-2U *Kingfisher* floatplanes off the Battle Cruiser *Guam*."

"I will certainly do that."

Over the next several days, the task group cruised the coast of China on lookout for any signs of an imminent invasion of Formosa. Although they stopped and interrogated fishing boats and coastal freighters and gathered visual and electronic intelligence, they saw no signs of any Chinese invasion forces or anybody's man-o-war.

Evidently, Admiral Joy, CINCNAVFE decided that the *Helena*'s 8-inch guns could be more effectively utilized bombarding Korea. On August 1, the 5-inch gunned light cruiser *Juneau* (CL 119), the destroyers *Moore* (DD 747) and *Maddox* (DD 731) and the fleet tanker *Cimmaron* (AO 22) arrived in the Formosa Straits to relieve the *Helena* Task Group. After a brief transfer of documents to *Juneau*, *Helena*, *Percival* and *Radford* headed north. *Helena* was bound for Sasebo for a quick replenishment stop and then on to the east coast of Korea to rejoin Admiral Hartman's East Coast Support Group of Cruiser Division Three and Destroyer Division 3. *Percival* and *Radford* were bound for

Sasebo for ten days of tender availability and replenishment.

In the meantime, reinforcements continued to arrive in Japan and Okinawa. The First Provisional Marine Brigade had been debarked in Pusan and was now in the frontline. The Escort Aircraft Carriers *Sicily* (CVE 118) and *Badoeng Strait* (CVE 116) with embarked Marine Air Wings had arrived and were operating in the Yellow Sea to provide close air support for the Marines. The aircraft carrier *Phillipine Sea* (CV 47) arrived and joined Task Force 77. The USS *Boxer* (CV 21), with it's cargo of Air Force P-51's and Navy *Corsair*'s arrived in Yokusuka, Japan after having set a trans Pacific speed record of eight days and 16 hours from San Francisco. Three AD *Skyraiders* loaded with pilots flew in to Yokusuka to ferry the *Corsairs* back to *Valley Forge*. A steady stream of destroyers, minesweepers, landing craft and auxiliary ships were arriving every day. Help was finally here!

24 – Sasebo Redux

Shortly after dawn on August 3, *Percival* came through the gate in the anti-submarine net and headed for the Josco Fuel Docks on the west side of the Sasebo channel.   Shortly after she moored at the fueling dock, an LCVP came alongside with several large bags of mail that caused big smiles among the crew.   While the ship was being refueled, Captain Brown held a Division Heads meeting in the wardroom.

Brown opened the meeting.   "We have to take maximum advantage of this tender availability and our time in Sasebo as we may not get another maintenance opportunity anytime soon.   With the shortage of destroyers and the high level of activity in Korea, we are probably going to be spending a lot of time at sea.   If you have any problems at all with your equipment, get the parts and the help that you need to get them fixed this week.   For tough problems, civilian tech reps are available through your contacts on the tender."

"On the other hand, I want to make sure the crew gets an opportunity to get ashore as much as possible while we are here because they need to blow off some steam before we go back to sea.   Liberty for the section coming off a duty day will commence at 1000   The other section goes ashore at 1500.   Liberty today will be 1500 for everybody – we need to get all of our maintenance tasks started.   As soon as we finish refueling we will be going alongside the Destroyer Tender USS *Dixie* AD 14. Make sure that you have all of your work orders ready to submit to the tender as soon as we are moored. That's all. Dismissed."

Murphy and Hutch walked out of the wardroom together. Murphy said, "We both have liberty tonight what are your plans?"

"I thought I might go over to the O Club, see if I could call Peggy, have a steak and get a little drunk."

"Sounds like a plan to me. I've still got some stuff to do – how's 1630 for you?"

"That works – see you then."

Hutch turned left at the ladder and climbed up to the sonar shack. Leading Sonarman Johnson was there and was going over some papers. Hutch said, "Have you got all of your tender work orders ready to go?"

"Yeah, I want them to put a diver down to see if there is anything that could cause the QDA sword transducer to jam."

"That's a good idea, we already have a diver coming to check the zincs[26] on the hull – while he is under there, he can check the QDA." said Hutch, "I doubt that they'll find anything though – everyone seems to have problems with their QDA."

"I also requested some Tech Rep support on the Mk4 Attack Director. It seems to have a problem getting a solution when we are on a curving course. Our Fire Control Techs helped us work on it and the techs from *Piedmont* worked on it when we were in Buckner Bay – no joy.

---

26 Zinc plates are bolted on to the hull near the bronze propellor to prevent galvanic corrosion. The "zincs" are eroded in the process and have to be replaced.

"Good. We really need to get that fixed."

"I agree, we'll see if the techs in *Dixie* can do any better than those in *Piedmont*. Dodge and O'Connell are working on a problem with the Attack Plotter. We think that it just needs some tubes replaced. If they don't get it fixed by tomorrow, I will cut a tender work order."

"OK," said Hutch, " I will take these orders over to *Dixie* and see if I can get a schedule from them. Let me know how you come out on the Plotter."

"Yes sir. Oh, one other thing. We are short some critical spare parts for the QHB and the Attack Plotter. Miller and MacDonald are going to try to scrounge them from *Dixie*. If not successful there, they are going to get a boat over to the USS *Electron,* that LST that's been converted to an electronics parts supply ship. It just arrived from the states and hopefully has a good supply of parts."

"Excellent. Good thinking and good luck."

At 1630 Hutch and Murphy went to the quarterdeck, marked themselves ASHORE on the Officer Status board, saluted the quarterdeck and the ensign and went across the gangway to *Dixie*. They went through *Dixie* to the accommodation ladder on the opposite side and boarded the waiting LCM liberty boat. The unwritten rule was that officers rode the LCM standing around the pilot house; the white hats rode down in the well deck. Arriving at the Fleet Landing Hutch and Murphy took a taxi up to the Sasebo Officers Club. The Sasebo Officers Club had previously been the Imperial Japanese Navy Officers Club and local folklore had it that the plot for the December 7, 1941 Pearl Harbor attack had been hatched in one of its private dining rooms.

186

Their first stop was the telephone center. They both went to the desk and placed calls; Hutch to his wife Peggy and Murphy to his fiance' Emily and then took a seat to wait. Hutch's call came through first and he went to one of the numbered phone booths.

"Hi honey"

"Oh Dave, it's so good to hear your voice."

"Peg, I really miss you – It seems like such a long time since we were together in Hawaii."

"I miss you too and so does your son – he took a few tentative steps this week. I wish so much that you were here to share in his life."

"So do I. This being away from my family is much tougher than I ever thought it would be."

"I'm so worried about the war – it doesn't seem to be going well. Have you been in action?"

"We have fired our guns but no one as yet has fired back and I hope it stays that way. We are in Sasebo for about another week but I don't know where we are going after that. Hopefully we will be back with Task Force 77 escorting aircraft carriers. Of course, we never know where they will send us and we could well be doing shore bombardment."

"Well, I hope not.. I hate to think of *Percival* coming under fire. Well, I know that this call is expensive so I will go now. I love you very much. Take care of yourself."

187

"I love you too and think of you all the time. Give my son a kiss for me. Goodbye."

As Hutch came out of the booth he could see Murphy talking in an adjacent booth. In a few minutes Murphy came out and they headed for the dining room. Neither said a word until they were seated.

"Boy that was tough." Said Hutch, "I really miss her and she is having a hard time without me."

"So is Emily. She was crying through most of the call. She is sure that I am going to be killed."

A waiter arrived and gave them menus. Hutch ordered a Jack Daniels and water and Murphy ordered Johnny Walker Red and soda.

Hutch said, "You know Frank, I grew up with the Navy. My grandfather and father were both academy graduates. My father still serves and I always knew that I would. I've lived all over the US and overseas at my Dad's duty stations. And now with all that and after 4 years at the Naval Academy, I'm not sure that this is what I want to do for the rest of my life. I've gotten excellent fitness reports and a commendation and I guess I'm pretty good at this but I'm really having trouble being separated from my family. I've got four more years to go on my academy commitment and I'll have to hang in there but then I will have to see."

"Well Dave, as you know, I went to Fordham on an NROTC Scholarship. My family could have afforded the tuition, but I guess, I wanted to assert my independence a bit. I have two more years of required service and I am not staying in, that's for sure. I'm not too sure what I'm going to do beyond marrying Emily. Maybe I'll go back to school on the GI Bill and get a law degree. Growing up, my mother always wanted me to be a priest – you know 12-years of Catholic School, altar boy, the whole nine yards. I guess I just liked girls too much. I do have a very strong faith, however, and I hope that in some way I can use that to do some good in this world. God knows it needs it."

They ordered steak dinners and another round of drinks. Murphy said, "Dave what do you think of the skipper?"

"Good man and a fine officer. Quiet but decisive and gives us junior officers opportunities to learn. If I were him, I might have taken the conn when I was doing that cowboy maneuver to put the whaleboat in the water to pick up the pilot from the Valley – but he didn't. I heard him get to his feet behind me but he left me alone. From all accounts, his actions during the sinking of *Hoel* during the battle of Leyte Gulf in War 2 and being in the water afterward was nothing short of heroic. I like him and I think that we will be glad to have him as our CO should we get into a real shooting war."

"And the XO?"

"He's a good man and a good navigator and he is also the CO's enforcer with us officers as Harris has found out. At heart, he is still an enlisted man. He and Chief Swenson go ashore in civvies and get drunk at the CPO's hangouts. Ordinarily he is fair, but don't get involved with him when he's been drinking which happens quite a bit when we are in port."

Yeah that's been my experience too. So do you have any idea what is next for us?"

189

"Not really. The scuttlebut is that MacArthur wants to do a big amphibious landing at Inchon to cut off the Commie's supply lines. Boy is that ambitious --Inchon has 40-foot tides. That severely limits the time of day and time of the year that you can do a landing so the enemy probably knows when you are coming. If that invasion comes to pass you can believe that we will be in it."

"Boy that MacArthur has balls."

They ordered another round.

Murphy said, "The thing that really worries me is that if we start winning this thing and push the Reds back up north, the Russians and/or the Chinese will feel that they have to step in and help their North Korean allies. That could be the beginning of World War III."

"That's true, but even before we get to that point, those guys can help in less obvious ways than putting troops on the ground. I've heard that in the few encounters our flyers have had with *Migs*, our guys are convinced the *Mig*-15's are being flown by Russians. The thing that really scares me is that the Russians have evidently given the North Koreans tens of thousands of naval mines – most of them contact type but some magnetic. As much time as we are spending along the Korean coast, we would probably be the ones that find the mines by running into them.   The big-gunned ships can stay outside of the 100-fathom line, safe from mines, and do shore bombardment but we cans have to go in close. Can you picture what one of those mines could do to a tin can like *Percival* with our 3/8-inch thick steel hull?   I certainly don't want to find out."

"Oh boy," said Murphy, "You have just made my day. I think we need another round."

"Well," said Hutch, "I think that we have a really good crew, even if we have been a bit short handed. Now every time we pull into Buckner or Sasebo we pick up a few more Sailors that they have flown out from the states for us. We really have to work hard to integrate these new hands into the crew."

"I've been thinking about this a bit myself. It's no problem with the rated men – their rate determines where they will go. With the seamen, I need to put them where they can help the most but also where there are good petty officers that can train them."

Hutch said, "I think that we have probably gone about as far as we can go in solving the world's problems for tonight. We probably better start heading back to the ship."

"Let's have one for the road and then we can head back to the war."

"OK, but this is the last one."

Hutch and Murphy arrived back at the Fleet Landing about 2300. It was a mob scene of drunken Sailors waiting for their ship's name to be called. They made their way to the officers waiting area and finally boarded the LCM back to *Dixie*. Both leaned against the pilot house and hung on to the rail all the way back. It was going to be a long day tomorrow.

A few days later, George Johnson, SO-1, Bill Tubbs, SO-3 and Charlie MacDonald, SOSN took the LCM from *Dixie* to go on liberty in Sasebo. After converting some of their "scrip" dollars into Yen they hailed a pedicab and told him to take them to Paradise Alley. The driver complained about squeezing three sailors into the pedicab but relented when Johnson said they would give him 100 Yen extra. After a scary ride along the edge of the road that ran perilously close to the Benjo Canal they arrived at Paradise Alley. The large "Paradise Alley" electric sign arch identified the 20-foot wide entrance to one of the Sailor's favorite hangouts. Both sides of the alley were lined with bars each with the largest sign that they could manage within the narrow confines of the alley.

"Wanna go to the Manhattan Bar?" said MacDonald.

"Might as well," Replied Johnson, "Last time there was good."

"Sounds like a plan," said Tubbs, "Let's go, the beer's getting warm."

They went down the crowded alley and entered the Manhattan Bar. Michiko and Atsuko, the two hostesses, greeted them with big smiles. "Percival guys!" Michiko yelled and the bartender waved to them.

"That's us!" said Tubbs, as they sat down at one of the small tables.

The Manhattan, like most Paradise Alley bars, was small with a bar along the back wall and about 10 tables.

"Wot you drink?" said Atsuko.

"I think we need a round of Kirins." said MacDonald and Atsuko walked over to the bar.

"I see that their one liter bottle of Kirin is still 200 Yen -- that's about 56 cents US, what a bargain." said Johnson.

"Yeah," said Tubbs "And a liter is about 34 ounces so its worth almost 3 cans of Budweiser."

"Can hardly afford to stay sober." commented MacDonald.

Atsuko brought the beers and sat down at the table.

"Big time." she said "I sink so maybe three week. Last time you guys sukoshi stinko, ne?"

"I think maybe takusan stinko." said Tubbs, "we sure poured away a bunch of Kirin's."

"Yeah, good time, good time, joto,ne." said Atsuko, "Anything eat?"

"Not right now," said Johnson, and Atsuko walked back to the bar. "Did you guys get any mail since we were in Sasebo."

"I got a "Dear John"," said MacDonald, "Julie met this guy and I'm here and he's there and so she said sayanora."

"Gee and you are also getting fluent in Japanese." kidded Tubbs.

"Well, it's just the way it goes when you're in the service I guess. I remember at boot camp in Great Lakes, they had a huge bulletin board in the rec center where guys posted their "Dear John" letters. Some of them were pretty funny and I think that 90% of them contained the line "..but we'll always be friends"."

"Well," said Johnson, "it's going to be tough on all of us, because the way things are going we are probably going to be in the Far East for quite a while. Seventh Fleet is short of cans now and the ones on their way from the West Coast will be just about enough to bring the fleet up to wartime strength. I don't think that any destroyers are going to get rotated back to the US until they can get some East Coast cans out here to relieve us."

"Never thought of it quite that way, but I think that you're right -- we're probably going to be here for a while." said Tubbs. "Hey Atsuko, another round."

As Atsuko delivered more Kirins, he said, "What do you guys think of our Division Officer Mr. Hutcheson?"

I think he's a great guy." said Johnson, "These Annapolis guys are comfortable in their skin, not like those candy ass NROTC types. If he doesn't know something he isn't afraid to ask an enlisted man. He is firm but fair and he treats us with respect – you can't ask for more than that."

"Well, Mr. Murphy is NROTC and I think that he is pretty good." said MacDonald.

"I agree," said Johnson, "He's probably the exception to my rule. But then again Mr. Harris fits it to a tee."

"Boy, he scares the shit out of me." said Tubbs, "I swear, one of these days when we are doing high speed maneuvers with Task Force 77 he is going to get us into a collision. You ever notice how the old man spends a lot of time on the bridge when "Sneaky Pete" has the conn?"

"You're right" said Johnson, "for a Yale graduate, he doesn't seem to have much common sense."

As the discussion continued, Atsuko kept the Kirins coming. At some point they ordered hamburgers.

"Hey George," said MacDonald to Johnson, "When am I going go to Sonar School?"

"Probably not until we get back to States, whenever that is. You really need to go. I'll talk to Hutcheson about putting in a chit for you."

"Thanks, I really want to go."

"I enjoyed Sonar School." said Tubbs, "The school is pretty intense, but my math was good enough that I skipped the math night school.   The first six weeks of operations was interesting, particularly the two weeks of Sea Phase but I had a hard time with Morse Code. I really began to enjoy it when we got down to troubleshooting the sonar equipment.

"I here there's not much to do in Key West." said MacDonald.

"Well Key West is pretty isolated, it's about 130 miles at sea, but there was really quite a bit to do." said Tubbs.

"Yeah," said Johnson, " The Habana Madrid, Two Friends, Mardi Gras and Sloppy Joe's. Oh, and don't forget Mom's whorehouse on Stock Island."

"Naw, there was that nice USO Club on Whitehead Street where they had dances with girls from town. On the base there were swimming pools, the Enlisted Men's Beach, movies and a good EM Club with cheap beer.   And the best part was that there are lots of musicians in sonar school – I was playing in a great little combo there."

"That's true," said Johnson, "They like to make musicians into

195

sonarmen because they have good pitch discrimination and can hear doppler."

"The group that I played in had a couple of gigs in town – which as you know is against Navy regs. So when it came to the Friday that they had the monthly Happy Hour, with dancing, at the Echoasis Officers Club, our division officer told us we had to play for it or he would turn us in – so we played. The good part was that the Stewards Mates, that tended bar at the Echoasis, premixed Martinis and Manhattans and they would slip us a bottle of them."

During all of this discussion, the beers kept flowing. Michiko had brought over the leather cup and the bar dice and they played Tally Hold while drinking and talking.

Johnson said, "I was talking to Hutcheson and he said we are going up the east coast of Korea when we leave on Monday. We're going to support some raiders that are going ashore to blow things up."

"That should be interesting," said MacDonald. "I'm afraid that things are going to start heating up with a lot more action. You know when we sank that North Korean Torpedo Boat, I was really scared. I was thinking, I hope to hell we can sink this guy before he puts a torpedo in us. A torpedo in a fire room or boiler room in these cans could capsize us."

"Worse than that, said Tubbs, "I keep hearing stories about mines. We could hit one of those things while we're just steaming along and never know what hit us."

"Well guys, as enjoyable as this has been," said Johnson, "It's 2325 and we better jump a cab and get back to the Fleet Landing by midnight before we all turn into pumpkins."

They stumbled out of the bar and got to the end of the alley where they flagged a cab. When they arrived at the Fleet Landing, it was a sea of drunken Sailors pushing toward the gate. The Percival's managed to get checked in by 2355 then waited around in another mob until the boat to *Dixie* was called. The ride back to the ship in the packed well deck of the LCM was kind of a blur but the almost continuous fights and guys throwing up was unforgettable.

25 – Landing Party

Shortly after dawn on August 14, *Percival* had passed through the Sasebo anti-submarine nets and in company with *Radford* had headed north toward the Western Channel of the Korean Straits. Lt. j.g. Mark Benson was the OD and Ens. Joseph Hagerman was JOOD and had the conn.. Quartermaster Chief Swenson had just come out of the pilot house.

"Mr. Benson, I understand that we are headed for Pohang to help ROK forces. Do you have any further info?"

"The information that we have is that the North Korean Army has launched a fierce offensive against the ROK forces holding the northern end of the Pusan perimeter along the coast and that we may lose Pohang. The threat is serious enough that the Air Force has flown forty-five of their P-51 fighters out of the Pohang airstrip and back to Japan. The ROK 3rd Division has been driven down to Chongha just north of Pohang harbor and are surrounded with their backs to the sea. General Walker has ordered the ROK's evacuation by sea. In the meantime we are supposed to join the cruiser *Helena* to provide gun fire support to hold back the Commies until ships can be organized for the evacuation.

"Wow, what a mess." said Swenson, "The ROKs have been fighting pretty good but the North Koreans with those Russian heavy tanks have been hard to stop."

"I also understand," said Benson, "that it has gotten so bad that *Helena* has been using their helicopter to fly medical and other critical supplies in to the ROKs."

"Captain on the bridge." shouted the bosun.

"Change of plans." said the Captain, "*Percival* is going in to Pusan to pick up some 55-gallon drums of motor gasoline. We will use our whaleboat to deliver the gasoline ashore to the ROK troops that are trapped north of Pohang. They have vehicles that are completely out of gas and they don't want to leave them on the beach for the Commies. They need just enough fuel so that they can at least drive their vehicles on to the LST's when and if they get there to take them off."

"Mr. Benson, the XO is setting a course for Pusan and he will give you instructions."

Swenson said, "I'll go down and get the approach and harbor charts for Pusan."

The XO called out,"We will also need the charts for the Yongil Bay and the Toksong-ni area."

"Aye, aye sir."

As *Percival* approached the South Korean coast, the Special Sea Detail was set. As they approached the sea walls protecting Pusan harbor, they picked up a harbor pilot and Ensign Kim of the ROK Navy who would act as translator for the mission and liasion to the ROK forces. The pilot directed *Percival* to a large barge moored alongside an industrial pier. *Percival* moored port side to the barge so that they could use the motor winch to haul the 400-pound barrels aboard. A hoist was jury rigged from the whaleboat davit and in about an hour six 55-gallon drums had been loaded aboard and lashed down on the deck.

Shortly thereafter, Percival got underway and cleared the harbor about 30 minutes later. When the Special Sea Detail was secured, Lt. Murphy was OD and had the conn and Ens. Matthews was JOOD. The captain was in his port side chair and Ensign Kim of the ROK Navy was standing by on the port wing.

"Things are really a mess where we are going." said the Captain. "The ROK's are hanging on by their fingernails and *Helena* and the destroyers are bombarding the crap out of the Commies that are trying to push them off the beach. This morning here was a rumor that there was an enemy landing at Kuryongpo behind the UN front lines. *Helena* and the destroyers dashed down there at full steam, fired a few rounds and killed a small North Korean reconnaissance party on the beach. When they were convinced that there was no enemy landing in force, they charged back north at 25 knots and resumed bombarding the guys north of Pohang."

"Wow, so what are we going to do?" asked Murphy.

"Why don't you and Mr. Kim come in to the chart table in the pilot house. We will go to GQ as we approach Pohang and your GQ station is OD so you will continue as you are now. The XO has been plotting the course into Toksong-ni north of Pohang. Charlie, can you explain to Lt. Murphy and Mr. Kim what we plan to do."

"Certainly.   As you can see from the chart, Toksong-ni is on a little peninsula.   There are three small boat harbors around the town protected by manmade breakwaters.   The ROK's hold the town.   They want us to land the gasoline at the southernmost small boat harbor right next to the beach.   We will anchor out about a half mile from the harbor.   We will use a fire team from our Landing Party[27] to provide protection for the whaleboat.   We can fit three gasoline drums in the front section of the whaleboat so we will have to make two trips.   The course is marked on the chart as is the anchorage that is in about 50 feet of water with a sand bottom.   Navigation should not be hard – it will be in daylight.   The harbor is just to the north of the beach and the breakwater should be visible as we approach."

Mr. Kim spoke up. "I have just talked to our ROK headquarters at Toksong from your radio room.   They have assured me that although there is fighting a few miles away, the harbor where the gasoline is to be delivered is securely in our hands.   They have also said that there is a small crane on the pier that should make delivery of the gasoline easier."

"Very well," said the Captain, "Mr. Kim you will go in the whaleboat with the Landing Party."

"Aye, aye, sir."

"Mr. Murphy, the Anchor Detail will have to be on the foc'sle when we anchor.   I want them off the foc'sle and everybody aft of the foc'sle doors as soon as we are securely anchored in case we have to fire Mount 51. Have them stay right inside the doors ready to weigh anchor

---

27 All Naval vessels are required to maintain a Landing Party in proportion to
   the ship size. Destroyers are required to have a 13 man rifle squad
   consisting of a petty officer squad leader and three 4-man fire teams.

201

when needed."

"Aye, aye, sir. I will brief Chief Bosun's Mate Egan"

Down on the main deck under the whaleboat, Lt. j.g. Harris was organizing the Landing Party. Roger McMillen, Gunner's Mate First Class and also the Landing Party Squad Leader was detailing his plans to Harris.

"Chief Egan has given us a Coxswain and an Engineman to run the whaleboat who are also qualified with the M-1 Carbine. They will each have a carbine with a 30 round clip by their side plus two more clips. I will be in the bow as the Bow Hook armed with a Thompson submachine gun. My three other team members will be armed with Browning Automatic Rifles (BAR). We are a small force and I want to have as much firepower as possible in case we get into trouble. We have plenty of additional ammunition for all of the weapons."

"Very well,' said Harris, Radioman Jones will be operating the AN/PRC-6 radio and has extra batteries. Quartermaster Evans has a Signalling Light Gun and Signal Flags. He also has a First Aid pack. Ensign Costa will be in charge and Ensign Kim will be your translator. Ensign Costa will be carrying a 45 pistol, however, he is qualified with the carbine and would like to have one available."

"I will see that he gets one." said McMillen.

"Make sure," Harris added, "that as soon as the whaleboat is in the water, that you rig the radar reflector so that CIC can track you."

"Aye, Aye Sir."

Most navy ships jury-rigged a radar corner reflector for their whaleboat out of chicken wire and a piece of pipe because the wooden boat is too small to be skin tracked on radar.

Percival passed close offshore of the peninsula just south of Yongil Bay and then turned slightly left toward Toksong. The ship was at General Quarters. The XO was directing the quartermasters taking bearings on nearby mountain peaks as he piloted to a point about a half mile off the beach south of Toksong. The Anchor Detail was standing ready on the foc'sle.

Murphy had slowed the ship to five knots as she approached the anchorage. Helena and her destroyer division were a few miles north of Percival's location and their gunfire could be clearly heard.   Some explosions could be seen on inland mountainsides.

"All stop." Said Murphy.

"Engine room answers All Stop"

The Landing Party was in the whaleboat ready to be lowered away. As the ship lost way, Captain Brown turned to Murphy and said "Make absolutely sure that we are dead in the water before letting the anchor go – if we have any way on, you could drag the chain into the sonar dome and damage it."   About three months earlier, *Percival* had anchored with some headway on and had damaged the sonar dome. Repair required dry docking the ship in Sasebo for two days which probably had an effect on Brown's fitness report – his concern about anchoring was understandable and had become a legend in *Percival.*

Murphy called to the quartermaster. "Drop a wood chip." and the quartermaster threw a small piece of wood over the side.   The chip stayed at the same point alongside the ship showing that they were dead in the water.

Murphy said to the talker, "Let go the anchor."

On the foc'sle, one of the seamen swung a sledge hammer knocking the bale off the pelican hook chain stopper. The pelican hook flew open and the chain started to pay out with a roar. As sufficient scope of chain was paid out, the windless brake was applied and the stopper fastened on the chain. As the anchor dug in, the ship swung around until its head was into the light breeze.

"Away the Landing Party." said the Captain.

The whaleboat was lowered to the water and the engine started. All of the crew wore kapok life jackets and steel helmets. The whaleboat was held alongside as a hoisting line that had been rigged from the boat davit was used to load the drums into the whaleboat. Using the motor windless three 55-gallon gasoline drums were lowered into the boat's forward compartment. A manila line was passed over the top of the drums several times and secured under the gunwhale.

Jones checked the radio. "Sofahound this is Raider1. We have the gasoline on board and are manned and ready. How do you read?"

"Loud and clear Raider1. Shove off and report when you get to the breakwater."

"This is Raider1, we are underway."

As they left the ship, McMillen ordered. "Cock your weapons put them on safety."

The whaleboat proceeded toward the breakwater sheltering the small boat harbor. The sea was relatively calm with only a slight swell. All of the Sailors were quiet and focused on the shoreline. McMillen and Costa were surveying their destination through their binoculars.

"Mr. Costa I only see a few people along the breakwater. Do we know where we are supposed to go."

"Mr. Kim, advises that we should come right around the breakwater and head for the pier with a crane on it. I will conn the coxswain."

"Aye, aye. Listen up you guys! No safties off unless I tell you. And no one shoots unless Mr. Costa orders it. We do not expect resistance here."

As they came around the breakwater, McMillen yelled, "The crane is straight ahead."

"Sofahound, Raider1. We are rounding the breakwater and have the pier with the crane on it in sight. We are proceeding inbound. There appears to be a few ROK soldiers and a couple of civilians on the pier."

"Roger Raider1, stay alert. We were able to follow you all the way in on radar"

In a few minutes the whaleboat was alongside the pier and the soldiers were swinging the crane out.

McMillen called out. "Smith and Ryan get up on the pier to lookout and cover us. The rest of you lend a hand and lets get these drums unloaded." The coxswain and the engineman both remained at their stations but picked up their carbines and started scanning the surrounding buildings.

The Sailors and soldiers worked quickly with Mr. Kim helping with instructions and in about 15 minutes, the drums were unloaded and the lookouts returned to the boat.

As the whaleboat pushed off, Mr. Costa called *Percival.* "Sofahound this is Raider1, we have delivered the first load and are returning to the ship for the other three drums."

"Roger that Raider1, we have the next drum on the hoist and ready to load. Thus far we can see no indication of any enemy activity near the harbor."

"Roger, hope it stays that way."

The whaleboat came back alongside the ship and in about 20 minutes the other three drums were loaded. The whaleboat shoved off and headed back to the harbor where the gasoline was quickly unloaded. The soldiers on the pier were already busy pouring gasoline from the drums into 5-gallon jerry cans to take to their stranded vehicles.

Mr. Kim said, "The soldiers thank you for coming in here to bring them this gas. They are most appreciative because they very much want to get their vehicles out of here and on to the LST's."

Kim turned to Costa, " Their officer also said that North Korean patrols are probing the perimeter pretty hard and in some places are close to the beach -- we should be alert!"

"Tell him thank you." said Costa

As the whaleboat cleared the breakwater, McMillen who was watching the beach through his binoculars, called out. "There are about a half dozen guys with guns coming out out of the woods and on to the beach about 200 yards south. Safeties off!"

"Sofahound this is Raider1. We have company about 200 yards down the beach. Don't know if they are bad guys or good guys."

"Roger Raider1, we see them. We have Mount 31 covering them. Any indication of their intentions?"

About that time, the intruders opened fire on the whaleboat. Geysers appeared in the water near the boat and a couple of slugs thunked into the boat's oak hull.. The engineman put the boat's throttle as far forward as it would go and they surged ahead. The coxswain steered a sinuous evasive course toward the ship.

Mr. Costa yelled, "Open fire, open fire." followed by a fusillade of shots from all of the boat's weapons. The BAR's very loud 300 round per minute bursts were interspersed with the popping of the carbine's 600 round per minute bursts and the deeper sound of McMillen's 45 caliber Tommy gun. Empty box and stick magazines clattered into the whaleboat bilge as they were emptied.

"Sofahound, we are taking fire from the beach."

A few seconds later they could hear the rapid fire of the dual 3-inch 50's of *Percival's* Mount 31. Sand was blowing high in the air as the HE shells exploded near the enemy troops.

Every gun on the whaleboat except for the engineman's and the coxswain's were pouring bullets into the NPRK soldiers – some had already fallen. At the same time enemy shots were thudding into the side of the whaleboat. There was a loud scream and Ensign Costa pitched forward.

"Mr. Costa is hit in the arm," shouted Ryan. "Pass the First Aid pack."

The fire fight did not last long. The concentrated automatic small arms fire from the whaleboat and the 3-inch fire from Percival quickly decimated the NPRK fighters.

"Cease fire, cease fire," yelled McMillen. "We've got them all. How's Costa?"

"The bullet went through his left upper arm," said Ryan, "I'm holding compresses on it."

"It hurts like hell," said Costa, "but it's not bleeding too badly.

"See if you could find something in the pack to wrap tightly around the compresses and his arm," said McMillen.

"Smith's got a pretty deep cut over his right eye from some flying wood splinters from bullet hits on the gunwale." said Evans, "We're holding a thick gauze pad on it and it looks like the bleeding is almost stopped."

McMillen picked up the radio handset, "Sofahound, Raider1. We are returning to ship with two casualties. Mr. Costa has a bullet through his left arm and Smith has a cut over his right eye."

"Roger, will have corpsmen standing by."

The whaleboat made *Percival*'s port side by the boarding ladder near the quarterdeck.   As they came alongside, Chief Hospital Corpsman Ed Cosgrove dropped down into the boat with a medical pack. Corpsman Cleary remained on the deck. Cosgrove told Smith, "Climb up to the deck, Cleary will take care of you."

Mr. Costa was slumped in his seat, obviously in pain. Evans had placed thick gauze pads on both sides of the wound and wrapped an Ace bandage around Costa's arm to hold the pads in place.

Cosgrove quickly examined Costa and said, "Good job Evans, he doesn't appear to be bleeding too badly, let's get him to sickbay."

Cosgrove called out, "Pass down the Stokes stretcher."

Hands on deck passed down the stretcher and Costa was carefully loaded into it and strapped in. The stretcher was passed up to the deck and taken to the sickbay.

Cleary examined Smith's cut, poured some peroxide on it and did a more professional bandage with wrappings around his head.

"This is going to take some stitches," he said to Smith, "Come on with me to the sickbay and I will get it sutured up."

As soon as the casualties were cleared, the guns were quickly handed up to crew on deck and the Landing Party and Mr. Kim clambered aboard. The Anchor Detail had the anchor at short stay and were waiting instruction from the bridge to weigh anchor.   The Deck Force moved the whaleboat forward and it was hoisted aboard.

On the bridge, Mr. Murphy turned to the Captain. "The whaleboat is aboard and Chief Egan is inspecting the battle damage. Request permission to weigh anchor and get underway."

"Let's get out the hell of here before we get some better armed company." said Brown

Murphy turned to the talker. "Tell the foc'sle to take in the anchor and let me know when it's aweigh."

A few minutes later, the phone talker called out: "Anchor's aweigh."

Murphy replied. "Aye roger. All ahead one. We'll pull ahead slowly and get turned around while they get the anchor stowed. Steer zero-four-five."

"All ahead one, steer zero-four-five aye."

About twenty minutes after the ship was underway, Chief Cosgrove came up to the bridge and reported to Captain Brown. "Mr. Costa is very lucky, the bullet went cleanly through his upper arm without hitting anything vital. I sutured up the wounds and gave him a shot of penicillin and a some morphine for the pain. I think he will heal up OK. I will check on it every day to be sure there is no infection. He will need to be on limited duty for a week or so.

"Very well, how's Smith?"

"That piece of wood made a nasty gash, however, Cleary is good with sutures and there shouldn't even be much of a scar. We will keep an eye on it as it heals."

A little while later, Lt. j.g. Harris and Chief Boatswains Mate Egan came up the ladder   at the rear of the bridge and came over to the Captain.

"The Chief and I have looked over the whaleboat.   There are some bullets imbedded in the sides of the boat and a couple came through -- we found them laying inside.   None of the buoyancy tanks were penetrated. A couple of rounds split pieces off the gunwale like the one that hit Smith. The Chief can explain how it will be repaired."

We are going to make wood pegs to plug the holes." Chief Egan said. "We'll cover them with caulking, drive them in, sand them off and paint over.   We'll just have to trim, sand and varnish the gunwale until we can get to a boatyard where it can be fixed right. We were very lucky that those guys weren't better shots. They had automatic weapons and fired a helluva a lot of rounds and somebody could have been killed."

"We certainly were lucky chief ," said Brown, "but the fact that we were prepared and responded with a lot of firepower certainly contributed to the outcome. It's good that our boat can be made seaworthy. When will the repairs be finished?"

"We expect to have the hole repairs finished later tonight. We'll paint tomorrow."

As Percival cleared the harbor, they secured GQ, set the Normal Steaming Watch and headed south.

The Bosun piped All Hands and Captain Brown went to the 1MC. "I want to commend all hands for a job well done. Mr. Kim advises me that the gasoline we delivered to the ROK troops enabled them to get all of their stalled vehicles down to the landing area ready to be evacuated. The whaleboat crew and the Landing Party did an outstanding job, some of it under fire. Mr. Costa and Seamen Smith were wounded but are going to be OK. We have orders to proceed to Pusan to escort the evacuation ships from Pusan into the beach at Chongha where the ROK 3rd Division is to be extracted.

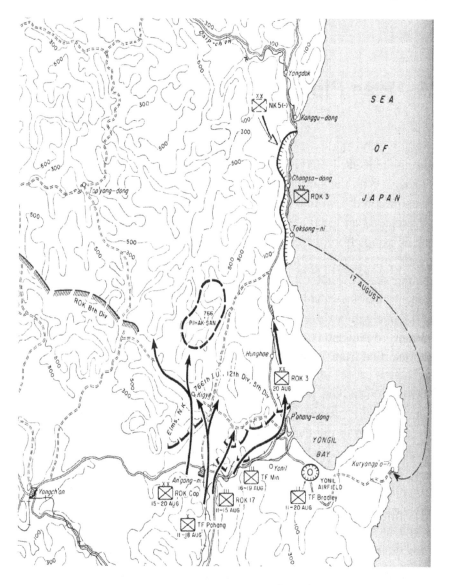

**The Pohang situation as the ROK 3rd Division evacuated
Toksong and redeployed to Kuryongpo on August 17, 1950.**

26 – Pied Piper

Getting the ROK 3rd Division exfiltrated from the Chongha beaches was not easy. With the shortage of ships it was uncertain whether adequate transport could be found in time for the evacuation. Admiral Hartman had prepared an alternate evacuation plan that involved removing the Korean troops from the beach on rafts towed by whaleboats out to naval vessels off shore. Fortunately, that wasn't necessary. At Pusan, Commander Michael J. L. Luosey, USN, who was Acting Commander of the ROK Navy, had rounded up four civilian Landing Ships, Tank (LST), one with a Korean crew and three with Japanese crews. By late morning of August 16, the LST's were ready to go and they and their escort sortied from Pusan.

Percival was tasked with leading these ships, now designated as Task Element 96.51, as expeditiously as possible to Chongha, Korea and directing them to the beach. Chongha was about 5 miles north of the beach where Percival's whaleboat had been engaged in a firefight yesterday. With Mr. Kim relaying commands on the radio, Captain Brown had formed his four charges into a box formation spaced about 500 yards apart with *Percival* 500 yards in front. Under the best of circumstances, an LST can make about 12 knots. One of the four LST's could do no more than 10 knots so that set the Task Element's speed.

As TE 96.51 proceeded slowly northward, *Helena* and destroyers shelled the North Korean front lines. Throughout the day, *Corsairs* and *Skyraiders* from the aircraft carriers *Valley Forge* and *Phillipine Sea*

214

bombed and strafed the North Korean troops that were beyond the range of naval gunfire.

The sun had set and it was getting dark as TE 96.51 finally arrived off Chongha. In *Percival*, Lt. j.g. Hutcheson was the OD and Ens. Langan was the JOOD and had the conn. Captain Brown was on the bridge. By 2030, as darkness approached, with *Percival* in the lead followed by the LST's, TE 96.51 was about 2 miles offshore and headed toward the beach at 5 knots.

There were flashes in the sky and the rolling thunder of heavy guns as Helena and the destroyer division, about a mile north, continued pounding the North Korean forces pushing on the beachhead.

Just before last light, the XO had the quartermasters take cuts on several geographic landmarks to establish *Percival*'s exact location. There were no lighthouses or light beacons operating in this part of the coast so once it was dark they would have to plot their position by dead reckoning backed up by radar data and depth sounder readings.

"By the chart, it looks like we can go in toward the beach about another mile before it gets too shallow." Hutcheson said to the Captain.

"That's right, we can't lead the LST's any further than that. They will then have to feel their way into the beach."

Mr. Kim came out of the pilot house and over to Brown. "Captain, sir, I have been in radio contact with the ROK HQ on the beach. They are very concerned about how the LST's are going to find their way to the right place on the beach in the dark."

"So am I." said Brown

"They have told me that they are going to park some of their jeeps in pairs with their headlights pointing out to sea to mark where each of the LST's has to beach."

"That's a great idea."

Hutcheson called. "I am seeing some headlights on the beach now."

"Mr. Kim" said the Captain, "Get on the radio and coordinate with your people on the beach about where they want the LST's. Then you can tell each of the LST's which pair of headlights they should go toward. Also tell the LST's that they should continue to follow us until they can clearly identify their destination. Also let them know that we are going to go about another half mile closer to the beach and then will bear off to the north and they will be on their own."

Aye, aye sir," answered Kim.

"Commander," called Hutcheson to the XO, "how much farther to our turning point?"

"About five hundred yards, that will be about 3 minutes from now. You should still be in about 30 feet of water."

"Aye, aye, planning to turn at 2110 and increase speed to 10 knots to get out of the LST's way."

"Very well." said the Captain.

"Mr. Kim, tell the LST's that we will turn at 2110."

"Aye, aye."

At 2110, *Percival* turned northward and then, when clear of the LST's turned out to sea taking up a southbound course, parallel to, and about two miles off the beach. The LST's continued on toward the beach. About 200 yards from the beach, the LST's released their stern anchors that, along with deballasting, would help them get back off the beach.

At Captain Brown's direction, the Gunnery Liasion Officer in *Percival*'s CIC contacted the US Marine, Air Naval Gunfire Liasion Company (ANGLICO) embedded with the ROK 3rd Division and notified them that *Percival* was now available for 5-inch and 3-inch gunfire support missions.

On Percival's bridge, Hutcheson turned to the phone talker. "Tell Plot1 and Plot 2 to standby for shore bombardment assignments from the Gunnery Liasion Officer."

The Bridge Phone Talker: "Gunnery Liason Officer reports that they have designated night time harassment targets in the North Korean rear area. Also, Plot1 reports solution plot for Mounts 51 and 55. and Plot 2 reports solution plot for mounts 31 and 32."

Captain Brown said, "Fire when ready."

All mounts began firing with a load roar. The muzzle of Mount 51 was less than 50 feet from the bridge and everyone felt a large concussive force as it fired. Firing continued at irregular intervals during the night. Further up the coast, the *Helena* Group also continued their planned schedule of harassing fire through the night.

Starting at 0415 on the 17th, the loaded LST's started to clear the beach

217

and by daylight all 5800 ROK troops, the members of the American Korean Military Assistance Group (KMAG), and 1200 civilian refugees had been evacuated along with about 100 vehicles. *Percival* led the four LST's on their leisurely sea voyage to Kurypongpo where, in mid afternoon, the LST's were once again beached to put the Koreans back in the fight.

Percival turned northward to join Gunfire Support Group 96.5 for shore bombardment assignments. On the morning of the 18th, Percival caught up with the task group, consisting of the Heavy Cruiser *Helena* and a division or more of destroyers. The task group was in the process of refueling from the Fleet Tanker USS *Cacapon* (AO 52). *Helena* was fueling from *Cacapon*'s port side and *Percival* joined the line of destroyers waiting to fuel on the starboard side. When Percival and Radford completed fueling, they were directed to proceed north to bombard the town of Uljin.

27 – Gunslingers

Because of the high level of operations in the Gunfire Support Group the ships in the group stood watches at Readiness Condition II, Wartime Cruising, in which battle stations are only partially manned. Sufficient manning is provided to carry out shore bombardment assignments without requiring everyone to be at Condition I, General Quarters. On August 19 at 0510, as they steamed north in the Sea of Japan, *Percival* and *Radford* approached Uljin, South Korea. Uljin had been captured by North Korean troops in July and and since then supplies for their army in the south had been flowing down the railroad and highways that ran through the town. On *Percival*'s bridge, Lt. j.g. Mitchell was OD and Ens. Moore was JOOD and had the conn. *Percival* turned to a southerly course parallel to and about 1 mile off the shoreline and about 5 miles north of Uljin. *Radford* was on the same course about 500 yards behind *Percival*. Captain Brown, as the senior of the two captains, was Officer in Tactical Command (OTC).

Uljin is in a mountainous area and is not a seaport -- there is a small range of mountains between the city and the Sea of Japan There are two small boat harbors on the Sea of Japan connected to the city by roads that run through passes in the mountains. The commercial city is tucked into a valley on both sides of the winding Gangbyeon River. At this time of the year the river is mostly dry with just a small water flow in the middle of a wide river bed. At the southern edge of the city is the flowing Uljinbuk River that drains into the Gangbyeon about 1200 yards from where it flows into the Sea of Japan.. There were rail and highway bridges crossing both of the rivers. *Percival* and *Radford*'s mission was to cut those bridges and thus stop the flow of NK's supplies to the south. Because of the mountainous geography, it would not be easy.

Mitchell turned to the pilot house. "Mr Moore, slow to five knots."

"Five knots aye."

Mitchell picked up the TBS handset. "Gypsy Prince, this is Sofahound, slowing to five knots."

"This is Gypsy Prince, slow to five."

Captain Brown turned to Mitchell and Moore, "This mission is tricky because of the mountainous terrain. Captain Ogle, of *Radford,* and I agreed that the best approach would be to approach from the north. That way we can first use direct fire to shell the bridges on the Uljinbuk River that are shielded by the mountains on their south side. We will take out the highway bridge and *Radford* will take out the rail bridge. Because of the bends in the Gangbyeon River and the mountains, we will not be able to see the bridges, about a mile upstream, until we are several miles further south. As we proceed south, there is a possibility that we can bear on the Gangybeon River bridges through a pass running westward from the boat harbor. We will only go fast enough to maintain steerage way as we come to bear on the bridges because the field of view is not very wide.

At about 0545, the sun was just peeking over the horizon. Captain Brown, Lt. j.g. Mitchell, and Ens. Moore were peering through their binoculars at the Uljinbuk River highway bridge.

Brown said, "It is a three span steel box girder bridge. We will work on the center span first."

Quartermasters were at both peloruses taking angles on an old lighthouse and the railroad station near the Uljinbuk River rail bridge. The XO, Lt. Cmdr.. Cook, was navigator.

In the Mark 37 Gun Director, Lt.. Murphy had located the target highway bridge in his Slewing Sight and was slewing the director over to it.

"Control in Local -- you should have the bridge in your sights." he called out to the Pointer and the Trainer.

"Rangefinder, sight in on that post in the center of the bridge. Radar give me range to the bridge."

The Mk 25 radar operator in the director reported, "Seven two two zero yards range to the bridge."

The XO came out of the pilot house on to the bridge and addressed the Captain. "Mike, we have been piloting on some well defined landmarks around Uljin and I feel that we have a good track of our position. In addition since the Mk 37 Director is tracking on the center of the bridge, I plotted their data and it fits right on our track. I think that we will have good ship's position data in case we need to use indirect fire on the Gangbyeon River bridges."

"Thanks Charlie."

From Plot1, the Plotting Room Officer reported, "Solution Plot."

Murphy called out to director crew, "Solution Plot, Control to Automatic."

The Mark 37 Gun Director was pointed at the highway bridge, and Mounts 51 and 55 were following the director while the ship continued slowly southward.

Murphy keyed the 17MC Battle Announcing Circuit, "Mounts 51 and 55, Director Control, High Explosive, One salvo for effect, Standby."

Mr. Murphy, "Fire when ready." said Captain Brown.

Murphy called into the 1JP sound powered phone, "Fire, fire" followed by large booms as both 5-inch guns fired.

A few seconds later Murphy called to the director crew, "Hits are short and left. Right deflection 2 mils and add 20 yards in range."

Murphy keyed the 17MC, "Mounts 51 and 55, Director Control, High Explosive, One salvo for effect.

Murphy called into the 1JP, "Fire, fire" followed by booms.

A few seconds later Murphy called to the director crew, "Excellent! - two hits on the bridge, no changes."

Murphy keyed the 17MC, "Mounts 51 and 55, Director Control, High Explosive, Rapid Fire."

Murphy called into the 1JP, "Commence fire." This was followed by continuous fire about every five seconds.

After about four minutes of Rapid Fire, Murphy called on the 1JP, "Cease Fire, Cease Fire, the center span has fallen."

Fire was shifted to the north span and then the south span until both had fallen. In the meantime *Radford* was having similar results. The railroad bridge had four spans of riveted built up steel girder construction. Two spans had fallen and one had been blown off its concrete pedestal foundation.

As they continued southward, both ships slewed their gun directors to the northwest to see if they could acquire the Gangbyeon River bridges through the pass in the mountains. As *Percival* passed the more southern boat basin on its starboard beam, Lt.. Murphy reported, "I have a clear shot through a pass to the railroad bridge."

"Control in Local -- you should have the bridge in your sights." he called out to the Pointer and the Trainer.

"Rangefinder, sight in on the concrete pedestal in the center of the bridge. Radar give me range to the bridge."

The Mk 25 radar operator in the director reported, "Three one four zero yards range to the bridge."

The gun crews got off a salvo for effect, made their corrections and began firing rounds into the three span, steel deck truss bridge. Captain Brown ordered the ship stopped and then backed down slowly to hold the favorable angle through the mountains.

Radford had come down close astern of *Percival* and also began pouring fire through the valley into the railroad bridge. After about a half hour two spans of the bridge had collapsed and both ships got underway southward to the point where they had sight lines directly up the Gangbyeon River valley to the highway bridge.

To get the best angle Percival had moved in closer to shore as they passed the mouth of the Gangbyeon River. It was now 0910 and the bridge watch had changed. Lt.. j.g. Hutcheson was OD and Ensign Langan was JOOD and had the conn. Lt.. j.g. Benson had replaced Murphy in the Gun Director. Captain Brown was in his chair on the starboard side of the bridge.

"Sonar, how deep is the water?" asked Hutcheson

Sonarman SeamanYork was at the NMC Depth Finder in the director room just off the pilot house and he called back, "Fifty five feet under the keel."

Hutcheson walked into the pilot house to the Chart Table and looked at their penciled track on the chart that showed that they were about one half mile from shore. "Fortunately that agrees with the chart." he said to the Captain.

"In this mountainous area the bottom drops off sharply from the beach." said the Captain.

"I have to admit." said Hutcheson, "that I get pretty nervous being this close to the shore. We are doing all this shore bombardment and thus far no one has fired back. One of these days we may get a surprise."

"Well," said Brown, "we have both 3-inch gun mounts manned and ready to provide rapid counter fire should we get some from shore – but you are right, thus far we have gotten off easy."

224

Hutcheson looked up to the flying bridge. "Lookouts, keep an eye out on the shore and the roads for any NK Army troops or anything that looks like heavy weapons approaching."

"Aye, aye, sir."

As they continued south from the river mouth they could gradually see further up the valley. The Mk 37 Gun Director was now pointed straight up the valley.

In the Mark 37 Gun Director, Benson had located the south end of the target highway bridge in his Slewing Sight and was slewing the director over to it.

"Control in Local -- you should have the left end of the bridge in your sights. The rest is obscured by the mountains," he called out to the Pointer and the Trainer. "We should get a better look in a few minutes."

"Rangefinder, sight in on that concrete pier on the left edge of the bridge. Radar give me range to the bridge."

The Mk 25 radar operator in the director reported, "Six nine two zero yards range to the bridge."

"Okay", said Benson a minute later, "We now have the whole bridge in view and our point of aim is the middle of the center span. I am also seeing trucks going across the bridge."

From Plot1, the Plotting Room Officer reported, "Solution Plot."

Benson called out to director crew, "Solution Plot, Control to Automatic."

Benson keyed the 17MC, "Mounts 51 and 55, Director Control, High Explosive, One salvo for effect.

Benson called into the 1JP, "Fire, fire" followed by booms.

A few seconds later Benson called to the director crew, "Excellent! Two hits on the bridge including a truck – no changes."

Benson keyed the 17MC, "Mounts 51 and 55, Director Control, High Explosive, Rapid Fire."

Percival's gunfire decimated the old bridge and it wasn't long before two spans had collapsed. Gunners then transferred their fire to a line of trucks that had stopped on the bridge approach road when the shooting started. Their barrage destroyed three trucks including a fuel tanker that blew up causing an enormous fire that spread to two nearby buildings. Loud cheers erupted throughout the ship.

The Bridge Phone Talker turned to Hutcheson, "Starboard Lookout reports what appears to be an   Rifle Platoon double-timing down the road to the beach bearing relative zero six zero."

Hutcheson looked at the beach through his binoculars, checked the pelorus and said to the talker, "Plot 2 engage troops at waters edge bearing approximately two six zero true."

The starboard lookout yelled down to the bridge, "One of those guys has something that looks like a bazooka."

Talker replied, "Plot2 has them. Will engage with Mount 31."

By this time, the troops were spreading out in the woods along the beach and firing their rifles. There were some splashes in the water but none were anywhere near *Percival*.

"Commence fire." said Hutcheson.

Immediately, Mount 31 opened up with a steady stream of 3-inch projectiles. Soldiers went down in a fusillade of explosions as Mount 31 worked its way down the line of trees at the edge of the beach. The 3-inch fire took out all of the soldiers but not before the "bazooka" man got off one shot. The rocket, trailing white smoke, fell harmlessly into the water about 300 yards offshore and well short of Percival.

Captain Brown said, "Mr. Hutcheson, get us underway out of here and headed north, we have just received orders from 7th Fleet to go to Chongjin up close to the Russian border. The Navigator will give you the course and speed."

"Aye, aye sir. Are we going alone?"

"Yeah, they are sending *Radford* to blow up some other coastal town. And when we get clear of the shore, the gun crews can stand easy and get all of the spent brass picked up and struck below. I will be in my cabin."

"Aye, aye sir," Hutcheson replied.

A few minutes later, as Percival pulled away from Uljin, the XO came out on the port bridge where Hutcheson and Langan were standing.

"Mr. Langan, our new course will be zero-one-three at eighteen knots. We should arrive off Chongjin around noon tomorrow."

"I will make that so." said Langan.

"Commander," said Hutcheson, "Why are we going after a target way up north?"

"Evidently, sixty-three B-29 Heavy Bombers from Far East Air Force bombed Chongjin from 18,000 feet early this morning while we were blowing up Uljin. Air Force Bomb Damage Assessment reported that, despite the bombing, there are still undamaged targets in the city that are within destroyer gunfire range. The USAF 19th Bomb Group dropped hundreds of bombs but all of the highway and railroad bridges are apparently still intact and operable. Also, the locomotive repair facility, one of the primary targets, was only slightly damaged. We are going to go up there to finish the job.

"Well, so much for the Air Forces strategic bombing prowess." said Hutcheson.

"Actually," said Cook, "It's pretty complicated. There has also been a high echelon change of thinking in the utilization of naval forces in Korea. Up until now, the Navy has concentrated on close support for the troops but has been frustrated by the overloaded and untrained Air Force Controllers that we have to use because of the mandate in the Key West Agreement. At the same time, the Air Force has not been able attack and destroy the strategic targets that are rightfully theirs under that same agreement -- like Chongjin. And in fact, the other day nine Air Force B-29's dropped 54 tons of bombs on the railroad bridge at Seoul and didn't even damage it. The next day, planes from *Philippine Sea* and *Valley Forge* dropped both spans of the bridge. Admiral Joy, COMNAVFE has now come around to a semi-strategic approach for utilization of naval forces that has, at least tacitly, been agreed to by

MacArthur.   That's the reason that Task Force 77 has been attacking strategic targets in the north and it's one of the reasons we were blowing up bridges in Uljin and why we are going north to Chongjin."

"Commander," said Hutcheson, "Chongjin is only about 150 miles from Vladivostock, Russia which is a major naval and air base and we will be up there all by ourselves. As I remember it, Chongjin was captured by Russian Marines in 1945 in the only amphibious operation in their short war against Japan.   Supposedly, some Russian naval units have been stationed there from time to time. I sure hope that there are no Russkies still hanging around."

"I don't think that there will be," said Cook, "We will still be within 50 miles of the Blockade Limits, declared by the US and sanctioned by the United Nations. I don't think that the Russians as UN Charter Members will cross that line lightly."

"Let's hope not." said Hutcheson.

By early afternoon of the 20th of August, Percival was approaching Chongjin and some smoke could be seen from yesterday's B-29 bombing raid.   Lt. j.g. Mitchell was OD and Ensign Moore was the JOOD and had the conn. The ship was at Condition 2.

Mitchell and Moore were standing at the chart table in the pilot house. "As you can see," said Mitchell, "Chongjin is located in a river valley, surrounded by mountains, at the head of a small bay. The eastward flowing Sosong River is on the south side of the valley and the Sonam Stream, that becomes a canal, is parallel to it on the north side.   There are north/south highway and railroad bridges over both of those waterways.   Between the two waterways, and to the east of the rail lines, is a large industrial area including some iron works, a railroad marshaling yard and the locomotive repair facility. Also between the waterways, down close to the Sea of Japan is, what looks to be a manmade excavated ship harbor. There is another industrial area and a larger ship harbor on the south side of the Sosong. This port is evidently a major coal and lumber export center. Our plan is to stand off the shore about two miles and bombard the industrial, rail and highway targets."

"Boy, it sure looks like there are plenty of juicy targets close to the shore." said Moore.

"Captain's on the bridge," shouted the bosun.

"Mr. Mitchell," the Captain said, " We will run parallel to the shore about two miles out at five knots. The plan is to have the Mk 37 Director and the 5-inch guns concentrate on the bridge and rail targets while the Mk-56 Director and the 3-inch guns work over ship, industrial and oil storage targets. There is particular interest in the railroad locomotive repair facility that the Air Force guys couldn't get. It was damaged but not destroyed in yesterday's B-29 raid. That will become the primary target after the bridges are destroyed."

"Understood, sir."

The city of Chongjin, with a population of about 200,000 was now clearly visible as Percival approached at 18 knots and maneuvered into position to conduct shore bombardment.

"Mr. Moore, make speed five." said Mitchell.

"Aye, aye, sir."

"Mr. Mitchell," called the Captain, I really just want to maintain headway and steering control. We can go like this for now and if it looks like there are no problems with currents, you can slow to three.

"Aye, Aye sir."

"The first target for the Mark-37 and the 5-inch guns is the rail bridge over the Sosong that is a seven span steel truss bridge. We hope that we can drop all seven spans. We will use the Mark-56 and the 3-inch guns against industrial targets along the shore. Just south of the harbor near the Sosong there is a large oil tank farm that the 3-inchers can start on."

"Captain," said Mitchell, "Both Gun Directors report manned and ready and that they have Solution Plot for their initial targets."

"Fire when ready." the Captain ordered.

Five inch and three inch guns began firing; first for effect and then rapid fire as they corrected. Five inch rounds were hitting the lower structure of the first span of the rail truss bridge. Suddenly the span collapsed and fire was transferred to the second span.

"Mr. Mitchell," said Brown, "A truss structure is a group of steel triangles that transfer the loads to the foundation – you pop a few of those triangles and it goes right down."

"So I see," said Mitchell as he scanned the shore through his binoculars. "The three inch have got that big oil tank on fire and now they are working their way down that row of smaller tanks – big fire, good shooting."

"Mr. Moore, slow us to three," said Mitchell.

231

"Three aye," said Moore.

"I see that they have finished off the rail bridge and have dropped back to get that highway bridge just upstream." said Mitchell.

'The highway bridges are concrete and they will be harder," said Brown, "we will use armor piercing shells."

With the oil tanks burning furiously, the three-inch guns shifted their fire to two small freighters in the harbor near the Sosong River. One had started to list and the other was on fire.

The highway bridge center span dropped and 5-inch fire was shifted to the big railroad locomotive repair facility between the rivers. The land from the shore to the rail yard was absolutely flat allowing the gunners to easily see and target the rolling stock in the rail yard and shop buildings. The gunners gave locomotives highest priority and in a short time three had been dispatched with large explosions and enormous clouds of steam. As they continued, the yard became littered with burning tank cars, shattered box cars and torn up tracks. In one case a box car exploded with a huge ball of fire and a concussion felt on *Percival* – undoubtedly an ammunition explosion that damaged other rolling stock in the yard and the locomotive repair building.

"Good shooting," said Brown, "You can't have supply trains without locomotives.

Three-inch fire was now directed at a small ship in the middle harbor and industrial buildings and cargo handling facilities around it. The five-inchers were working over the smaller rail and highway bridges over the Sonam Canal. Clouds of smoke rose high into the sky.

The XO walked out of the pilot house and over to the Captain. "Mike, it is obvious that this is a major coal shipment port. There are mountains of coal stored just to the north of the canal. Now, I know that it isn't easy to ignite coal with gunfire, however, why don't we fire some Willie Peter[28] rounds into those piles as we leave and see what happens?"

"Good idea, we're just finishing up our primary targets and we can put some WP rounds into the coal as we get underway. Now that we have blown up the place, I don't want to loiter here any longer than necessary. We haven't had any counter fire yet, however, it is Sunday and the NK artillery guys may have slept in. I don't want to hang around and find out that they woke up. Actually, I don't think that there is any North Korean artillery in Chongjin. I think that the North Koreans never expected such a fast US response to their aggression especially to a city this far north. I'm sure that they are now scrambling to get some protection for these ports that we have been blowing up."

Percival turned northeastward and picked up speed to 10 knots. Mounts 51 and 55 dropped 10 widely spaced rounds of White Phosphorus into the huge coal piles. A large cloud of white smoke immediately arose from the coal. Percival turned southward and increased speed to 18 knots.

On the bridge Captain Brown and Lt. Cmdr.. Cook were looking back at Chongjin through their binoculars.

"Charlie,' said Brown, "At first there was so much white smoke that it was hard to tell if the coal caught fire, but now the smoke is getting

---

28 Jargon for white phosphorus a chemical that burns intensely at high
   temperature and makes clouds of white smoke.

darker and I believe that we got a fire started."

"That's sure what it looks like. Once it gets going good in all that fuel, they will play hell putting it out."

"I certainly hope so."

At about 1800, Percival received a message from Commander 7th Fleet commending them for a job well done at Chongjin and ordering them to proceed to Songjin, North Korea for more shore bombardment.

Percival arrived off Songjin at about 1900 on the 21st. The city of Songjin straddles a medium size river in a valley with the industrial and shipping part of the city spread along the Sea of Japan. It is a major mineral and lumber export center. Port facilities were built along a peninsula south of the river and were protected by a breakwater. There were many warehouses and industrial buildings along the seafront. There was a two track rail bridge and two highway bridges over the river. There was a railroad marshaling yard just south of the bridges.

The sun was setting as *Percival* approached on a course parallel to and about 2 miles off the coast. Lt. j.g. Hutcheson was OD and Ensign Langan was JOOD and had the conn. The Captain had just come up on to the bridge as Songjin was sighted.

"Mr. Hutcheson, with it now dark, we will use Plot 1, Mount 51 for illumination firing and Mount 55 for bombardment. Plot 2 and Mounts 31 and 32 will also be used for bombardment. The bridges are the first priority followed by the railroad marshaling yards and the port."

"I understand, sir. Directors and gun mounts report manned and ready."

"Fire when ready."

Mount 51 fired and a few seconds later the city was illuminated with the bright white light of the parachute flare. Almost immediately Mount 55 began firing for effect and correcting their fire until they were hitting the steel rail bridge. Mounts 31 and 32 were doing the same thing on the small highway bridge downstream from the rail bridge.

Mount 51 kept two illumination flares in the air at all times. As Mount 55's rounds hit the railroad bridge there were great showers of sparks and blue flames – it was evidently an electric rail line. In a short while two spans of the bridge were down and the 5-inch fire shifted to the rail yard just to the south of the bridge. Two electric locomotives were destroyed and a large amount of rolling stock blown up including some tank cars that burned fiercely.

Meanwhile the 3-inch fire had taken down the light concrete bridge and their fire shifted to the port facilities and a collier that had been loading coal. The collier was listing and coal conveyers and loading equipment was heavily damaged. Bombardment continued for about an hour and caused severe damage to industrial facilities throughout the port area.

As the gun fire ceased, the officers on the bridge were surveying the city through their binoculars and making notes for the Action Report.

"Captain," said Hutcheson, "Because the city is surrounded by mountains, there is a rail tunnel at both the north and south ends of the city. The Gunners would like to see if they could put a few rounds into the tunnels in case a train is hiding in there. The Mk 37 Director and the Mk 56 Director radars are both locked on the south tunnel entrance."

"Tell them to have at it."

Both 5-inch and 3-inch rounds hit around the south tunnel and then in it. Although they caused some damage, there were no secondary explosions. They then shifted fire to the north tunnel and after several hits in the tunnel there was a huge explosion and a ball of flame rolled out of the tunnel – followed by cheers and applause on Percival.

"Wow," said Brown, "they must have hidden ammunition cars in there. Good job."

"Mr. Hutcheson, when we get clear of the shore, the gun crews can stand easy and get all of the spent brass picked up and struck below. Get a course from the navigator and let's head for Sasebo."

"Aye, aye sir," said Hutcheson enthusiastically.

Brown went over to the 1MC and pushed they key. "This is the Captain speaking. First of all, I know that you will be happy to hear that we are headed for Sasebo. We will probably be there for a just few days to refuel and rearm but we will see that everyone gets some liberty. I want to tell you what an outstanding job all of you have done in the last couple of weeks. We were called upon to do some very different things like being the gas station for the ROK Army, and you pulled together and got it done and killed some bad guys in the process. Your performance in shore bombardment has been outstanding. The last time we did any shore bombardment exercises was many months ago at San Clemente Island back in the states but you rose to the occasion and did a great job. As we head southward, and are now about 20 miles away, you can still see smoke from the fires burning in Songjin. A *Skyraider* photo plane from the *Phillipine Sea* did a damage assessment on Chongjin yesterday and said that there are still fires burning in the fuel tanks and the rail yard and that our Willy Peter did, in fact, set the coal piles on fire.   In Uljin and the others we cut the rail lines and highways that have been used to send supplies south to the NK Army.   We have a message from 7th Fleet commending *Percival* for a job well done.   To that I add my well done and tell you that I am proud to be the CO of this fine crew."

28 – Back To 77

In mid morning on August 22nd, *Percival* entered Sasebo harbor and went directly to the Josco fueling pier.   When fueling was complete, *Percival* got underway to the inner harbor and moored alongside USS *Grainger* (AK-184) to replenish ammunition.

Rearming is an all-hands evolution.   That means that, other than essential watch standers, the entire crew loads ammo.   It is back breaking work. Before any ammunition can be loaded, however, the first task is to unload the spent 3-inch and 5-inch brass shell casings. The AK lowered empty cargo nets to *Percival's* deck. The crew, formed human chains, and passed the spent brass up to the main deck and into the nets.   Loading live ammunition is a much tougher job. No human chains here – the ammunition is heavy and obviously can't be dropped. As the crane on the AK lowered pallets of ammunition to the deck, crew members carried individual 3-inch rounds, 5-inch projectiles or 5-inch powder cases down to the magazines.   All are heavy loads, a 5-inch projectile, for instance, weighs 54 pounds. The magazines are in the bottom of the ship so the ammo must be carried down steep ladders. Although it was heavy work, the crew turned to, inspired by the fact that there was no liberty until the ammo was loaded.   The job was finished in about three hours and *Percival* then moved to Buoy 3 and tied up alongside *Radford*.   Liberty for Section 1 and 3 was called away at 1600.

The next morning, at Officers Call, there were a few officers, the XO included, looking a bit worse for the wear of liberty in Sasebo. After the officers had finished their reports, the Captain announced, "You have probably heard rumors that there are plans afoot for an amphibious operation somewhere north of the current Korean battle lines. Admiral Sherman, Chief of Naval Operations, and Admiral Radford, Commander in Chief Pacific Fleet, just completed a visit to Korea and arrived in Sasebo yesterday. One of the purposes of their visit here was to appoint Admiral Struble commander of the amphibious operation. Rear Admiral Ewen, Commander Carrier Division 1, with flag in *Phillipine Sea,* will replace Struble as Commander Task Force 77. It is of course, hard to keep a large landing operation such as this a secret – anyone seeing all the ships in this harbor and other Japanese ports has to know that something is up. As a result, there will probably be lots of diversionary air strikes and shore bombardments to try to confuse the NK leaders in Pyongyang as to where the landing will actually take place. *Percival* will get underway on Friday with Task Force 77 for operations off both the east and west coasts of Korea. Some of these will be in support of the landing and some will be diversions. It doesn't matter which they are because all of them we are striking at the enemy. I think that we can count on a high level of operations for the next month or so. Make sure that all of your equipment is operable and ready to go. Current plan is that we will take on stores tomorrow and get underway on Friday. That's all."

Over the next two days Percival took on stores, completed maintenance that could not be done at sea and allowed the crew liberty. On Friday August 25, 1950 the ships of Task Force 77 got underway from Sasebo and headed for the East Coast of Korea. The task force consisted of the aircraft carriers *Phillipine Sea* (Flagship) and *Valley Forge,* two light cruisers *Worcester* and *Manchester* and 14 destroyers.

Up to this point in the war, naval ships had not been attacked by North

Korean aircraft. Three days earlier, two Russian-supplied, North Korean IL-10 Sturmovick fighters had surprised and lightly damaged the British destroyer HMS *Comus* in the Yellow Sea.[29] Their 23mm cannons, however, killed a stoker in Comus's fire room. As a result of this incident, a plane towing a cloth target sleeve on a 1000 foot cable rendezvoused with the task force in the Korean Straits. The task force lined up in two columns and conducted anti aircraft practice on it's way to the Sea of Japan. However, practice was cut short when one of the destroyers reported a sonar contact. The contact initially appeared to be a submarine but as the ship approached datum, it proved not to be.

The next morning, planes from both carriers attacked enemy communication lines, and attempted to contact Air Force ground controllers to provide support for ground forces. If they were unable to contact ground controllers or if the controllers couldn't handle them or were busy, the planes attacked targets of opportunity. Flights of F4Us and ADs from *Valley Forge* attacked troops, tanks and trucks along roadways leading to Pohang. Air Group II from *Phillipine Sea* made a jet sweep that attacked North Korean troops trying to hide in a highway tunnel north of Pohang. The F9F's fired rockets into the tunnel and dropped bombs at the tunnel mouth. Following that, Corsairs and Skyraiders from *Phillipine Sea* attacked vehicles in a NK troop concentration west of the Naktong River near Sonsan. Another jet sweep northwest of Pohang attacked a North Korean infantry battalion strafing the troops and their trucks with their machine guns and rockets. Although there were improvements in ground control, Admiral Ewen felt that the overall troop support effort was ineffective due to inadequate communications, poor radio discipline and poor control.

As the task force passed near the island of Ulleung-do off the Korean

---

29 The North Korean government claimed that they had sunk *Comus*.

east coast, sonarmen on many of the destroyers in the screen (including *Percival)* were reporting suspicious contacts. It turned out that the contacts were whales which frequent the neighborhood of the island.

Overnight the task force steamed northward and on the morning of the 27th attacks were launched in the Wonsan-Chongjin coastal strip. The flights concentrated on railroad bridges and highway bridges along the narrow coastal plain. In a one instance they surprised a convoy of large trucks on a bridge and decimated the trucks in addition to dropping the bridge. Other flights attacked maritime targets in Wonsan Harbor. The harbor was filled with ships, barges and junks that were being loaded with war material destined for their troops in the south. Many were sunk or set on fire. One innocuous looking junk blew up with a tremendous explosion when hit with cannon fire. It was probably being loaded with mines to seed the inshore waters around Wonsan. These junks masquerading as fishing boats or coastal freighters had been caught laying mines a number of times. The aviators and task force commanders considered that these attacks were much more effective than the sorties assigned yesterday for troop support..

On the morning of the 28th, the task force was in the Western Channel between Tsushima Island and Pusan, Korea. The Fleet Tankers USS *Passumpsic* (AO 17) and USS *Cacapon* (AO 52) had sortied from Pusan and, at first light, both tankers had started refueling operations.

Percival was now next in line to refuel and was slowly closing the distance to *Cacapon* at 20 knots.

Matthews, the JOOD looked up from the pilot house Radar Repeater and called out: "One thousand yards to the tanker."

Murphy turned to the Bridge Talker. "Ask both fueling stations and the

241

highline station their status."

"All stations report manned and ready."

Chief Swenson, as usual, asked the Captain if he had any preferences in movies.

"Yes Chief, see if they have "Asphalt Jungle"."

"Will do sir," as he walked to the bridge aft to negotiate with the tanker by wig-wag.

The quartermaster reported. "Tanker has Roger two-blocked on starboard yardarm."

Percival was about one ship length behind the tanker. Murphy called out. "Turns for one seven knots."

All of the crew above decks had helmets on to protect them from line throwing projectiles. Those at the fueling and highline stations also had lifejackets on.

As *Percival* slowed and came even with tanker, the red helmeted line thrower on the tanker blew his whistle and fired the gun sending a light nylon line over to the forward fuel station on *Percival*. At the same time, a similar procedure took place at the aft fueling station.

About a minute later, the phone talker called to Murphy, "Aft fueling station reports that the line throwing projectile hit Seamen Chavez and is sticking out of his back."

Murphy turned to the bosun, "Pass the word – Corpsman to the aft fueling station – on the double."

Despite the accident, both fueling stations were soon connected to the tanker and fuel was flowing.

About ten minutes later, Lt. j.g. Mayer, the Engineering Officer, who had been at the after fueling station came to the bridge and addressed the Captain and Murphy, "The corpsmen have moved Chavez to Sick Bay. The eight inch projectile is in his back about 4-inches. Chavez is not bleeding badly, that they can see, and he is talking to the "docs" but is in a lot of pain and may be bleeding internally. Chief Cosgrove, has given him morphine and says that he needs a doctor to remove the projectile and examine him for possible internal injuries."

The Captain turned to Murphy, "Message to Com TF 77 that we have a seriously injured man who requires a doctor."

"Aye, aye sir."

The Captain said, "Mr. Mayer, where was Chavez when this happened?"

"He was wearing a life jacket and helmet and was crouched behind a table. The projectile had passed over the 01 level and hit him from behind – he was doing what he was supposed to do."

"Very well, a doctor is on the way. Ask him to let me know Chavez's condition."

Aye, aye sir."

Within a few minutes, a helicopter from *Phillipine Sea* lowered a

243

medical officer onto *Percival's* fantail. The doctor examined Chavez thoroughly, carefully removed the projectile from Chavez's back and inserted a drain. He discussed aftercare with Cosgrove and prescribed antibiotics. When he finished, he went to the bridge.

"Captain, I'm Doctor Sanders. I believe that Chavez will be OK. He was very lucky that the projectile did not hit any vital organs or break any ribs. I did not see any signs of excessive internal bleeding and hopefully the antibiotics will prevent infection. Chief Cosgrove did a good job and he and I discussed the prognosis and continuing care. In a day or two, after the drain is removed, Chavez should be up and around, however, he is going to have a sore back for some time."

A short time later, the helicopter returned and picked up the doctor as *Percival* returned to her position in the screen.

Refueling continued until mid afternoon. At that point, the task force turned into the wind and prepared to land aircraft. Replacement AD *Skyraider* and F4U *Corsair* aircraft were being flown out from Japan to *Phillipine Sea* and *Valley Forge*. These planes had been ferried from San Diego, CA to Yokusuka, Japan by the *Essex* Class carrier USS *Boxer* (CV 21) on the last of her three high speed trips between the US and Japan. On each of these trips she carried Air Force planes, Navy planes, huge stocks of maintenance parts and equipment and Navy and Air Force personnel. In a few days, *Boxer,* her transport duties done, would join Task Force 77 to bring the aircraft carrier total to three.

Over the next two days there were few requests for close air support at the front lines. Since the Marine Brigade had entered the fight and the Army 24th Division had enlarged the Pusan perimeter, there had been a temporary lull in the fighting. As a result, the carriers took this opportunity to strike other targets directed by CINCFE. In a message to

General MacArthur, Admiral Joy had said, "..North Korea contains a multiplicity of targets which are well suited to to carrier strikes, whereas, in the south, targets are few and well hidden. After August 25, I strongly recommend that Task Force 77 be employed north of the 38th parallel."

On the 29th flights from both aircraft carriers were directed at the Seoul-Inchon area. *Skyraiders* and *Corsairs* hit railroad bridges, airfields and highways and caused great damage. On the 30th, enjoying their new found freedom, the carriers attacked the port of Chinnampo and the North Korean capital city of Pyongyang. They destroyed or damaged bridges, docks, shipping and water works in both cities and then worked over road and rail targets further north. Altogether an effective and rewarding few days for the aviators. As aircraft were recovered on board, the task force turned south to refuel and rearm off southwestern Korea.

On the morning of August 31, the task force again rendevoused with Fleet Tankers *Passumpsic* and *Cacapon* and the Ammunition Ship USS *Mt. Katami* (AE-16). With the recent high level of air operations, the aircraft carriers were in need of bombs, rockets and machine gun and cannon ammunition. Refueling and replenishment continued until late afternoon when the task force turned northward into the Yellow Sea toward North Korea.

The next day at 0800 the carriers launched strikes on rail and highway facilities in and around Seoul. Planes from Valley Forge destroyed a railroad bridge near Sariwon and attacked rail and highway targets near Hwangju. Bombers from Phillipine Sea hit rail targets around Pongyang including bridges, marshaling yards and rolling stock. The planes also sighted many flatcars loaded with steel girders that was proof of the effectiveness of previous attacks on rail and highway bridges. As the first wave returned to the carriers at 1120, a second wave of Skyraiders and Corsairs were taking off to hit North Korean bridges and marshaling yards.

As they departed northward, an emergency teletype message was received by ComTF77 from the UN Joint Operations Center (JOC) in Taegu:

"MAJOR ENEMY ATTACK LAUNCHED ACROSS RIVER FROM TUKSONGDONG SOUTH TO COAST X   ALL AVAILABLE EFFORT FOR CLOSE SUPPORT REQUIRED SOUTHERN SECTOR IMMEDIATELY X SITUATION CRITICAL X REQUEST ARMED RECCO FROM BEACH NORTH TUKSONGDONG TO DEPTH 10 MILES WEST OF BOMB LINE X   REQUEST IMMEDIATE ACKNOWLEDGEMENT X

Admiral Ewen acknowledged the message and notified the JOC that Task Force 77 was headed south to provide the requested support. As the task force turned southward and built up speed to 27 knots the recently launched strike missions bound for North Korea were recalled. A combat air patrol was vectored out to help the returning planes find the task force as it steamed south at high speed. Shortly after noon, ComTF 77 advised the JOC by Flash message   that his first strike would be on station in about two hours. At 1315, 12 Skyraiders loaded with three 1000 pound bombs each and 16 Corsairs armed with a 1000 pound bomb and four 5" HVAR rockets each took off for the front. About ten minutes later, the recalled aircraft from the north were safely landed on board.   ComTF 77 sent JOC a Flash message that within the hour a second strike of identical composition to the first would be launched.

As the first wave arrived over the battlefield they once again

246

encountered the usual problems with ground controllers. One *Phillipine Sea* strike group was directed to attack a group of tanks. As they approached the designated area, they observed that the tanks had large white stars on them and none of the troops were running for cover – obviously American tanks and troops. They then went looking for targets on their own and attacked NK troops and a bridge on the Naktong River. Planes from Valley Forge had to orbit for 45 minutes because the controller had no targets he could give them. They were finally ordered to attack villages on the Naktong front.

The second wave had better luck destroying much of the town of Haman, destroying trucks nearby and bombing an enemy occupied ridge. Other flights could not raise a controller and attacked targets on their own.

Because of the criticality of the situation, Marine Air Squadrons from the recently arrived Escort Carriers USS Sicily (CVE 118) and USS Badoeng Strait (CVE 116), that had been put ashore at Ashiya Airfield, Japan, were put on alert to possibly reinforce the effort.

On the morning of September 2nd the weather was deteriorating with rain and low ground fog. Despite that, Task Force 77 launched 127 close support sorties while Fifth AF and Ashiya based Marine aircraft added 201 more. Although some flights aborted because of targets obscured in fog, most of them found controllers and made succesful attacks. As the fog lifted and the sun broke through, the situation improved dramatically. Flights from Task Force 77 claimed that they destroyed 4 tanks, 14 trucks and 3 barges. In addition 18 North Korean troop concentrations were broken up with large numbers of casualties and troops scattered. The concentrated troop support missions obviously were helping out because the last flights of the day were attacks on enemy troops retreating northward across the Nam River near Sanch-ong.

In normal cruising operations, destroyers operate with two of their four steam boilers on line. The 25 to 30 knot high speed maneuvering during recent flight operations required that the destroyers keep all four boilers on line at all times – and boilers require feed water. By the second day of these ops, *Percival* was running low on water. Unlike the later *Sumner* and *Gearing* class destroyers, that had two water evaporators, *Fletcher* class cans such as *Percival* had only one. This caused imposition of "water hours" -- the boilers had priority over showers. Padlocks were placed on the shower handles and were only removed by the Master At Arms for one hour at the four to eight and the eight to twelve watch change periods. This of course made the crew rather surly because the "ON" times did not work well for all of them. As a result, if you went into the after head in the evening you would see two rows of naked men filling sinks with water and taking "bird baths" by throwing the water over themselves. Some felt that leaving the showers on and calling for conservation would be more effective than half of the crew taking "bird baths" and throwing water all over the deck. The command didn't agree and water hours remained in force. The XO also pointed out that the salt water showers were always on – they remained unused.

Sunday September 3rd was not a day of rest. Task Force 77 was refueling and rearming in the southern Yellow Sea just off the city of Mokpo. It was squally and raining from the effects of Typhoon Jane that was then centered over Honshu Island, Japan. All of the Marine and Air Force planes were grounded by the weather. At 1404, ComNavFE instructed Task Force 77 to give "all practicable support" to the Eighth Army that was falling back under a heavy NK counterattack. As soon as possible the task force broke off refueling and reconfigured for flight operations. At 1547 Admiral Ewen reported that his first planes would be off in an hour and over the battlefield by about 1745. *Phillipine Sea* and *Valley Forge* launched 46 flights that successfully contacted controllers and provided close air support for Marine and Army units helping them to stop the NK advance.

As soon as the aircraft were recovered on board, Admiral Ewen turned northward with the objective of going further north in the Yellow Sea than any 7th Fleet carrier had ever gone. During the night, the task force went through the narrows between the Shangtung Peninsula and Korea's western tip and into Korea Bay north of the 38th parallel. Two combat air patrols (CAP) were established to protect the task force. CAP1 consisting of four F4U Corsairs was at 12,000 feet about a third of the way between the task force and the Korean coast. CAP2, also consisting of four F4U's, was at 10,000 feet about 30 miles north of CAP 1 and closer to China.

Percival had been detached from the task force and was assigned radar picket duty at a station about 60 miles north of the task force operating area. Their mission was to detect any aircraft flying out from the Chinese mainland or from the Russian controlled Port Arthur about 70 miles away. Percival's CIC was fully manned with active radio circuits to the CAP aircraft and ComTF77 (Jehovah). Morning flight operations from both carriers against targets in the North Korean capital of Pyongyang and its port of Chinnampo proceeded uneventfully. Other than the strike aircraft, going to and from their targets, Percival had detected no other radar contacts.

At noon, the watch changed on the bridge. Lt. j.g. Hutcheson was OD and Ensign Langan was JOOD and had the conn. Captain Brown was in his cabin. Percival was steaming on a triangular course centered on its picket station at about 10 knots. Chief Swenson was on the bridge checking that all was well with his afternoon quartermaster watch.

"Mr. Hutcheson," he said, "Does it make you nervous to be in Korea Bay surrounded by North Korea, China and a Russian naval base?"

"Not a bit – this is what we do.   We are in international waters, operating under a United Nations mandate fighting an aggressor who invaded a democratic sovereign country."

"That's true.   One of the the things that I don't understand about all of this is how the Russians got control of such a huge naval base in China."

"Actually, it goes back to the 19th century when western powers extracted many concessions from from a weak Qing Dynasty government, including control of a number of seaports,. Russia needed ice-free access to the Pacific Ocean and made a deal with the Chinese to lease and fortify Port Arthur, even though the Chinese had previously agreed to cede the port to Japan. This was the basic cause of the 1904 Russian/Japanese War.   In a series of horrific battles the Japanese recaptured Port Arthur and Admiral Togo destroyed the Russian Pacific Fleet in the Battle of the Yellow Sea."

"I thought that Admiral Togo sank the Russian fleet at Tsushima, down near where we have been refueling recently."

"That was later. After Togo sunk their Pacific Fleet in the Yellow Sea, the Russians sent their Baltic Fleet all the way around the world to replace it.   Admiral Togo met the Russian Baltic fleet in the Tsushima Straits and annihilated it.   He sank eight battleships and killed 5000 men."

"Wow. So, if the Japanese won, how did the Russians end up back in

Port Arthur?"

"As you probably remember, in the last months of WW-II, Russia suddenly declared war on Japan and occupied North Korea, Manchuria and the Liaotung Peninsula where Port Arthur is located. They are still there."

"Very interesting. Do you think that the Russians will intervene in this thing?"

"Probably not directly. We are pretty sure that the submarine we sank a couple of weeks ago was Russian and our aviators have been telling us that they are convinced that the Migs they are encountering over North Korea are flown by Russians."

Langan, the JOOD, called out, "Coming to new course two eight zero."

"Very well" said Hutcheson.

This course change put them on the westward leg of their triangle. It was a pleasant afternoon with light winds and a slight sea and the ship rode easily on its patrol.

Suddenly, the TBS came alive with the voice of *Percival*'s CIC Officer.

"Jehovah, this is Sofahound, Bogey bearing three zero zero, range four five miles. Estimated course one five five. May be multiple targets"

"Sofahound, Bogey designated Able, Sofahound tracks. Provide vectors to CAP2."

"Roger, will do."

251

The Bosun called out. "Captain on the bridge."

As the Captain settled into his chair, the CIC Fighter Director came up on the Primary Air radio.

"Ripper this is Sofahound, Bogey Able bears three one five from you range four one miles. May be multiple targets."

"Roger, Ripper, Flight of four turning to three one five."

"Ripper this is Sofahound, Bogey Able now estimated on course one six zero, speed one eight zero knots, altitude twelve to thirteen thousand feet."

"Roger – looking."

"Ripper, Sofahound, be advised target has separated into two parts. First part has turned and appears to be retiring toward Port Arthur. Part 2 continues toward you."

"Roger, still looking."

About six minutes later. "Sofahound, Ripper – Tally ho! Have twin engine bomber in sight with a big Red Star on the wings. We are splitting into two sections to box him in."

"Sofahound, Roger."

"This is Ripper, I think this guy made a big mistake, he's diving and heading for North Korea."

252

"This is Ripper, Bogey Able just fired at my Dash Two.   Request permission, FOX Guns."

"Ripper this is Jehovah. Guns Free!"

"This is Ripper Two, I hit him at the wing root and the wing came off. He is falling in a flat spin and is on fire. For the record, that plane was an old, American Douglas A-20 -- must have been one of the ones we Lend-Leased to the Russians during War 2."

On *Percival*, a lookout on the flying bridge called out, "Just saw a flash in the sky and there is a smoke trail going down."

Captain Brown called out, "I want to get over there as soon as possible to pick up anything that's floating."

Hutcheson was looking through his binoculars. "I see it – I followed him all the way down and there was another explosion at the surface. I have the conn! Come left to two six zero, make turns for twenty-two knots."

He turned to the phone talker. "Whaleboat crew to the whaleboat and standby to launch. Tell them to make sure that they have grappling hooks and boat hooks."

As Percival approached the crash scene, there were floating pieces of an airplane and some fuel was burning downwind.

Hutcheson called to the pilot house, "All back two."

"Engine Room answers all back two."

The ship vibrated as the reverse screws slowed the ship. The ship came to a stop about 30 yards from the wreckage.

"All stop," said Hutcheson, "Away the whaleboat away."

In a short time the whaleboat was in the midst of the wreckage. A minute later, the quartermaster was standing up in the boat, sending a wig-wag message to Chief Swenson on the bridge.

Swenson turned to the Captain, "They've found a body in the water and he seems to be alive."

"Good Lord," said the Captain, "Get him back aboard here as quickly as possible."

He turned to the Bosun, "Pass the word for Doc Cosgrove to lay down to the quarterdeck on the double."

As the whaleboat came alongside, the body of the Russian aviator was put into a Stokes stretcher quickly lifted up to the deck. Chief Cosgrove listened to his heart with his stethoscope. "He's still alive, get him up to sickbay."

Hands grabbed the stretcher and quickly carried the Russian to the sickbay on the starboard side of the Main Deck. He was transferred to the examining table and Cosgrove and Hospitalman Cleary removed his outer clothing. There was a gash above the Russians right eye, large bruises over the chest area and the right arm and right leg were at odd angles.

As Cosgrove was assessing his injuries, Cleary put the blood pressure cuff on him and checked the pressure. "He is bad,"Cleary said, "BP is about 70 over 40 and his pulse is 130 and irregular. Also his breathing is weak, thready and labored."

Cosgrove prepared a hypodermic syringe with a long spinal needle and filled it with adrenalin. "I've never done this before." he said, "But he is severely traumatized and dying and I don't know what else to do." He pushed the needle between the ribs and into the ventricle and injected the adrenalin into the Russians heart. His breathing seemed a bit improved but within five minutes, he died.

While all of this was going on, Ensign Solodar, the Supply Officer, was going through the aviators flight suit and jacket.

He said to Cosgrove, "I found an ID card. He apparently is Lt. Mishin Tennadii Vasilebiu, Serial Number 25054. Not much else in his clothing -- some Russian coins and some other pocket litter, a pen and a piece of paper that may be a flight plan."

"Sorry I couldn't save him," said Cosgrove, "But beside his injuries, he had been in the water awhile and was quite cold. I'm really surprised that he wasn't killed in the crash."

Solodar said to Cosgrove "Wrap him in a blanket and put him in a body bag. Take his clothing and this other personal stuff and package it up and put it in the body bag. The Captain said that we are going to highline him over to *Phillipine Sea*. Fill out your standard paperwork for an on board death."

Later that day, *Percival* returned to the task force and highlined the body of the Russian and the salvaged airplane wreckage over to *Phillipine Sea*. They then took their place in the bent line screen.

The next morning an AD weather flight was launched from *Valley Forge* that reported heavy rain and low ceilings caused by Typhoon Jane over all of North Korea. As a result, Admiral Ewen turned Task Force 77 southward towards Japan to prepare for the next big event; the amphibious landings at Inchon. Plans had been debated for several different landing sites, however, General MacArthur decided that the landings had to be made at Inchon despite it's 33 foot tides and the misgivings of many of his subordinates.

At this point, Admiral Ewen was comfortable leaving Korea for Japan feeling that Task Force 77 had done what had been asked. Despite continued heavy fighting and a powerful North Korean offensive, the UN forces had held the perimeter owing in no small part to Task Force 77's support operations. Despite continued problems with ground controllers, the aviators of *Phillipine Sea* and *Valley Forge* had acquitted themselves very well. The situation was well enough stabilized that the Marine units required for the Inchon landing could be pulled from the front lines and redeployed. The buildup of forces with ships and men from the States continued. Two Escort Carriers with their Marine Air Groups were in theater and available for support. *Badoeng Straits* was today underway for the Yellow Sea. *Sicily* was still in the shipyard in Sasebo, however, it's Marine Air Group was ashore at an airfield in Ayshia, Japan and available for support in South Korea. Com7th Fleet officially changed the name of Striking Force Task Force 77 to Fast Carrier Task Force 77.

Commander Naval Forces Far East (COMNAVFE) issued an order changing the Fleet Base from Buckner Bay, Okinawa to Sasebo, Japan. Just another sign that the higher commands now felt that they had gained control of the situation and did not have to fear Russian bombing raids against Japan. Although the danger of Russian long range bomber raids had receded, the downing of the American, Douglas A-20

Attack Bomber flown by Russian pilots introduced a new concern. It turned out, from examination of the wreckage and intelligence data, that the A-20 was a G model that the Russians had converted into a torpedo bomber. This aircraft, particularly if deployed from Port Arthur, could pose a serious threat to the ships of Task Force 77 operating in the Yellow Sea.

29 – Getting Ready

Shortly after dawn on September 7, *Percival* arrived in Sasebo with Task Force 77.   After refueling at Josco she proceeded to Buoy 20 and moored to a nest of four destroyers alongside USS *Piedmont* (AD 17). In preparation for the Inchon invasion, the harbor was filled with US Navy ships and the gin mills, whorehouses and other entertainment enterprises in Sasebo were filled with Sailors. For the next three days, Percival did maintenance operations (with help from the tender), took on stores, conducted training, enjoyed liberty and otherwise prepared for another intense period of operations in Korea.   When ships are at sea for extended periods there is nowhere for Sailors to spend their money so when they get back to port they spend it with a vengeance. There were bargains to be had in Japan. Many Sailors bought Nikon 35mm cameras with an F1.2 lens that in the states sold for $450 that in Sasebo were $125.   Noritake China was a fraction of what it cost in the US and the Sasebo stores delivered it to the ship by water taxi. After a while all of the void compartments in the bottom of the ship were filled with crates of dinnerware. That Christmas, many girl friends and wives received very fancy Japanese kimonos.   And of course, the Asahai, Kirin, Sapporo and Nippon breweries benefited enormously from the thirsty Sailors.

One afternoon, Lt. j.g. Hutcheson went ashore in Sasebo. He really didn't need anymore liberty in Sasebo, his only objective was to see if he could talk to his wife Peggy on the phone. Arriving at the Officers Club, he went immediately to the Telephone Center.   It took about a half hour but the operator finally got through to Peggy in Columbus.

"Oh God," Peggy said, " it's so good to hear your voice. Everyday the papers are full of news about Korea and none of it seems to be very good for our side. I heard that Sam Costa was shot in the arm."

"Yeah that was a few weeks ago, he was in a landing party that got fired on."

"This is awful, those guys have finally started shooting back at you. I lay awake nights worrying that something may happen to you."

"Well fortunately, for the past week or so we have been with Task Force 77 away from the shooting. How is Dave doing?"

"He's good. He is really walking around now – I have to keep an eye on him to make sure he doesn't get into something. It seems like he sprouts up a little more each day. Where are you now?"

"I'm in Sasebo. We are going to get underway again later this week. There are rumors about a big amphibious operation somewhere north of the battle line but we still don't know if we will be involved."

"Well, I think of you every day and am really worried about what is going to happen over there."

"You are in my thoughts every day and I am certainly looking forward to the day that *Percival* heads for San Diego."

"So am I. Take care of yourself and I love you."

"I love you too. Goodbye."

Hutch had a double Bourbon at the bar and then headed back to the ship.

At 0900 on September 10, a meeting was held in *Percival*'s wardroom for all of the ship's officers. The Mess Stewards were sent away. Captain Brown opened the meeting. "First of all, this briefing is classified Confidential. Within the next week, there will be a major amphibious landing at Inchon, the port for Seoul, Korea. To preserve the element of surprise, the site of the landing is classified and attacks are being conducted against other potential landing sites to confuse the enemy. Inchon has 33 foot tides that limit the time of year and the time of day that the actual landing can take place so some of the element of surprise is lost. The navigable channels into the port are narrow, surrounded by mud flats at low tide and have strong current flows during flooding and ebbing tides. Mr. Mitchell will you put up the Inchon chart, please."

Lt. j.g. Mitchell put up a nautical chart of the Inchon harbor area on an easel.

"As you can see," Brown continued, "The island of Wolmi-do sits smack between Flying Fish Channel and the port itself – it has been referred to as the "Cork In The Bottle" for good reason. The North Koreans and their Russian benefactors have heavily fortified Wolmi-do with many artillery pieces in well dug-in bunkers. The channels around the island are narrow and shallow at low tide. As you may have guessed by now, we will be one of six destroyers whose mission is to destroy those fortifications on Wolmi-do before the invasion. We will have help. Today, even as we speak, Marine Air Squadrons from *Badoeng Straits* and *Sicily* are in the process of dropping about 50 tons of napalm on the western half of Wolmi-do. Air strikes will continue on Wolmi-do and at the same time there will be diversionary air strikes on other possible landing sites. When we go into the harbor, we will be backed up by heavy gun cruisers firing from Flying Fish Channel in addition to continued air support. Destroyers got the call to do this mission, because only they can navigate and maneuver in the narrow, shallow approaches to Wolmi-do. At some point in this operation, we may be as close as 800 yards to the enemy. I like to think that *Percival* was chosen for this mission because of our recent excellent shore bombardment record. At this point, I will pause for any questions."

Lt. Murphy spoke up, "It looks like they picked the toughest place to land on the coast of Korea – why was that?"

"It was General MacArthur's decision. I believe that he feels that from Inchon and Seoul, the Marines can strike across the peninsula and cut off the supply lines for the NK forces in the south. Anyone else?"

Lt. j.g. Hutcheson asked, "How are we going to maneuver six cans into and out of such a tightly restricted waterway?"

"That was my next topic, so I will continue. We will go in on a 5 knot flooding tide that occurs in early afternoon. We will anchor off Wolmi-do on short stay so that the ship will swing around and face the incoming tide. By keeping our anchors underfoot it will steady the ship's head and position and we will be headed out of the channel ready for a fast exit if required. Also at low tide, the close-in targets will be within the depression range of our guns. Part of this plan is that being anchored we will be sitting ducks and probably draw enemy fire, thus revealing the NK gun positions."

Audible groans around the room.

261

"This will not be easy. We will have the Sea Detail team on the bridge because we will have to pilot our way in and out and do some tricky maneuvering. We will also need the Anchor Detail standing by just behind the doors to the foc'sle. They can't be on the foc'sle when Mount 51 is firing. When we get to our firing location, they will drop the anchor and then return behind the foc'sle doors ready to weigh anchor when we have to. It is possible that one of our ships may become immobile because of enemy fire and another DD will have to tow them out. I want our towing wire laid out and faked down for towing. Just make sure that the tow wire and the shoring timber used to hold the faked down sections are lashed securely so that muzzle blasts don't blow anything loose. Also, we need to have fenders rigged so that we can go alongside another ship if necessary. We are going to be close to land and extensive mud flats and it is conceivable that we may have to repel enemy boarders -- particularly if we happen to go aground.. The Repair Parties will be armed and briefed on that possibility and will have to make sure that their weapons are close at hand. We are going to be doing almost continuous shore bombardment while we are anchored. The Gunnery Department needs to insure that all Ready Service Ammunition storage is completely filled and that our magazines are topped off. Given the unique requirements of this shore bombardment mission in intertidal waters, we are going to need a somewhat different GQ watch bill. The XO has started on one, and as soon as I finish, I want you to work with the XO to make sure that we have all the right people in the right jobs. One last word on security. You are going to have to brief the crew on some of the special requirements for this mission. Under no circumstances mention Inchon, Wolmi-do or anything about a port with very high tides. Carry on."

The officers continued meeting among themselves for about another hour finalizing the watch bill and planning how to accomplish all of the tasks outlined in the Captain's orders.

The next morning, working parties moved ammunition from *Percival's* magazines and filled all of the 5-inch and 3-inch ready service storage. In the early afternoon, *Percival* got underway and went alongside the USS *Mt. Katamai* to take on ammunition to top off the magazines. When the ammunition was aboard and struck below, *Percival* got underway and moored to Buoy 10 alongside *Radford*. The Gunners Mates had the Small Arms Lockers open and were cleaning and checking out the weapons. They were also going over weapons procedures with the members of the Repair Parties that would be armed.

On the morning of September 12, the Deck Force started rigging the towing cable to be ready to tow another destroyer. The cable was heavy and unwieldy and required most of the deck force to accomplish the task. The one-inch diameter towing cable is stored on a reel on the fantail of each destroyer. Preparations involved removing all of the cable from the reel, shackling the bitter end to the towing pad on the fantail, faking out the cable on deck and lashing it in place to pieces of shoring timber. The bitter end is passed out a fair lead and led up to the foc'sle outboard of the lifelines. Pieces of small stuff are used to lash the towing cable to the lifeline. Should they have to tow another destroyer, the lashings are cut to make the cable free for running as it is paid out..

At 1300, the XO had a meeting of department heads out on deck to review all of the preparations. When finished, he went to the Captain's cabin.

"Mike, I have reviewed all of the preparations with the department heads and have walked around the ship and checked everything out. We are ready in all respects to go to sea."

"Very well Charlie, this promises to be an interesting few days and I am sure that this crew and the ship will acquit itself well no matter what comes up."

"Yes sir, I am sure that we will."

About 1500, *Percival* got underway and joined the line of destroyers standing out from Sasebo and headed for Inchon. *Mansfield* was in the lead of Destroyer Element 90.62, commanded by Capt. Halle Allen, followed by *DeHaven, Percival, Collett, Gurke* and *Henderson*. They were part of the Gunfire Support Group commanded by Rear Adm. John Higgins that also included the four ship Cruiser Element and the three rocket firing ships of the LSMR Element.

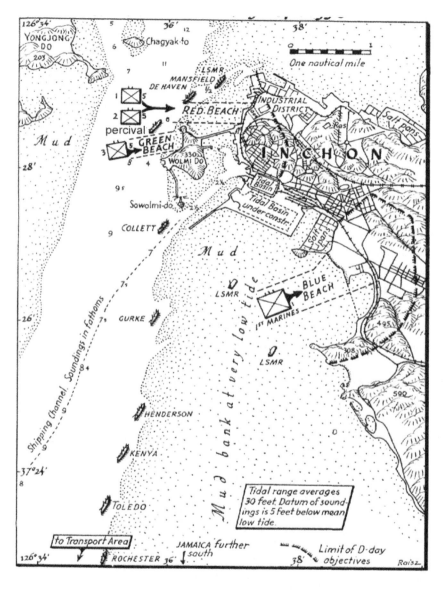

Gunfire Support Group TG 90.6 disposition off Wolmi-do and Inchon on September 14, 1950.

265

30 – Inchon

Dawn of September 13 found the Gunfire Support Group entering Kyonggi Bay from the Yellow Sea. During the night, the destroyer *Gurke* had arrived from Task Force 77 bringing yesterday's aerial reconnaissance photos of Wolmi-do -- copies had been distributed to all ships. At 0700 the destroyers started up the Flying Fish Channel toward Inchon in column; *Mansfield, DeHaven, Percival, Collett, Gurke* and *Henderson.* Following them were the cruisers USS *Toledo* and *Rochester* and HMS *Jamaica* and *Kenya.* Vice Admiral Arthur Struble, Commander, Attack Force 90, broke his flag in *Rochester.* Rear Admiral John Higgins, Commander, Gunfire Support Group 90.6 broke his flag in *Toledo.* Captain Halle Allan, Commander, Destroyer Element 90.62 was in *Mansfield.*

Percival was about 700 yards behind *DeHaven* and the crew was at their modified General Quarters. Material Condition Able was set throughout the ship to preserve it's watertight integrity. All of the crew were wearing helmets and life jackets. Lt. j.g. Hutcheson was OD and Ensign Langan was JOOD and had the conn. Captain Brown was on the bridge. Lt. Cdr. Cook, the XO, was at the emergency conning station on the forward side of the aft stack where he could take over control of the ship if the bridge was put out of commission. Lt. j.g. Mitchell and Chief Swenson were navigating from the chart table in the pilot house. Quartermasters manned the port and starboard peloruses to take bearings on landmarks on shore for navigation. The sonar equipment was secured and the transducers retracted into the hull to prevent damage in the shallow water. Two sonarman were taking sonar depth sounder readings and recording them on an Inchon harbor chart for reference. Two sonarmen were assigned to assist quartermasters on the bridge and two were assisting radarmen in CIC. Chief Cosgrove and Hospitalman 3C Cleary had set up their medical aid station in the wardroom. Two Sonarmen, Seamen York and O'Connell, were also in the wardroom as assistants and litter bearers. The Anchor Detail was standing by behind the foc'sle doors. The anchor hawse pipe covers had been removed and the starboard anchor was at the weigh with about four feet of chain out. Heavy mooring fenders were out on both sides of the ship. Both the whaleboat and the gig were rigged inboard in case *Percival* had to go alongside another ship. The aft repair party had their weapons stashed just inside the door to the after living compartments – near the screw guards that would be the most likely point for any attempted boarding. Flying overhead was a Combat Air Patrol (CAP) of four F4U *Corsairs* from *Philippine Sea.*

The quartermaster called out, "Dehaven showing speed flags One Zero."

"Aye, aye," said Hutcheson, "Make it so Mr. Langan. The column is slowing as we are getting into the approaches to the Inchon outer harbor."

It was a little after 1000 and the column was on the right side of the channel close by the mud flats and about 2000 yards east of the main shipping channel. The water was about 40 feet deep as they proceeded slowly toward Wolmi-do. As they advanced north, the channel was gradually getting narrower.

Hutch was on the starboard side of the bridge, scanning the shore with his binoculars. "Well that naplam attack sure burned away the trees and underbrush -- I can see gun emplacements all over the shore. Despite the continued bombing, a lot of the guns look operational and capable of shooting at us. It's one thing to be lobbing shells into a far shore and no one shoots back – it's something completely different to be so close that you can almost see your enemy and he is firing right at you. And this whole thing about repelling boarders is surreal – it's almost like the War of 1812. Lord, I have to tell you, I'm just a little bit scared."

At about 1145, the port lookout on the flying bridge reported "Floating objects on the port bow about half mile – could be mines."

Captain Brown, looking through his binoculars, said, "They sure look like mines to me – I think I can see a horn on one of them."

Hutcheson picked up the TBS Handset, "Kingpin this is Sofahound, There are floaters about half mile off our port bow. They appear to be moored mines that have been uncovered by low tide."

"This is Kingpin," answered Com 90.62, "Understand mines on the port bow. Break, Life Blood this is Kingpin."

"This is Life Blood" answered *Henderson.*

" This is Kingpin, You are the last ship in the column, see if you can sink those mines."

"This is Life Blood, will do. We are getting closer now and believe that we have them in sight. "Don't really want to go in close enough to sink them with rifle fire – there may be other mines in there that we can't see. We will probably use the quad 40's on them."

"Roger that."

Shortly thereafter there was the steady thump of Bofor fire and Captain Brown said, "There go *Henderson*'s forty's."

A cloud of spray engulfed the mines that were now about three quarters of a mile off *Percival*'s port quarter. A few seconds later there were two enormous explosions as mines blew up followed by two more in short order.

"Kingpin this is Lifeblood, we believe there were about 12 mines in there. We were only able to get four before the rising tide covered them up.

"This is Kingpin, Roger that, maybe we can get somebody in there to take a look on next low tide.

"You know," said Hutcheson, "I have heard that Navy ships have reported an increasing number of mines in the last few weeks."

"That's true;" said Brown, "And in fact, I understand that Admiral Struble and Admiral Joy are very concerned that the North Koreans may be about to launch unrestricted mine warfare. They have asked Washington for all available minesweepers to be sent over here as soon as possible. Given the severely reduced size of the Mine Force there aren't many ships available so they have also asked for the reactivation of mothballed minesweepers."

"Well I hope that happens soon because even old fashioned contact mines could wreak havoc with these thin-skinned destroyers."

As they were speaking, flights of *Corsairs* and *Skyraiders* from Task

Force 77 were dropping tons of bombs on Wolmi-do that was now directly ahead of *Percival*. There were enormous explosions with huge amounts of dirt and rocks blown in the air. It was just past noon as the destroyers passed Wolmi-do, as the bombing continued, and they headed for their assigned positions. Some of the positions were less than a half mile from the heavily fortified island. As they approached, *Percival* had her engines stopped and was riding the 5-knot current as she came up on her assigned location.

Captain Brown said to Hutcheson, "Is the Anchor Detail on the foc'sle and ready to let go."

"Yes sir – all it takes is a swing of the sledge hammer."

"OK, put on right rudder before you let go the anchor so that the chain won't get dragged through the sonar dome by the current."

"Aye, aye sir. I have the conn, right standard rudder." and as the ship slowly started to swing, "Let go the anchor."

The anchor chain roared out and the bosun braked it as soon the anchor hit bottom. Ready hands quickly connected and locked the chain stopper and the ship started to swing around in the current as the anchor dug in. Bosun Sopchick yelled, "Clear the foc'sle." Everyone ran for the foc'sle doors.

Percival had swung around 180 degrees and was now headed into the current. All of her guns were trained out to port toward Wolmi-do. The planes continued bombing Wolmi-do for another 10 minutes. As the bombing stopped, Hutcheson said, "Captain, there is some small boat traffic in the harbor and I see some activity in Inchon but there is no sign of life on Wolmi-do."

"Well after that bombing, I would expect their heads are down, but they are dug into pretty deep holes and may well come back to life quickly when they see us."

Phone talker: "Optical range finder operator has spotted artillery men scurrying into their gun pits -- he is concerned that they may start shooting before we do."

At 1245 Captain Allen two blocked the flag Hoist "Execute Assigned Mission".

"Standby, expect execute at 1300." called out Captain Brown.

At 1255, with a manned enemy gun position squarely in his sights, and unable to wait any longer, *DeHaven*'s Mount 51 fired with both barrels. The Wolmi gun battery exploded with parts flying in every direction.

"Commence fire," said Brown.

All of Percival's 5-inch and 3-inch guns started firing at the island's batteries in Red Circle Two, an area to be designated as Red Beach in the upcoming invasion..   Their fire was deliberate, aimed at individual gun emplacements and bunkers.   All of the destroyers fired continuously causing a great roar and billows of smoke.   At regular intervals there were larger explosions on the island caused by incoming 6-inch and 8-inch rounds from the big guns on the cruisers in the lower bay.   For a few minutes there was no counter fire from the island and then the enemy batteries opened up with their fire concentrated on the ships closest to them, *Gurke, Percival* and *Collett.*

Geysers erupted around all three ships as enemy fire hit the water short of their targets. Two rounds hit about 30 yards from Percival's port side. The air was filled with the smell of cordite as Percival's 5-inch and 3-inch guns fired continuously.

"Looks like 75 millimeter stuff." said the Captain. "It's hard to hit those guys because the guns are really dug in."

On the TBS: "Kingpin this is Rifleman" called *Collett,* "We have taken several 75mm shell hits over the last 20 minutes without serious damage. Just now, however, we have suffered a broken low pressure steam line in the forward fireroom and a hit in the Plot Room that destroyed our firing selector switch and wounded five men. We are continuing to fire all of our guns in Local Control. I am going to shift my anchorage position slightly because they sure have this one zeroed in."

"This is Kingpin, roger that."

"They are certainly shooting at us," said Hutcheson looking at the splashes to port, "but so far their rounds have been landing short. Our gunners are good and they have been hitting those gun emplacements again and again but they are still shooting back at us."

On the TBS: "Kingpin, this is Roadhouse," called *Gurke,* "We had shells falling all around us for a while and were hit twice with no serious damage. I believe that we either got the gun that did it or they have turned their attention elsewhere. We haven't had any incoming for a while."

"This is Kingpin, Roger."

Hutcheson and Langan were standing in the forward part of the port bridge scanning the island with their binoculars. The Captain was doing the same thing from the aft end of the bridge near the flag bag. A number of shells had landed short of the ship on their port side and were gradually getting closer. Then two shells raised geysers of water close by on the other side of the ship.

"Oh shit," said Hutcheson, "first they were short, now they're long, they've got us bracketed."

Two more rounds hit close aboard the port side blowing water on the ship but causing no damage. A round struck the port side just aft of the bow and exploded in the bosun locker starting a fire in the paint storage.

Hutcheson yelled to the Bosun, "Pass the word, Repair Party One to the Bosun Locker."

Just then, a shell exploded in the air forward of, and above the bridge. Shrapnel rattled off the splinter shields and shattered the plastic windscreen. Hutcheson and Langan were both knocked to the deck and lost their helmets. The bridge phone talker, screamed and was spun around but was still standing although bleeding profusely from his shoulder. One of the quartermasters was standing in stunned silence with blood streaming from a slice in his cheek. The messenger was crouched behind the splinter shield, frightened but, apparently unhurt. The Captain, although stunned and shaken and leaning against the splinter shield, appeared OK and called out, "I have the conn -- continue firing." The Bosun was on the 1MC "Corpsmen to the bridge on the double, Corpsmen to the bridge on the double, multiple casualties." *Percival*'s guns continued firing.

Corpsmen Cosgrove and Cleary and the two litter bearers came up the aft bridge ladder and the corpsmen immediately went to the two

273

downed officers. A minute later, Cosgrove turned to the Captain and said, "Sir, Mr. Hutcheson is dead. A piece of shrapnel went through his helmet and into his brain."

"Oh dear God," said Brown, "What a terrible loss."

Corpsman Cleary was working on Langan as Cosgrove turned to the other wounded. Cleary turned to the Captain, "Mr. Langan's helmet was struck by shrapnel that knocked him down and unconscious. He is awake now has a bump on his head and some lacerations – we'll have to keep an eye on him for a while."

He called to the litter bearers, "Get that stretcher off the aft bulkhead and lets's get Mr. Langan down to the aid station."

"Aye, aye, sir."

Percival's guns fired continuously and rounds from the enemy continued to drop in the water nearby.

Cosgrove said, "Smith, the phone talker and Barton, the QM will need stitches and have lost some blood, but should be OK."

"Very well, take good care of them." said Brown

He turned to the Bosun, "Pass the word for Mr. Benson and Mr. Theobald to lay up to the bridge.

The Bridge Talker turned to the Captain, "Repair One reports that the paint locker fire is out."

Chief Cosgrove and other crew members put Hutcheson into a Stokes stretcher and carried him below. His body would have to be kept in the refrigerated Butter and Egg Locker until it could be transferred to a larger ship.

When replacements arrived on the bridge, Smith and Barton with compression bandages on their heads walked down to the Aid Station. The quartermasters cleaned up the blood. Through all of his, Percival kept up a continuous barrage. Enemy fire from the island continued to land in the water near the ship

Benson and Theobald arrived on the bridge and reported to the Captain.

"As you have undoubtedly heard, Mr. Hutcheson was killed and Mr. Langan wounded by enemy fire. Mr. Benson you are now the OD and Mr. Theobald, you are now the JOOD. We are presently anchored at short stay and continuing to fire on the enemy. Read the log and then Mr. Mitchell and Chief Swenson will brief you about our current location and the course out of here. I will remain on the bridge until we are clear of Inchon. Any questions?"

"No? – Very well, carry on."

A short while later, Com90.62 ordered all ships to cease fire. By 1400 all of the destroyers had weighed anchor and were slowly steaming out of the restricted waterways off Inchon and Wolmi-do. The guns on Wolmi-do, although greatly subdued, continued to fire erratically at the departing destroyers. As the destroyers withdrew, the cruisers continued their heavy fire on Wolmi-do. When the ships were several miles south down Flying Fish Channel and well clear of Inchon, they hove to and *Percival* came alongside *Toledo*. A hastily formed honor guard in undress whites, carried the stretcher with Hutcheson's flag-

275

draped body to *Percival*'s quarterdeck. All of the crew, not on watch, manned the rail of the main deck and the 01 deck. At the quarterdeck, as the crew stood at present arms, the stretcher was carefully passed to an honor guard of Sailors and Marines on *Toledo*. Shortly thereafter the all of ships got underway and resumed their passage to the open sea.

When the Task Group reached the lee of an island in Kyonggi Bay the task group again hove to and Rear Admiral Higgins and Captain Allen went on board *Rochester* to confer with Admiral Struble. The meeting convened in Struble's cabin.

"Gentlemen," said Struble, "Hutcheson's death is a terrible loss.   He was a fine young man and a good officer. You know, he accompanied me on my hurry-up trip to Formosa to talk to Chiang in July. He acted as my aide, took notes and wrote an excellent report.   His Dad, Vice Admiral Hutcheson, is an old friend and I plan to write him a note about his son."

"Yes sir, you are right," said Allan, "Captain Brown thought that he was one of his best young officers."

"Unfortunately," said Struble, "all of these ships are going to be out here in combat conditions for some time. We are going to have to bury Hutcheson at sea tomorrow before we go back into Inchon."

"Aye, aye sir."

"John," Struble said turning to Rear Adm. Higgins, "Your gunfire support was accurate and   effective today – good job. The destroyer's action in close quarters in dangerous waters, is a tribute to the aggressive spirit of the US Navy. As good as it has been today, however, I believe that we have more work to do. You know, in War II in the   Pacific, we had the experience that we thought that we had blown the hell out of   someplace and then we landed to heavy opposition. I think we are going to have to give Wolmi-do a second day of bombardment – basically the same plan as today."

"Yes sir, I agree." said Higgins

"The Marines had asked us to take some care in our aircraft bombing raids so as not to take out the causeway between Wolmi-do and Inchon. They will be landing tanks on Wolmi-do at Green Beach and they are going to need the causeway to get their tanks over to Inchon on the mainland.   However, that restriction has limited our bombing effectiveness and I am going to direct Task Force 77 to change the attacks from southward, as they were today, to westward and accept the risk of some bombs possibly hitting the causeway."

Both Allan and Higgins agreed and the meeting broke up.

O n *Percival*, a pall of silence had fallen over the ship.   An announcement had just been made about Mr. Hutcheson's burial at sea tomorrow.   Everyone continued doing what had to be done, however, when Sailors talked together it was in low voices almost whispers. Mr. Hutcheson had been admired by his fellow officers and respected by the crew.   They all felt that he was smart guy who knew what he was doing but he was also honest and fair and was willing to listen to other points of view in his dealings with both officers and enlisted men – a good man. He would be missed. Many of them also thought about his wife Peggy – it was hard enough to deal with a spouses death when you had a body and a funeral to give some closure – how would she handle Hutch's death when his body was at the bottom of the Yellow Sea?

Task Group 90.6 cruised in the Yellow Sea overnight.   Spent brass was collected and struck below.   Ready service ammunition was replenished from the magazines. Tomorrow would be another all day operation so sandwiches were prepared so that the crew could be fed on station.

The next morning, before standing up Flying Fish Channel, the task group hove-to to bury Mr. Hutcheson. *Percival* was about 150 feet abeam of *Toledo* so that the crew could observe the burial ceremony. All of *Percival's* crew, not on watch, manned the rail. The Burial Party was assembled on *Toledo*'s quarter deck.   Hutcheson's body in a weighted canvas bag covered with an American Flag was on a table at the ship's edge. On all of the ships, colors were lowered to half staff. On *Percival* and on all the ships the Bosun piped All Hands followed by: "Now All Hands Bury The Dead".

The chaplain's words of the Episcopal burial service were carried by radio to all of the ships.

"Unto Almighty God we commend the soul of our brother David departed and we commit his body to the deep in the sure and certain hope of the Resurrection unto eternal life through our Lord Jesus Christ, at whose coming in glorious majesty to judge the world, the earth and the sea shall give up their dead; and the corruptible bodies of those who sleep in him shall be changed, and made like unto his own glorious body; according to the mighty working whereby he is able to subdue all things unto himself.   I heard a voice from heaven saying unto me, henceforth blessed are the dead who die in the Lord: even so saith the Spirit; for they rest from their labors.."

The Burial Party upended the table and the body slipped from beneath the colors and into the sea. In *Percival*, there were sobs and tears for a good man who bore the ultimate cost of war.

The chaplain continued, "We commend to Almighty God our shipmate David Michael Hutcheson III and we commit his body to the depths. Ashes to ashes, dust to dust. The Lord bless him and keep him. The Lord make his face to shine upon him and be gracious unto him. The Lord lift up his countenance upon him, and give him peace. Amen

May the angels lead you into paradise. May the martyrs greet your arrival and lead you into the holy city, Jerusalem. May choirs of angels welcome you and with Lazarus, who once was poor may you have rest eternally.

The Marine Honor Guard on *Toledo* fired three volleys. The bugler then played Taps. As the last note sounded all of the ships hauled their colors close up and the task group got underway.

On Percival, as Taps faded away, an impromptu choir led by Lt. Murphy started to sing.

"Eternal Father, strong to save,
Whose arm hath bound the restless wave,
Who bidd'st the mighty ocean deep
Its own appointed limits keep;
Oh, hear us when we cry to Thee,
For those in peril on the sea!"

The ships picked up speed and headed down the approach channel toward Inchon. Because of her battle damage, *Collett* had been detached and was assigned, with the Fleet Tug Mataco (AT-86), mine destruction duty. As a result, only five destroyers entered Flying Fish Channel. As *Henderson, Mansfield, DeHaven, Percival* and *Gurke* steamed northward, a few mines left from yesterdays minefield were

279

spotted and were taken under fire by *Collett*. The five destroyers resumed their positions around Wolmi-do and anchored. After another massive bombing attack on the island by planes from Task Force 77, the naval bombardment resumed. The rhythmic pounding of the 12 round per minute 5-inch guns was interspersed with the much faster firing of the rapid 3-inch fire and the almost machine gun-like bursts of the 40-millimeter guns as all of the ships hit the island with concentrated fire. There were also larger explosions on the island from the big guns of the cruisers USS *Toledo* and *Rochester* and HMS *Kenya* and *Jamaica* firing from Flying Fish Channel. Initially there was no counter fire from the island. After about 45 minutes, a few desultory 75mm rounds splashed near the destroyers with no hits. After 75 minutes of continuous fire that rocked the island, the ships ceased fire, weighed anchor and left without being hit by even one retaliatory shot from the wounded island. The destroyers work had been done and Wolmi-do was now about to be invaded. The ships proceeded west to the Yellow Sea to prepare for tomorrow's invasion.

Shortly after midnight on September 15, *Mansfield, DeHaven* and *Percival* entered Flying Fish Channel followed by the 3rd Battalion Landing Team, 5th Marines embarked in the Landing Ship Dock USS *Fort Marion* (LSD 22) and three high speed transports *Bass* (APD 124), *Diachenko* (APD 123) and *Wantuck* (APD 125). The ships coasted in on the flooding tide, navigating by radar along the winding narrow channel. Their navigation was assisted by a beacon on Palmi-do island lighted by the intrepid Lt. Eugene F. Clark, USN who had been secretly ashore behind the lines for two weeks before the landing. With Wolmi-do no longer a menace, the three destroyers anchored on the north side of the island. At 0545, *Mansfield* and *deHaven* opened fire on Wolmi-do and *Percival* began shelling the northern shore industrial area of Inchon.

On *Percival* Lt. j.g. Benson was OD and Ensign Theobald was JOOD and had the conn. The Captain was on the bridge and the ship was on the same watch bill as yesterday.

"Lots of good targets in here," said the Captain, "Warehouses, factories, oil storage."

"Sure are," said Benson, "Right now we have been concentrating on the buildings along the shore at Red Beach where the 5ᵗʰ Marines are supposed to land. Did you notice over there by Green Beach on Wolmi-do, three of those rocket launching LSMR's are moving in to fire. I would of thought our two days of bombardment together with the air attacks wouldn't have left anything worth shooting at."

"There may not be, but after some of our island experience in the Pacific war no one wants to take a chance. Wow, there they go – that must be 1000 of those 5-inch rockets – sure wouldn't want to be on the receiving end of that."

Benson had been checking his watch. "Captain, the bombardment is supposed to end at 0615 so that the boats can start in for the beach – I make it 0614 right now."

"I concur -- I'm sure that they will stop on time.."

"Small Boys, this is Kingpin, Cease Fire, Cease fire."

At that moment, at the exact time planned, LCVP Landing Craft full of Marines began pulling away from the APD's and heading for the beach just as the sky in the east was getting light. At the same time, the LSD, that had flooded down it's dock area, released three large LSU Landing Craft carrying tanks and more Marines. The Marines stormed ashore

281

on Green Beach on Wolmi-do to light resistance. The three days of air and surface bombardment had left the 500 or so remaining defenders of the island shell-shocked and frightened. Some units of a North Korean artillery regiment and a NK marine regiment had escaped across the causeway to Inchon during the night. The US Marines advanced up the hilly cratered slopes and 42 minutes after landing, the US flag was flying from the highest point of Wolmi-do. The Marines spent the rest of the day mopping up stragglers and securing the island..

Despite the difficulties caused by having to wait for high tide to bring ships into Inchon, the operation proceeded relatively smoothly. Using Wolmi-do as a launching point, reinforced Marine units landed on Red Beach and Blue Beach and took the lightly defended Inchon in the next two days and with the support of Marine Air Wings from *Sicily* and *Badoeng Straits*, pushed on toward Seoul. By the 17th they had overcome stiffening resistance and taken Kimpo airfield on the outskirts of Seoul and five days later the city itself had fallen.

The Inchon landing had been a resounding success and the credit for its success was certainly MacArthur's. Despite almost every one else's misgivings, the Emperor persisted and he was proven right. He also roundly refuted Army General Bradley's oft-quoted statement "that amphibious operations are a thing of the past". The Inchon amphibious landing cut off the enemy supply lines to the south and reversed the course of what had been a seemingly hopeless situation.

It was widely recognized that, despite its severely depleted forces, the United States Navy did a superb job of fighting back against the surprise North Korean invasion. It was also a fact that the undersized US Navy would not have been able to hold on as long as it did without the rapid deployment of Her Majesty's naval units to Korea. Early on, it quickly became apparent that not only was the Air Force concept of close air support for ground troops seriously flawed but that they had never seriously implemented the concept, or trained for it – no wonder it was so bad.   The superiority of Navy/Marine close support operations was clearly demonstrated first at Inchon and, later in the war, during the retreat from Chosin. All of these factors sharply changed US military policy and brought the Navy back to the place it deserved in the US Armed Forces. As a result, in the next three years, 540 ships were recommissioned from the reserve fleet to bring the Navy back to strength and undo the damage inflicted on it by Louis Johnson and a complicit Congress.

31 – Epilogue

On September 19, 1950 President Truman fired his Secretary of Defense, Louis Johnson and replaced him with 5-star General George C. Marshall. Truman blamed Johnson for the Armed Forces being short of both men and equipment when he ordered them to intervene in the Korean War.

The destroyers of Task Element 90.62 later received a Navy Unit Commendation for their close-in two-day bombardment of Wolmi-do. *Percival* continued to provide gunfire support to the Marines in the week after they landed at Inchon until they moved inland out of destroyer gun range. During the rest of September and into October, *Percival* continued to operate with Task Force 77 and units of Task Force 95. On October 30, 1950 *Percival*, streaming a Homeward Bound pennant, departed Sasebo for San Diego stopping in Pearl Harbor on the way. On November 21, 1950 *Percival* arrived in San Diego to a hero's welcome with fire boats spraying red, white and blue water, a band on the pier playing Anchors Aweigh and a huge crowd of parents, wives, lovers and friends waiting eagerly for their Sailors, home from the sea. Fully a third of the crew left for a couple of weeks of leave. Lt. Murphy, Lt. j.g. Harris and Ensign Langan stopped in Columbus, Ohio to see Peggy Hutcheson and Dave IV.

Three weeks after arriving home, *Percival* went into the Mare Island Naval Shipyard for a much needed overhaul. She continued to serve in the Pacific Fleet, including a number of deployments to East Asia, until she was decommissioned in August of 1969. She was sold for scrap in February 1972.

Commander Brown was passed over for promotion to Captain and immediately put in papers to retire. He went into his father-in-laws real estate business in San Diego. Lieutenant Commander Cook, having put in 30 years in the Navy, retired to Washington DC and five years later died of cirrhosis of the liver. Lt. Murphy married Emily, completed his remaining six months in the Navy and returned to Long Island. He went back to school and obtained a law degree. He and Emily had four children and in 1968 he was ordained a deacon in the Catholic Church. Lt. j.g. Harris completed his navy time, went back to school, received a PhD in medieval history from Harvard and taught at Hamilton College in Clinton, NY. Ens. Langan recovered from his wounds, received a Purple Heart and was promoted to Lt j.g.. Two years later, when his Minimum Service Requirement was complete, he resigned his commission and joined his father's Kaiser/Frazer Automobile dealership in Benton Harbor, Michigan.

Chief Quartermaster Swenson applied for selection as a Limited Duty Officer (LDO) and was commissioned Lieutenant j.g. the following year. Lcdr. Swenson retired in 1962 while XO of a *Dealey* class Escort Destroyer. After completing six years in the Navy, Sonarman 1st Class Johnson returned to New Jersey where he taught music and played in a heavy metal rock band. Sonarman MacDonald returned home to Ohio, reconnected with and married Julie, who had written him the "Dear John" letter.

It would be almost three more years and 36,516 US military deaths before the Korean War ended. After the successful Inchon landing, the Marines and Army fought their way northward across the 38th parallel driving the North Korean forces before them toward the Yalu River. On October 25, 1950 the Navy landed the Army's X Corps at Wonsan North Korea, for the third landing of the war, again belying General Bradley's claim of the end of amphibious operations.   On the same day, two hundred thousand Chinese Peoples Liberation Army (PLA) troops crossed the Yalu River from China into North Korea and joined the battle, driving the outnumbered United Nations forces back south.

In one of the epic battles of any war, the 25,000 Marines at Chosin, North Korea surrounded by 120,000 Chinese PLA troops fought their way out of the trap and down a 78 mile winding two lane dirt road in below zero, snowy, weather bringing their equipment, wounded and dead with them and defeating seven Chinese divisions in the process. Instrumental to their success was the close air support provided by Navy and Marine aircraft operating from Navy carriers and directed by Marine controllers. Marines on the ground later kidded that the support was so close that they were kept warm in the snow by the burning napalm dropped on their nearby Chinese adversaries.

Hutch's worst fears were realized as the North Koreans and their Russian helpers planted 12,000 mines in the waters around Korea. Four US minesweepers and a tug were sunk and four US destroyers were severely damaged with heavy loss of life.

The Chinese drove the outnumbered UN forces back down the peninsula and once again captured Seoul. The US Eighth Army finally regrouped, pushed north and recaptured Seoul.   On June 23, 1951, Jacob Malik, the Russian delegate to the United Nations, proposed a truce. The war then entered a sort of stalemate between the UN Forces and the combined Chinese and North Korean Armies just north of the 38th Parallel. After protracted negotiations, an armistice agreement was finally signed on July 27, 1953 and the fighting stopped.

And thus ended the war that the US had not planned for and was ill equipped to fight but one that it rearmed for and managed to battle to a stalemate.   It also proved that strategic air power has very limited usefulness in post World War II regional conflicts.

"No war involving the United Sates exemplified the value of sea power better than the Korean War.   The need for a strong, balanced, and adequate U. S. Navy for controlling the oceans for our purpose and for denying them to an enemy was made elementarily clear."[30]

---

30 The Sea War In Korea – Malcolm W. Cagle and Frank A. Manson – Naval
    Institute Press, 1957

Author's Notes

The Forgotten War Begins is a work of fiction, however, I have placed my story, as much as possible, within the framework and timeline of actual events in the first three months of the Korean War.   I have, however, taken some liberties. There never was a USS *Percival*, DDE-452 in commission in the United States Navy. The Navy did assign the name *Percival* and the hull number 452 but the ship was never built. John "Mad Jack" Percival, however, was a real naval hero of the War of 1812 and, was in fact, larger than life.

On June 25, 1950, the USS *Valley Forge* was actually in the South China Sea on its way to Subic Bay in the Phillipines, having left Hong Kong the day before. It suited the purposes of my story, for her to still be in Hong Kong.

Vice Admiral Struble traveled to Formosa in a destroyer to talk to Chiang Kai Chek at the request of General MacArthur   The discussions in the meeting between Admiral Struble and Chiang Kai Chek were documented in a report of the meeting by the then United States Charge d'Affairs in Taipei Robert C. Strong.

In my story, Percival sinks the North Korean patrol boat PB-21, the sole survivor of the real life sinking of a group of four North Korean patrol boats by the USS *Juneau* and HMS *Black Swan*. In fact, the actual PB-21 is today in the Museum of Victory of the Fatherland Liberation War in Pyongyang, North Korea and is celebrated for having escaped the United States Navy.

Percival's sinking of a Russian submarine is fiction, however, it is based on an actual incident just west of the Sasebo harbor entrance on December 18, 1950 involving the USS *McKean* DD 784 and what is widely believed to have been a Russian submarine.

US destroyers picked up gasoline in Pusan and ferried it ashore by whaleboat to the ROK 3rd Division in mid-August 1950. A destroyer also lead four LST's into Chongha to evacuate the ROK 3rd Division and was guided by jeep headlights on the beach.

Uljin, Chongjin and Songjin (now Kimchaek) were bombarded by destroyers operating independently in late August 1950

The Lyman K Swenson (DD 729) was part of the Gunfire Support Group bombarding Wolmi Do Island in September 1950 just before the Inchon invasion. Shell fragments from a North Korean near miss on the Swenson killed a Lt. j.g. And wounded another officer. The dead officer was buried at sea from the USS Toledo (CA 133) on the following day.

US Navy fighters from Task Force 77 shot down a Russian twin engine bomber on September 4, 1950 and a US destroyer on radar picket duty off Port Arthur recovered the body of the Russian pilot.

President Truman did in fact fire his Secretary of Defense, Louis Johnson, blaming him for the Armed Forces being ill prepared to intervene in the Korean War.

290

The author served as a Sonarman in USS *Wren* DD 568, a Fletcher Class destroyer, operating in the Korean War Zone with Task Forces 77 and 95. Those experiences are certainly reflected in this story.

Archie T. Miller
archbook111@gmail.com
May 2, 2014

Acknowledgements

I am deeply indebted to my wife Judy for her understanding and encouragement and for putting up with my endless hours seated at the computer. My thanks to Colleen Kehler for her critical comments on the early draft of the book. To former shipmates and and many other "old salts" who shared their experiences during the hectic buildup of the Navy during the Korean War, my thanks.

Over the years my reading about the people, events and ships of the period described in this book included:

Alexander, James Edwin *Inchon to Wonsan.*
      Annapolis: U.S. Naval Institute Press

Cagle, Malcolm & Manson, Frank *The Sea War In Korea.*
      Annapolis: U.S. Naval Institute Press

Field, James A. Jr. *A History of United States Naval Operations: Korea.* Naval Historical Center

Forrestal, James *Functions of the Armed Forces and the Joint Chiefs of Staff* – Memo 4/21/48 (Key West Agreement)

Friedman, Norman *U.S. Destroyers: An Illustrated Design History.* Annapolis: U.S. Naval Institute Press

Hornfischer, James D. *The Last Stand of the Tin Can Sailors*
Bantam Books February 2004

Korean War: Chronology of U.S. Pacific Fleet Operations, June-Dec. 1950. Naval History & Heritage Command

Lewis, Andrew L., Lcdr. USN *The Revolt of the Admirals*
Air Command and Staff College 1998

McGraw Hill Book Co. *Jane's Fighting Ships 1953 - 1954*

Marolda, Edward J. *Invasion Patrol: The Seventh Fleet in Chinese Waters.* Naval Historical Center

McGarty, Terence P. *DD 649 USS Albert W Grant.* Self Published

US Naval Institute Press *The Bluejackets Manual 14th Ed. 1950*

Raven, Alan *Fletcher Class Destroyers.* Annapolis:
U.S. Naval Institute Press

Spector, Ronald H. *At War At Sea.* Viking 2001

Strong, Robert C. U.S. Charge in Taipei *Report 794.00/7-1050*
Meeting Struble/Chiang July 10, 1950

USS Fletcher Deck Log .June 15, 1950 to October 31,1950

Made in the USA
Coppell, TX
13 June 2021